TALK TO THE PAW

TALK TO THE PAW

MELINDA METZ

KENSINGTON BOOKS
www.kensingtonbooks.com

KENSINGTON BOOKS are published by

Kensington Publishing Corp.
119 West 40th Street
New York, NY 10018

All Kensington titles, imprints, and distributed lines are available at special quantity discounts for bulk purchases for sales promotion, premiums, fund-raising, educational, or institutional use.

Special book excerpts or customized printings can also be created to fit specific needs. For details, write or phone the office of the Kensington Sales Manager: Kensington Publishing Corp., 119 West 40th Street, New York, NY 10018. Attn. Sales Department. Phone: 1-800-221-2647.

Kensington and the K logo Reg. U.S. Pat. & TM Off.

eISBN-13: 978-1-4967-1217-2
eISBN-10: 1-4967-1217-X
First Kensington Electronic Edition: February 2018

ISBN-13: 978-1-4967-1216-5
ISBN-10: 1-4967-1216-1
First Kensington Trade Paperback Printing: February 2018

10 9 8 7 6 5 4 3 2 1

Printed in the United States of America

For Gary Goldstein, with thanks
for the oppurrtunity and inspurration,
and in memory of the real
Al and Marie Defrancisco, best of neighbors

CHAPTER 1

MacGyver opened his eyes. He lay snuggled with his belly against Jamie's soft, warm hair, his favorite sleeping spot. He purred with contentment. His person's scent, one of the few familiar ones in this new place, comforted him.

Except . . . there was still that tang. It wasn't the smell of illness, but something about it reminded him of that scent. Mac suspected he knew the cause. He hated to think it, but humans were more like dogs than cats, at least in some ways. They needed others of their kind close around them, a pack.

Mac was more than fine being the only cat in his home, surrounded by his food, his water, his litter box, his toys, and his person. Jamie wasn't like that. Mac thought she should just go out and find a human for herself. There were humans everywhere to pick from. But sometimes Jamie missed the obvious. Like she just didn't understand that her tongue was made for washing. There was no need for her to endure submerging her body in water.

His purring faded. Now that he'd noticed the tang, it was bothering him more and more. He stood, abandoning his comfortable spot. It was time for action! He rubbed Jamie's head a few times with his own, so that anyone who smelled her would know she was his, then he jumped to the floor and padded through the living room and out to the screened front porch. Earlier he'd noticed there was a small rip at the bottom of the screen.

He stared out into the darkness. In this new place there had to be someone who could belong to Jamie the way Jamie belonged to him. But she wasn't going to find that person on her own.

Not a problem. MacGyver was on the case.

Mac squeezed through the rip in the screen and paused. It was his first time out in the outside world, at least without a car window or the mesh of his carrier between it and him. There would be dangers out here, but that didn't worry him. He knew he could handle himself in any situation that came up.

Ears forward, tail high, he slipped into the night, taking in the mix of scents—spicy tomato sauce, chocolate frosting, tuna steak, and dozens of other food smells; the waxy odor of the purple flowers that grew up the side of his house; a whiff of something sweet and rancid from the garbage cans along the curb; an intriguing hint of mice droppings; and the overwhelming aroma of dog piss. Mac gave a hiss of disgust. Obviously, there was a dog in the complex who peed on *everything*. The bonehead clearly thought that meant he owned the place. Wrong.

MacGyver trotted over to the tree the dog had doused most recently. He gave it a good clawing, and when he was done his scent was much stronger than the mutt's. Satisfied, he took in another breath, this time opening his mouth and flicking his tongue. It let him almost taste the air.

Jamie wasn't the only human in the area who was emitting that tang of loneliness. Going with his instincts, Mac decided to follow the strongest strain. He stopped a couple times to claw over the disgusting smell of dog, but quickly reached the source of the scent he was tracking, a little house with a rounded roof.

Other than the lonely smell, he liked a lot of the other scents around the house—bacon, butter, a little sweat, freshly mown grass, and nothing sharp, like the stuff Jamie liked to spray in the kitchen, interfering with his complete enjoyment of his food. Now, how to get Jamie to realize that there was a good choice for a packmate here? Mac thought for a moment, then he decided he should bring something from the house to his person. Her nose wasn't nearly as sensitive as his, but he was sure once she had something right in front of her and got a blast of the mix of scents, she'd know what to do.

There wasn't a screened-in porch, like the one at his new house, but he wasn't worried. Mac's upper lip curled back as he continued his surveillance. The bonehead dog had been around, that was for sure. He managed to ignore the reek by reminding himself he was on a mission. His eyes scanned back and forth, searching, searching. Then he saw it, a small circular window standing partway open on the second floor.

Getting up there—no problem. The big tree growing beside the house seemed designed as his personal staircase. He quickly scrambled up, gave the window a head butt to open it wider, then jumped inside. He landed on top of the perfect thing to bring back to Jamie. It was saturated with attractive odors, plus the scent of loneliness that would make Jamie realize the smell came from a person who needed a packmate as much as she did.

Mac snatched the wad of cloth up in his mouth, enjoying the tastes that went with the smells. Filled with triumph, he jumped back to the windowsill, then into the night, his prize flapping behind him.

A high, demanding meow woke Jamie the next morning. "I'm coming, Mac," she mumbled. She climbed out of bed, only about a quarter awake, took two steps, and smacked into the closet door. Well, that got her to at least the halfway-conscious mark.

Okay. Got it. She was in her new place, and in her new place the closet was on the other side of the bed than it had been in her old apartment.

Meooooowwrr.

"I. Am. Coming," Jamie told her cat as she walked the short distance to the kitchen. Mac gave another of his *I-Want-Food* yowls. It was like he had studied her to decide which of the sounds in his repertoire made her eardrums throb the most and now he used them to request meals.

"I keep telling you, if you learned to work the coffeemaker, it would make both our mornings more pleasant," she reminded him. She didn't bother attempting to make her coffee before serving His Majesty. MacGyver had her too well trained for that.

But even jonesing for caffeine, she couldn't help smiling as Mac began weaving around her ankles the moment she took a can of cat food out of the cupboard. She thought her kitty was brilliant, but there were some things he just didn't get. Like that she'd be able to get the food into his bowl a lot faster if he didn't try to tie her feet together with his body.

"Here you go." She managed to get the food into Mac's bowl without dumping any of it on his head. She watched while he took a few sniffs, then a bite, then another bite. It seemed like Alli-Cat was still on his approved foods list. She couldn't believe she was feeding her cat alligator. But the vet had said wild food was good for him, and he liked it—for now. She amused herself by imagining Mac, all eight and a quarter pounds of him, bagging breakfast by twining himself around a gator's big ankles until it went down.

Jamie took a step toward the coffeemaker, one of the few essentials she'd unpacked last night, then sank down in one of the kitchen chairs, suddenly overwhelmed. She'd just trashed her whole life. Quit her job and moved about as far away as she could while still staying in the United States. She wrapped her arms around her knees. What had she been thinking? She was thirty-four. When you were thirty-four, you were supposed to be settling down, not attempting a complete reboot. Her friends had. They were all married now, all as in *all*, and more than half of them had kids—and not just babies. One of Samantha's was an actual teenager.

"Don't do this. Do not do this. This is not how you start." But how *was* she supposed to start? She thought for a moment. First, she had to stand up. She shoved herself to her feet. Now what?

The answer hit her almost immediately. She was going out! And that meant she needed to get dressed. She hurried to the living room and unzipped her biggest suitcase before she could change her mind. She pulled on her favorite jeans and the upcycled top she'd found on Etsy. She'd only worn it once, even though she loved it. It just didn't seem to fit with Avella, PA. It *was* a little crazy, most of it coral with black roses, but with long pieces of colorful fabric in a mishmash of patterns around the hem and green leaves appliqued here and there.

The top was perfect for LA, or at least she thought so. And who cared if it wasn't? Jamie had declared that 2018 would be "The Year of Me." She'd declared it silently, but she'd declared it. She'd gone through The Year of the Self-Absorbed Man, The Year of the Forgot-to-Mention-I-Was-Married Man, The Year of the Cling-Wrap Man, The Year of the Non-Committal Man. And, the worst year of all, The Year of the Sick Mother.

The Year of Me wouldn't involve men of any kind. It would involve wearing clothes she thought were gorgeous, even if no one else did. It would involve following her dream, as soon as she figured out what her dream was. She knew for sure it wasn't teaching high school history.

The Year of Me would involve living in a place where she didn't know anyone and where every place she went was a fresh start. The Year of Me would change her life! She shook her head. Give herself one more second and she'd be bursting into song like Maria leaving the convent in *The Sound of Music.* She grabbed her purse and started for the door, then stopped. Probably she should brush her hair. And her teeth.

That done, she headed out. Her gaze snagged on something crumpled on top of the doormat. She picked it up. It was a plain white terry-cloth hand towel. She was sure it hadn't been there yesterday, and it wasn't hers. She didn't go for plain white anythings.

She started to open the screen door so she could toss the hand towel on the porch. She'd only opened it about three inches when suddenly Mac was there—darn those silent little cat feet—and then out.

Jamie bolted out the door after him. Mac had never been outside. Her brain jangled with a dozen horrible things that could happen to him. "MacGyver!" she yelled. He kept going—big surprise. She tried again, knowing it wouldn't work. "MacGyver!"

"The voice of authority," someone said, with a snort. She turned and saw Al Defrancisco weeding the little flower patch that ran beside his porch steps. She'd met him and his wife, Marie, when she'd arrived yesterday. They lived in one of the twenty-three bungalows—bungalows, how glamorous Old Hollywood was that?—making up Storybook Court. It was named for the 1920s storybook-style architecture of the little houses. That architecture, which gave the complex its historical-standing status, was the only reason Storybook Court hadn't been torn down and replaced with a high-rise. She'd so lucked out that one of the adorable houses had become vacant on the very afternoon when Jamie had started searching for a place.

"He comes when he's called . . . sometimes. When I have a can of food in my hand. Or when I'm eating a tuna sandwich," Jamie told Al. At least Mac hadn't gone too far, not yet anyway. Her tan-and-brown tabby was using one of the palm trees near the courtyard fountain as a scratching post.

There were palm trees by her house! How cool was that? This couldn't be her life. But it was. Thanks to the inheritance her mother had left her, she could spend a year here. She didn't even have to get a job. Not for this once-in-a-lifetime year. She had no intention of being a slacker, though. She knew, for sure, she didn't want to teach. But she was going to find out what she did want to do—and then do it!

"Al, I told you to wear a hat." Marie came out of the house next door and threw a straw fedora down to her husband. She was small and frail, both she and Al probably in their eighties, but her voice was strong and commanding.

Al put on the hat. "The voice of authority," he muttered, jerking his chin in Marie's direction.

"Where are you off to?" Marie asked Jamie.

"Once I corral my cat, just out for coffee. I saw that Coffee Bean & Tea Leaf a few blocks away when I was driving in," she answered.

Marie gave a huff of disapproval that seemed to be directed at Jamie and went back inside. Jamie was used to everyone knowing her business in Avella. The town didn't have even a thousand residents. She'd been sure LA would be different, but it was seeming like she was mistaken.

Jamie glanced over at Mac, trying to act like she wasn't checking on him. Knowing her cat, the best way to get him to come home was to act like she didn't care whether he did or not. He was sunning himself beside the palm. "I can't leave him out here. He's an indoor cat. He has zero car sense," she told Al, then added, "He likes it in the courtyard. Maybe I should get him a leash and walk him around."

Al only grunted in response. Jamie debated going inside for a can of food. But Mac had just eaten. She didn't think it would work. Maybe the feathered cat toy . . . Before she could decide, Marie came back out. "Coffee," she said to Jamie, holding a cup over the porch rail. "Twenty-seven cents a cup. It's probably ten times that at your Bean."

"Thanks. That's so sweet of you," Jamie answered. She took a sip. It was perfect.

"Take this over to Helen." Marie handed a second cup to Al. He walked over to the bungalow on the other side of his and Marie's.

"Helen. Coffee," he hollered, not bothering to climb the two steps to the porch.

A few moments later, a woman, maybe ten years younger than Al and Marie, came outside. Helen took the coffee, drank some, then glared over at Marie. "You forgot sugar. Again."

"You don't need sugar," Marie shot back. "You're getting fat." Helen continued glaring. "Nessie still has a lovely figure. You could—"

"I told you not to talk to me about—" Helen stopped. "I'm putting in sugar," she declared, then noticed Jamie. "You! You're Jamie Snyder. I wanted to see you. I have a godson just about your age. You're not exactly his type. He usually goes for exotic, not blond girl-next-door types. But he's a teacher, too. I'm going to give him your number."

Blond girl-next-door type? Was she the blond girl-next-door type? She wasn't exotic. She knew that. But blond girl-next-door type sounded extremely wholesome and extremely boring. Okay, she was wholesome, but not extremely. And she—

"Number?" Helen prompted.

"No. I mean, thanks, but I'm not interested in meeting him. In meeting any guys," Jamie protested, the words coming out too fast and too loudly to be polite. "I mean, I just got here. I want to get settled in." She took another glance at Mac. Still sunning himself. "How'd you know I am—used to be—a teacher?" she asked. She was almost positive she hadn't mentioned it to Al and Marie yesterday, and she hadn't talked to anyone else in the complex yet.

"If it was on the credit check or rental agreement, these two know it," Al said as he returned to his weeding. Jamie was sure it was illegal for a landlord to share that info, but she decided not to make an issue of it.

"Her godson's not right for you anyway," Marie said. "He won't even change a lightbulb for her when she needs it. I have to send little Al, our son, over. He comes every Sunday for dinner." She pointed one bony finger at Helen. "Besides, your godson is too young."

"Only five years younger than she is," Helen retorted.

"My great-nephew is three years older. The man should be older. They mature later." Marie returned her attention to Jamie. "He might be good for you."

Jamie began backing away slowly. As if sensing her discomfort, MacGyver trotted over and gave his *Pick-Me-Up* meow, which was softer and much more pleasant than the *I-Want-Food* one. Gratefully, Jamie scooped him into her arms. She traced the M on his forehead with one finger. The brown marking was one of the reasons she'd named him MacGyver.

"Your godson is allergic to cats, isn't he?" Marie called to Helen, her voice infused with triumph.

"I'm going to get sugar," Helen muttered and retreated inside.

"Just leave the cup on the porch when you're finished," Marie told Jamie and went inside herself.

"I really don't want to be set up with anyone," Jamie said to Al, since neither of the women had paid any attention to her.

Al gave another of his grunts. "You think that matters?"

It definitely mattered to Jamie. She was not letting The Year of Me start with awkward meetings with great-nephews or godsons or any other men.

"You told her about Clarissa, didn't you?" Adam demanded as soon as David sat back down at the table.

David didn't answer, just took a swallow of the sour IPA Brian, owner of the Blue Palm, had recommended. David was usually a Corona guy, but you didn't order Corona at the Blue Palm.

"You don't have to answer," Adam continued. "I know you did. I could see it. I could see the exact second it happened. You walked over to the bar, got a spot next to her and her friend, made some humorous and probably self-deprecating comment. She smiled. It looked good. The friend left for the bathroom, probably to give you two some privacy. She put her hand on your arm. *She put her hand on your arm.* And I'm thinking, this was so much easier than he expected it to be. Then the arm touch turned into an arm pat. A *sympathetic* arm pat. And I knew, I *knew,* you'd brought up the dead wife."

David felt his shoulders stiffen, but he forced himself to smile and lift his glass to his friend. "You nailed it."

"Sorry. I shouldn't have said it like that." Adam popped a pretzel ball into his mouth. "But you can't bring up Clarissa in the first five minutes you meet someone," he said while he chewed. "Not if you want something to happen."

"I don't even know if I want anything to happen. I told you that." His voice had come out with more of an edge than he'd intended, but he'd told Adam—repeatedly—that he wasn't sure he really wanted to "get back out there." Even though it had been three years.

"Well, I'm your friend. I've known you since before you had pubes, so at least five years. And I say that even if you're not sure you want anything to happen, you really do want it to happen."

Adam tried to take another pretzel ball, and David knocked his hand away. "Mine," David said.

His friend went in from another angle, grabbed the pretzel ball, and kept on talking. "Because if you don't do it now, it's just going to get weirder and harder, and then you're not going to be able to make it happen even if you're a hundred percent positive you want it to, and you'll end up a sad, lonely old man."

"I'll end up a sad, lonely old man? You sound like you're writing dialogue for your next episode," David told him.

"I'm serious," Adam said. "It's been long enough. Lucy thinks you should go on counterpart.com."

"This is what you and Lucy talk about when the kids are finally asleep? No wonder you never get sex," David answered.

"Online dating makes sense. You can take it slow. Get to know each other before you meet. And you can think about what kind of impression you want to make. I'm not telling you you can never mention Clarissa. Just not in the first five. You want more of these?" Adam pointed to the empty appetizer plate.

"More?" David protested. "Don't you mean *any?*

"We'll get more." Adam signaled to their waitress, pointed to the plate, and gave her a pleading look, complete with hands clasped to his chest. She laughed and nodded. "We'll also get more drinks. And before we leave here, we're getting you up on Counterpart. I'm a writer. I'm sure I can find a way to make even you sound appealing." He studied David. "People are always saying you look like Ben Affleck, but that's not the vibe we want, what with the cheating and the gambling. And, actually, since you're supposedly writing this, it would probably sound egotistical to describe yourself like a celebrity anyway. So, we'll just go with the basics: thirty-three, brown hair, hazel eyes, six-foot-one, what, about one-eighty?"

David nodded. His friend was on a roll. There was no stopping him now.

"We have to put in that you're a baker. Women will love that. They get you and your hot fudge sundae cupcakes. Maybe your profile pic should have you kneading dough or something. It would be like that scene in *Ghost*, but dough instead of clay," Adam went on.

"I'm not asking why you've seen *Ghost*." Actually, David had seen it himself. Clarissa had watched it for the first time when she was about twelve and it had made an indelible impression. Whenever it came on TV, it was like she'd become hypnotized and had to watch to the end.

The waitress appeared with another plate of appetizers and took their new beer order. "Okay, what else? What else?" Adam muttered. "Get out your cell and set up the account while I think."

David got out his phone, because Adam was Adam and he was relentless. But he just looked at the site without signing up.

"We'll put in that you have a dog. Shows you can at least keep a living thing alive." Adam was scribbling on a napkin now.

"How desperate are we thinking these women are?" David asked.

Adam ignored him. "We'll leave out your silent-movie obsession for now, because that will limit your dating pool. You like long walks on the beach, right?" Adam asked.

David tried to remember the last time he'd gone to the beach. Not since Clarissa. Less than an hour away, a lot less if the traffic was good, and he'd been acting like he lived halfway across the state. "You can't say I like long walks on the beach. That's the biggest cliché ever. I wouldn't want a woman who would want a man who said he liked long walks on the beach."

Adam grinned. "Just wanted to make sure you were paying attention. You're getting into this. Admit it."

Was he? Maybe he was. A little. Maybe Adam was right. Maybe even if he didn't feel like meeting anyone, he needed to try. Try more than that lame attempt he'd made with the woman at the bar, which had been all Adam's idea. "Maybe say I volunteer with Habitat for Humanity," he suggested.

"I like. Makes you seem like a guy with a heart, and also like a guy who might be able to fix things around the house." Adam scribbled away. "We should also say something about what kind of woman you want, what you're looking for."

What he was looking for. Someone who was always up for trying something new. Someone who believed there was always something great out there to discover. Someone who—

He realized what he was looking for was Clarissa.

It felt like one of the salty pretzel balls had formed in David's throat. He couldn't believe this was happening. He struggled to fight down the grief that had had shocked him with its strength. Suddenly it felt like Clarissa's death had taken place yesterday.

"Look, I know you're right. It makes sense for me to try to meet someone new. But I'm not ready," he told Adam. David thought he'd managed to keep his tone casual, but Adam must have seen something of what David was feeling on his face. His friend crumpled up the napkin and jammed it in his pocket.

"I'm not saying forever." David shoved his hands through his hair. "Just not now. I don't know, maybe next year."

CHAPTER 2

Okay, Day Two of the Year of Me, Jamie thought. She wasn't counting the day she moved in. That wasn't a whole day, so how could it count? Besides if she counted it and this was Day Three, then she should have already come up with some kind of plan. But if it was Day Two, it was okay to still be working on one.

She grabbed her bag. It looked like something an old-timey grandma would carry, but in a good way, with flowers embroidered all over it and a wicker handle. It was nice and roomy, too, big enough for the notebook, where Jamie was writing—planning to write—her plan. She had nothing against her laptop, but for lists and plans, she was a pen-and-paper gal.

"I'm heading out, Mac. Don't tell Marie, but I'm going to Coffee Bean." She ticked the tabby under his chin. "I left you surprises." Jamie usually hid a couple treats for Mac when she went out so he'd have something to hunt.

She managed to slither out the door without Mac making a break for it. Then she managed to make it around the corner and out of sight without Marie appearing and asking where she was going. *Good start,* she thought. She decided to walk through the complex and out the other side. She was eager to get a look at the other houses.

The first one along the walkway looked like the house of a Disney witch, with a high-peaked roof that made the cottage look like it was wearing a witch's hat itself. The windows echoed the shape, and the doorknocker was a black iron spider with large eyes of faceted red glass. As Jamie studied the place, a woman came out and hooked a large candy cane over one of the legs of the spider doorknocker. She wore a short green dress that could almost have passed as an elf costume. Her black hair looked elfish, too. It was cut short, with bangs that almost touched her eyebrows. When she spotted Jamie, she waved and called, "I love Christmas, don't you?"

"Um, yes, I do," Jamie answered, though it was kind of a random question for September.

"I'm just getting out my decorations." The woman hooked another large candy cane on the small potted lemon tree on the porch. Jamie tried to guess her age. It was hard to tell. "I've also started baking," the woman added. "Want to come in and have a gingerbread man?"

Jamie tried to remember if she'd fallen into a rabbit hole or been taken up by a tornado recently. She felt like she'd entered another world. "Don't be scared," the woman said, with a smile, clearly sensing Jamie's hesitation. "I know it's September. I just think Christmas is too wonderful to be contained to a month or two. Oh, and I'm Ruby Shaffer. I forgot to say that. Gingerbread? It's good."

"Sure," Jamie joined Ruby on the porch and introduced herself. "I just moved in. My place is right around the corner."

"The one next to Al and Marie," Ruby said, and Jamie nodded. Now that Jamie was closer, she could see threads of gray in Ruby's black hair and decided she was probably fifty-something. "Aren't they a hoot? I love them," Ruby continued. "Marie tries to pretend she's a tough old bird, but she takes care of everyone in her orbit." She opened the door and ushered Jamie inside. She was greeted by an explosion of red and green, silver and gold.

"Like I said, I've started getting out the Christmas decorations," Ruby said as she led the way down a narrow path between piles of lights, ornaments, wreaths, and few dozen stuffed animals in holiday attire.

"Started?" Jamie murmured.

"I'm not a hoarder or anything like that. I keep them in a storage unit from January fifteenth through September fifteenth," Ruby told her. "Have a seat." She gestured to one of the chairs at the kitchen table. The only sign of Christmas in the room was the plate of gingerbread men clad in red and green icing. Ruby took the platter off the counter and set it down in front of Jamie.

"I always kind of hate to eat gingerbread men," Jamie admitted. "It makes me feel like a cannibal."

"Eat the head first, then it won't be staring at you," Ruby advised, then picked up a cookie and decapitated it with one bite. Jamie laughed and bit off the head of her own cookie. She was starting to like this strange woman. It wasn't as if Jamie didn't have a streak of strange herself, she just kept it slightly better hidden, especially when she'd been at the front of a classroom.

"Are you ready for the question?" Ruby asked. "I have this question I ask all new people I meet. It's a shortcut for getting to know them."

"O-kay," Jamie said. Because, really, what else *could* she say?

"What would be the name of the movie of your life?"

"It's hard to say, since I don't know the ending yet," Jamie answered. "I don't know if my movie is inspirational or terrifying or funny."

"Good point," Ruby said. "I've actually never gotten that answer before."

"My right-now movie title would be *The Year of Me*," Jamie blurted out. There was something about Ruby. She made Jamie feel like she could say pretty much anything with no judgments.

"How come?" Ruby bit one of the feet off her gingerbread men.

"I've just had this stretch of time, a long stretch, when my decisions were made based on who I was with. Guys, mostly. Then my mom was sick, and I wanted to make decisions based on her, but now . . ." Jamie pulled in a shaky breath.

"Now *The Year of Me*," Ruby filled in for her. "Nice. My movie would be called *My Amazing Untrue Adventures*. Because I work as a set dresser creating fake worlds. And my imagination is my best friend. I can always find a way to amuse myself. I have lots of mental adventures, some real ones, too."

"So, would you say your job is your passion?" Jamie asked.

"One of them, absolutely," Ruby said without hesitation. "I love the challenge of, say, deciding what a certain character would have in the top drawer of their nightstand. And I love being part of a team, well, mostly. When we're all working together, the director, actors, costumer, everybody, to create something, it's amazing."

That's what I want, Jamie thought. *I want to talk about my job like that.*

"What about you? How do you make your shekels?" Ruby ate the other foot of her gingerbread man. "Is there a word for taking off a foot? Dedepitation?" She shook her head. "Never mind. I want to hear about you."

"I was a history teacher. High school. Loved the history. Loved some of the kids. Hated the discipline and having to teach pretty much only what the kids needed to pass a standardized test. Also, the parents? Most of them were impossible to deal with. Give a kid an A and a parent will be in your office demanding to know why it wasn't an A-plus. And give a kid a C? Forget about it. Parents have gone insane," Jamie answered. "Uh, do you have kids?" she belatedly added.

"Nope. Forgot to ask my now-ex-husband if he wanted them before we got married. I just assumed he did. Stupid. By the time I found out he didn't and we untangled ourselves, it was too late for me. Not him. He now has a toddler and a six-year-old. Men have enough advantages. Do they have to have an unlimited supply of fresh sperm, too?" Ruby had managed to say all that in one breath, and now she sucked in a big one.

She plays fair, Jamie thought. *She doesn't just ask, she tells, too.*

"So, if you're not a history teacher, what are you doing?" Ruby asked.

"My Year of Me is financed by an inheritance," Jamie said. "I'm using it to figure out what I should be doing." She pulled the notebook out of her bag. "I was on my way out to have a brainstorming session."

Ruby stood up. "Then, go! I don't want to get in the way of you and inspiration. We'll talk more, unless you've decided I'm the Storybook Court crazy lady."

"I don't. I'd like that," Jamie answered, shoving the notebook back inside her bag.

"Fabulous purse," Ruby commented.

Yeah, Jamie was definitely liking her strange new neighbor. She promised herself she'd explore her new little neighborhood more thoroughly later, but now she wanted to get to work. She briskly walked through the complex, then made her way to Sunset. She paused to take a picture of the Gower Gulch strip mall.

It wasn't much to look at. Other than an old-style medicine wagon at one end of the parking lot, it could be a strip mall pretty much anywhere, on the shabby side with a Denny's and a Rite-Aid as the highlights. But she'd been reading up on the local history, and she'd found out that back in the day, cowboys looking for work in the motion pictures would gather over there. Just because she didn't want to teach history, didn't mean she didn't still love history, and her new city had some great stories. She'd actually taken a real tour yesterday. She'd decided she needed one day of R&R before she settled down to figuring out the rest of her life.

She walked a few more blocks, then stopped in front of a palm tree with purple morning glories twining around the trunk. She had to get a pic. She hardly ever did this. Some of her friends took pictures of every piece of food they ate, and of course, a bazillion baby pictures, but Jamie usually didn't bother. Maybe it was because back home she saw the same things every day. Here, everything was new.

Just as she photographed the palm, she noticed something moving up there where the fronds were *clack-clacking* together. A rat. Ick.

But not a bad picture. Beautiful flowers, glam palm, gleaming-eyed rat. Nice contrast. She took a couple, checked to make sure she had a keeper, then headed into the Coffee Bean. She ordered herself a large blended Black Forest, because figuring out the rest of her life required sugar—more than just a gingerbread man's worth—and lots of caffeine. She grabbed a table, took out her notebook and opened it to a fresh page, took out two purple Varsity fountain pens, her faves, then . . . sat there.

Sugar and caffeine, she reminded herself. She took a couple big swallows from her Black Forest. Too big and too fast. She now had—*ow, ow, ow, ow*—brain freeze. She rubbed her temples, waiting for it to pass. When it did, she returned her attention to her notebook, to that blank page in her notebook.

She wrote the words "Year of Me" at the top of the page, then scribbled over them. They sounded good in her head, and even as a move title, but they looked silly written down. She thought for a second, then wrote "Things I Like." That's how you were supposed to figure out your passion. Passion equaled what you liked, hopefully something you could make money at.

She underlined the words. Then she sat some more. Stared some more. Then she started writing things down as fast as she could:

Playing with Mac with the laser.
Watching old movies.
Things made out of other things.
Sugar and caffeine.
Smell of rain on hot pavement.
The way sheets feel against my legs right after I've shaved them.
Garage sales.
Old postcards with messages on them.
Old dolls—of varieties both creepy and not creepy.
History—but not teaching it.
Biographies.
Wonder Woman.

Wonder Woman? Where did that come from? Jamie guessed she liked Wonder Woman. She certainly had nothing against Wonder Woman. But she didn't expect Wonder Woman to show up that high on her List of Likes.

Maybe because on her tour yesterday she'd seen someone dressed up as Wonder Woman in front of Grauman's Chinese Theater? She knew it wasn't called Grauman's anymore, but she couldn't help thinking of it as Grauman's. Footprints of celebs equaled Grauman's.

Did that Wonder Woman impersonator make a living at it? Was it her passion? Maybe. If you truly loved and respected Wonder Woman, it could be your passion to be her all day. It made people happy. Everyone taking pictures with her had been smiling. Jamie hadn't taken a picture with her, but she'd taken pictures of people taking pictures with Wonder Woman. Wonder Woman had looked like she was enjoying every second of every encounter.

She'd taken more pictures in the last two days than she had in the last two years. She'd sort of fallen out of the habit, even though back in high school she'd actually taken pictures for the school paper, and she'd taken a couple photography classes in college, just for fun. Maybe she was getting back into it because there were so many new things catching her interest.

She added a few items to her list:

Taking pictures.
Seeing happy people.
Making people happy.

And . . . and nothing else was coming to her. She had to like more than—she did a quick count—fifteen things. But fifteen was a start. She read her list slowly, looking for similarities, connections, inspiration.

Apparently, she liked old stuff. Old movies. Old dolls. Old postcards. History. Garage sales. Even things made of other things, because lots of time the other things were old things. She'd known she absolutely had to live in Storybook Court the second she saw it, because it was straight out of another time. Even when the houses were first built, they wouldn't have looked modern. They looked like they'd been created in a fairy tale and then transported, like Ruby's little witch's house. Al and Marie's was like a miniature castle, complete with towers and turrets, and Helen's place felt like part cozy animal den and part human house.

So her passion had led her to her new home, even though she hadn't thought of it that way. Could it lead her to a new career?

Some people made good money selling old stuff on eBay,

but that didn't really appeal to her. She didn't want to look at fabulous old finds and have to calculate how much they were worth.

She wished she could upcycle clothes and make something like her favorite shirt, but she wasn't crafty. When she tried, the results were . . . not good. She'd actually superglued two of her fingers to her hair once. And not when she was in her single digits.

Jamie returned to sitting-and-staring mode. She was starting to feel like she had brain freeze again, even though she hadn't taken another swallow of her drink. "Thinking hard," she muttered, in her Frankenstein voice. Could you make a living in Hollywood with a somewhat-passable Frankenstein impression? Doubtful. She slapped her notebook closed and shoved it in her bag—another old thing she liked. She'd do more brainstorming when the inside of her head had thawed.

As she stepped back outside into the gorgeous day, she decided she really needed to get Mac a leash. He deserved to explore his new neighborhood, too, and not be stuck inside all the time, poor kitty.

Diogee greeted David at the door, leash in mouth, tail—make that his whole rear end—wagging. "Okay, Big D, okay." He took the slobbered-on leash out of his dog's mouth, and clipped it to his collar. As soon as he did, Diogee shoved his way past David and yanked him down the porch stairs.

David knew that he was supposed to be the alpha dog, not Diogee. And as the alpha dog, he was always supposed to go through the door first. But he'd decided that doing battle with a super-size dog multiple times a day went in the category of "life's too short."

First stop, the cedar tree that grew next to the house. Diogee gave it a good dousing of piss, but that didn't mean he was done. D regarded his urine as a precious commodity, and he'd spend the rest of the walk squirting here, squirting there, announcing "this is mine," "this is mine," "and that over there, also mine."

"Not on the fence," David warned him as he opened the gate. He'd built the fence himself when he'd gotten the dog, using twisty tree branches that he thought worked with what he always thought of as his Hobbit-hole house. "Not on the fence," he repeated. He pulled a piece of freeze-dried liver out of his pocket—yes, he bribed his dog routinely—and used it to get Diogee away from the fence before he could mark it.

Diogee galloped down to the wax leaf privet that grew at the side of his neighbor's bungalow and got down to business. He had a technique where he leaned away from whatever he was aiming at, which allowed him to lift his leg farther up and so launch the spray as high as possible. The mutt was almost the size of a pony, but he seemed to want to leave a mark that said a Clydesdale-size beast had been there.

"Excellent work," David told the dog as they continued down the cobblestone sidewalk.

"Diogee, hey!" Zachary Acosta called from across the street.

Diogee lurched toward the boy. David pulled back on the leash until he'd done a car check, then let the dog tow him over to Zachary. Diogee immediately put his paws on the kid's shoulders, and Zachary thumped the dog's sides, their version of a bro hug.

When Diogee finally dropped his paws back to the ground, David got a real look at Zachary's face. There was an angry red circle about the size of a quarter between his eyebrows.

David didn't ask, but he had to force his eyes away. It was so bright and so symmetrical. "What's the up?" he asked. That's the way the kid used to say it when he was little, and it had become part of the language of their friendship.

"School, whatever, nothing," Zach answered.

Sometimes David could hardly believe Zachary was fourteen. How could it have been almost ten years since they started making their trips around the neighborhood? David and Clarissa had only moved in about a week before, and David had made sure to go running at least every few days to work off all the samples he ate when he was developing new recipes. He'd just started down the street when the Acostas' front door had burst open and Zachary had come barreling out wearing an Oakland A's T-shirt, track pants, and tiny Puma sneakers. He'd looked like David's Mini-Me, right down to the color of the Pumas—red and white.

"Wait! Wait! I come!" he yelled.

His mom, Megan, caught up to Zachary before he reached the sidewalk and swooped him up. The boy immediately started trying to free himself. "Sorry, David. He saw you running the other day, and that's all he's been talking about. I thought the gear would be enough."

"Hey, I can use a running buddy," David told her.

"You sure?" Megan asked.

"Definitely. Let's hit it, Zachary." The kid insisted, then and now, on getting the full "Zachary" every time. No "Zach"s. Megan put him down and he hurtled toward David. From that day on, they'd been running together, or the last few years, walking Diogee, at least three or four times a week.

"School, stuff, whatever," David repeated. "Care to elaborate?" Zachary had just started his first year of high school. David was sure there was more to say.

"Squirrel at four o'clock," Zachary announced.

David wrapped the leash around his hand a couple times in preparation. A few seconds later, Diogee spotted the squirrel and gave what David thought of as the Shoulder Popper, a sudden jerk and yank. The squirrel scampered up the trellis of the closest cottage, and Diogee gave an explosion of barks, telling the squirrel exactly what he would have done if he'd been free.

When he finished, Zachary said, "I signed up for the track

team. Cross-country. I wanted to do football, but my mom had a freak-out."

Mom might have been right, David thought. Over the summer, Zachary had shot up in height, but he was still all legs and arms and feet. David remembered that stage. He'd hardly been able to walk across a room without banging into something. Not the best time to be on a football field. Not that he'd say that to Zachary. "You've been running since you were five. You're a natural," he said instead, forbidding himself to take another look at that red circle between the kid's eyes. Had it really been a perfect circle? Could he have gotten whammed by a golf ball?

David was pretty sure Zachary's dad played golf, but it didn't seem likely he'd take Zachary along. Zachary and his father had an every-other-weekend thing, which ended up being one night every other weekend way too much of the time. From what Zachary said, they usually went to some trendy restaurant his dad's current girlfriend liked, where there wasn't usually anything Zachary wanted to eat. To be fair, Zachary didn't like a wide variety of food. He seemed to live off of peanut butter and Slim Jims and those red Swedish Fish candies.

They paused while Diogee stopped to sniff repeatedly at a ginkgo tree. "Checking his pee-mail," Zachary called it. After he did his lean and squirt, leaving a message back, they continued on. When they reached the corner—or the closest thing to a corner Storybook Court had, since nothing in the place had a solid right angle—Diogee took a left. The alpha dog always decided which way to go.

They'd only gone a few steps when they heard Addison Brewer yelling. Like Zachary, she hated nicknames. It was the full "Addison" or she'd pretend she didn't hear you. Her voice got louder as they walked. "You said you were going to come over. And you're not in the kitchen eating directly out of the fridge. And you haven't declared yourself King of the Remote.

So you're not here. Oh, wait. You could be stinking up the bathroom. No, not there. So, you're not here when you said you'd be. Again. And you didn't look sick in gym. I could see you from Algebra. So, don't even try that."

"The girl is a shrew," Zachary muttered, twisting his head around so only the back of his head would be visible from Addison's house.

"Do you have any classes with her this year?" David asked.

"English." Zachary managed to pack the word with disgust.

"Impressive lungs. She didn't have to take one breath during all that," David said. Zachary didn't comment, just kept walking with his head turned toward the street.

There was a brief pause in the girl's rant. "How much traffic can there be? I'm home, and I take the bus. You said you only had to go home for one minute. Which means you should have been here twenty minutes ago. We're over. We're seriously over. Seriously. Do not ever come over here again. I don't care how close you are. Turn around."

One of the windows of what everyone called the Rose Bungalow—because of the yellow roses painted on the shutters—opened. A second later a purple cell phone with a rhinestone skull on the case came flying out.

Zachary glanced over, then turned his head away again. "Shrew."

"Remember when you gave her flowers for her birthday?" David asked. Zachary glowered at him. Sometimes David forgot how sensitive teenage boys could be. Sometimes he remembered, but he still couldn't resist teasing the kid.

"I was in kindergarten and my mom got to take home flowers from work, because they changed them every couple days."

"Oh, right," David said, deciding to give Zachary a break.

They passed the house with the drawbridge and moat filled with sparking aqua water. Sometimes David felt like he was living inside a miniature golf course. Clarissa's grandmother had given them her place as a wedding present. She'd decided to move to a luxury assisted-living place in Westwood. Storybook Court had felt too cutesy to David at first, but it wasn't like they could afford to turn down a free house when they were barely in their twenties. And it grew on him. Now it was so tied up with memories of Clarissa that he couldn't imagine living anyplace else.

Thinking of miniature golf made him think of that circle on Zachary's face, and this time David shot it a glance before he could stop himself.

Zachary caught him. "I kind of messed up my face."

"What? I didn't—" David stopped. There was no point in bullshitting the kid. "What the hell did you do?"

"You know those things you use to wash your face, with the spin-y brush on the end?"

David nodded.

"My mom has one. When I got home from school, I decided I was going to get rid of these zits. If you use it too long in one place—you get this." Zachary jabbed the bull's-eye between his eyebrows with one finger.

The was the last explanation David had expected to hear. Personal hygiene wasn't a big priority for the kid. Megan had asked David to tell him "real men wear deodorant" a couple years ago when Zachary started getting that ripe sock smell, and David would have thought that was about where his grooming stopped. *Gotta be a girl in the picture,* he thought, but he kept his mouth shut. He'd let Zachary bring that up if and when he wanted to.

"It just happened?" David asked.

"Couple of hours ago," Zachary answered. "I'm not showing up at school like this. The zits were bad enough." He poked the red circle again.

"First, keep your fingers off it," David told him, and Zachary jammed his hands in his pockets. "Maybe try some ice? That might help," he suggested as they continued walking, sometimes half-jogging, following Diogee.

"Did it. It's hopeless," Zachary answered, rubbing the circle.

"No!" David burst out.

"Sorry," Zachary said, jerking his hand away.

"Not you. Diogee. Diogee, no!" Diogee had started turning in those tight little circles that always preceded him taking a dump. And he was on the Defranciscos' lawn. "Marie will have my head. Make that my balls." He started trying to yank Diogee off the grass. Diogee dug in. He'd found the spot he wanted. He started to squat.

David leaned down, wrapped one arm around his dog's middle, and half-dragged him down to the next house. He didn't know who'd moved in there, but they'd have to be more tolerant of dog poop than Marie. It wasn't like he wasn't planning to clean up. Diogee let out a howl that probably reminded the whole neighborhood that he had a good amount of hound dog somewhere in the mix.

"Oh, come on," David said. "As if it matters that much which patch of grass you use." Diogee bayed again, and this time there was an answer, a high, long yowl from a large tan-and-brown-striped cat sitting in the house's screened-in porch. Its golden eyes were locked on Diogee, sending out lasers of hatred. Diogee snapped his jaws in response.

"That's enough, tough guy." David pulled out a liver treat. Diogee's attention immediately snapped over to him. He couldn't believe he'd forgotten to use one when Diogee had been about to bring down the wrath of Marie. He hurled the treat as far as he could, and Diogee ran for it, David and Zachary on his tail.

Diogee snarfed up the treat. He was an addict, and David was his supplier. That meant that, even though Diogee went out the door first, even though he chose which direction they walked, David would always be the alpha dog. Unless Diogee figured out how to obtain cash and get himself to Pet World.

"So, what do you think? Two days?" Zachary asked. He pointed to the red circle, but didn't touch it. "I don't want to miss too much practice. The track coach seemed pretty strict."

David could help with most of the problems that came up for a fourteen-year-old boy. He'd been one himself. But the skin-care malfunction was out of his league. "What I think is that we need an expert." He took out another liver treat. "Turn it around, Big D."

"Where are we going?" Zachary asked as they changed directions.

"Ruby's. She used to do makeup before she became a set dresser. She'll fix you up," David answered.

Zachary stopped dead. He looked as unwilling to move as Diogee had back on the Defranciscos' lawn. "I'm not wearing makeup to school. And anyway, I don't even really know her."

"Think of it as a special effect. And you know her well enough. Besides, I'm friends with her," David told him. Zachary didn't move. "Just let her try. If you don't like it, I'll teach you the best way to fake the flu. All you need is a can of extra-chunky soup."

Zachary didn't say yes, but he started walking toward Ruby's. "Chunky soup doesn't really look like puke."

"It sounds like it, though. You make sure your mom is close enough to the bathroom to hear, then start pouring it in the toilet," David explained.

Zachary snickered. "Sweet."

They followed the curve in the sidewalk, and Ruby's house came into sight. David felt like he'd been gut-punched. How'd he forgotten it was September fifteenth? It was one of Clarissa's favorite days, had been one of her favorite days. She'd never missed helping Ruby decorate the witch's cottage for Christmas.

Seeing something that made her so happy should have been a good thing. But it made him feel like a hole was opening right beneath his rib cage. For the second time in a week, he'd been surprised by how sharp his grief could still feel.

"You okay?" Zachary asked.

"Yeah," David told him. "Yeah," he said again, so he'd believe it himself.

He was okay. But he'd been right the other night with Adam. He wasn't ready to get something started with another woman. No matter what his friend thought, it was still too soon.

MacGyver left Jamie sleeping and made his way to the kitchen. He pawed open the cabinet under the sink and gave a short growl of annoyance. He reminded himself he had to be patient with his person. She was a human, and that meant that her nose was pretty much just a useless blob on her face. He hadn't been expecting this, though. She'd ignored his gift for almost two days. Then, finally, she'd picked up the hand towel. Yeah, she'd picked it up—then sprayed it with something that blocked out almost all the lonely smell he'd been trying to get her to notice, and rubbed it all over the table. He couldn't stop himself from letting out another little growl as he flicked the cabinet door shut.

Patience, he told himself again. He couldn't expect Jamie to understand with only one try. It had taken her a few times to find his favorite spot to be scratched. Right behind the whiskers. Pure bliss. It had also taken her a few times to realize she should never give his belly more than three rubs at a time. He'd had to give her a light bite to get that through her head. He hadn't liked to do it, but she'd had to be trained.

MacGyver just needed to put more effort into making his person see that what she needed to be happy was the right packmate. He was up for the challenge. Anything for Jamie.

She was flawed, true, but she was his. He trotted to the porch and slipped through the hole in the screen. Before he could do anything else, he had to deal with the stench. He went straight to the palm closest to the fountain and gave it a good scratching, obliterating the odor of dog piss with his own musky smell. There. Now he could focus on his mission.

He tilted his head back and flicked air into his mouth with his tongue, smelling and tasting at the same time. The loneliness was strongest in the same place it had been two nights ago. He wondered if he could train Jamie to use her tongue to get information about her surroundings, including his gifts. Doubtful. If her sense of taste was working correctly, she'd never eat grapefruit. He could hardly stand to watch her jab her spoon into the disgusting thing.

It didn't matter. Mac's nose and tongue were good enough for both of them. He started toward the lonely smell. Unfortunately, the reek of dog pee got stronger and stronger the closer he got to his goal, so strong he almost wished he had a human nose. Almost. He could never actually make the sacrifice. He slowed his trot and dropped into a stalk as the house with The Smell came into sight.

That dog Mac had seen earlier stood in the yard, a grotesque mishmash mutt with long, floppy ears, a long, wide body, long legs, an oversized head, and a mouth that excelled at slobber production. Mac knew he wouldn't have a problem eluding the bonehead, but he knew the mutt could bark as well as he drooled, and Mac didn't need a commotion when he was in stealth mode.

He decided he'd come back a little later. For now, he'd do some exploring. He caught a whiff of a different strain of loneliness, and decided to track it. It led to a house with a window in front open so wide it was like an invitation. Mac accepted by leaping inside. He landed softly, quickly assessing the room.

Even if he'd landed with the bang of a firecracker, he probably wouldn't have woken up the person sleeping on the sofa. Her scent was potent, an odor Mac had learned to associate with a human female who wasn't a little girl or an adult. Their sweat was especially strong, although they almost always tried to disguise it. This one's true scent was masked by something that smelled sort of like apples and melons and flowers, but sweeter and sharper at the same time. Mac could still make out the odor of anger coming off her, anger mixed with a little loneliness.

She wasn't the one producing the scent he was tracking. He followed that scent out of the room and down the hall. The girl inside was young. A young one shouldn't have such a powerful lonely smell. She still needed a pack leader to survive, and it didn't smell like she had one, at least not one who was nearby. Mac decided to find her one. He was a cat with skills to spare. They shouldn't be wasted. He leapt up on the bed and brushed his cheek against the girl's, a silent promise that he'd be back.

But now it was time to return to his primary mission. On his way out of the house, Mac paused to take a few licks of the potato chips lying on the table near the older girl. He didn't especially like chips, but he loved the salt.

When Mac got back to the house with The Smell, the bonehead was still in the front yard, sniffing around under the tree that Mac needed to climb to get into the house. The dog dropped into a squat, and Mac took the opportunity to race toward the tree. He scrambled straight up the otherwise-occupied dog's back and shimmied through the window.

The dog started yammering, but Mac didn't care. The opportunity to use the bonehead as an on-ramp had been too perfect to pass by. And anyway, dogs were always barking about something. They didn't have the brain power to decide what was important and what wasn't. "Diogee, shut it!" he heard a man call from downstairs. His voice didn't have any anxiety or fear in it. Clearly, he didn't rely on the dog for warnings. A sensible human, then. Except that he'd chosen to live with a bonehead.

It didn't take Mac long to find the perfect thing, ripe and rich with scent. Jamie would have to understand his message this time!

CHAPTER 3

"'Bye, Mac. I'll be bringing you a present when I come back," Jamie called, then edged her way out the front door and shut it behind her as quickly as possible. There was something black and yellow curled on the doormat. Snake! She jumped back.

Actually, now that she'd gotten a second look, she didn't think the thing really looked like a snake. She gave it a tentative poke with her foot, then when it didn't slither away or anything equally disgusting, she reached down and picked it up, using two fingers as tweezers.

Just a sock. Well, not just a sock. A black sock with rows of yellow sasquatches on it. Jamie smiled. Cute.

Her smile faded. This was the second time she'd found something she knew wasn't hers on the doorstep. How'd they gotten there? She'd heard about LA's legendary Santa Ana winds. They sounded strong enough to blow around a lot more than a sock and a hand towel. But there hadn't been much of a breeze, forget about the so-called devil winds, since she'd arrived.

Both items had been on the doormat, too. Not on the lawn. Not even on the two steps that led to the front door. They'd been right on the doormat. Had someone put them there? But, why? A sock and a hand towel? That was just random.

"Jamie, coffee!"

Al's voice pulled Jamie's attention away from her thoughts. "What?"

"Coffee," Al repeated. He was on his porch, holding a mug out to her. She'd barely stepped out of the house, and he had coffee for her. Did he—and Marie—do anything other than look out the window and watch the neighbors?

Maybe not. But it was harmless. There was nothing so bad about being offered delicious hot coffee. It was nice. Neighborly. Could Al or Marie have left the stuff on her doormat? Maybe they thought she could use a hand towel. But one sock? Maybe they'd left a pair and one had . . . disappeared . . . somehow.

Only one way to find out. Jamie walked across her lawn and over to the Defranciscos' porch railing. "Thanks," she said, taking the coffee. "You and Marie have been so sweet. Did you, by any chance, leave me this?" She held up the sasquatch sock.

Al peered at it. "Never saw it before."

"What about a hand towel? A white hand towel?"

Al peered at her.

"It was on my doormat the day after I moved in," Jamie added.

"Not me."

"Marie, maybe?"

"Marie!" Al hollered. "Did you leave a dish towel for Jamie?"

"Hand towel," Jamie corrected as Marie stepped out on the porch.

"You need a hand towel?" Marie asked.

"No, it's just that I found one outside my door. I thought maybe you left it," Jamie explained.

Marie frowned. "Why would I do that?"

Good question, Jamie thought. "Just checking," she said. "Maybe the person who moved out dropped it and I didn't notice it at first." But that wasn't how the sock got there. She would have seen it before that morning.

"I'm going to the pet store," she said. "Do you want anything while I'm out?"

Al grunted. "Got everything we need," Marie said, then returned to the house.

"I'll bring the mug back later," Jamie told Al. She started across the courtyard, then realized she was still holding the sock. She backtracked to her house and shoved it through the mail slot in her door. She'd deal with it later.

As she started for the street again, she heard Mac give a long, aggrieved yowl. Maybe getting outside would make him happier about his new home.

Jamie stood in front of the dog/cat leash display in Pet World, staring. The huge selection had left her paralyzed. "Stop being ridiculous," she muttered. "You're making some big life decisions right now, but this is not one of them." She flushed as she realized a tall guy with an enormous bag of dog food slung over one shoulder had come around the corner just in time to hear her talking to herself. "Can't decide if my cat is more of a superhero type or a pot-smoking Rastafarian monkey type," she told him. Why had she thought that would make the situation *less* embarrassing?

"You're picking the leash by your cat's personality?" the guy asked. "You're a better person than I am. I slapped a pink one on my beast. We're in a battle over who is going to be alpha dog, and I thought it would give me an edge. It's that one." He pointed to a light pink leash patterned with dog bones. "If I was really trying to emasculate him, although surgically he's already there, I guess I should have gone for the pink one with hearts."

Jamie laughed. "I think there's a flaw in your plan for dog dominion. Dogs are colorblind." What was she doing? Was she flirting? She shouldn't be flirting. This was not The Year of the Exceptionally Cute Guy. This was her Year of Me.

The guy shook his head. "Actually, they're more spectrum-challenged, like someone with red-green colorblindness. I actually have an app that lets you see in dog vision." He grimaced. "Can we just forget I said that last part? In any case, I think Diogee can feel the pink and that it makes it harder for him to try to dominate me."

"Because pink is a girly color and women are naturally submissive," Jamie said.

The guy's eyes widened. "I didn't mean it like that. I was just—Can we just forget I said anything at all?" He shifted the bag of dog food, looking uncomfortable.

"I wasn't trying to—I was just busting your chops," Jamie answered. Didn't matter if she *had* been attempting to flirt. She'd negated it with that gender-politics-of-pink comment. "But I'll wipe my brain of this conversation if you agree to forget you caught me talking to myself about which leash my cat would prefer."

"Done," the guy said. He stared at her for a moment, then slapped the bag of dog food. "Gotta go pay for this." He headed down the aisle. Jamie took a peek at his butt—nice—even though it was The Year of Me, and anyway objectifying men was as bad as objectifying women. She returned her attention to the wall of leashes and decided on a plain bright red one that would go great with Mac's tan-and-brown-striped fur.

About an hour and a half later, she stepped out her front door with Mac in her arms. Probably a third of that time had been used paying and driving home. The rest of the time had been used for getting the snazzy new leash and harness onto

Mac, which included yowling (him) and fighting back tears of frustration (her).

"Now, see," Jamie said to her cat as she plunked him down on her little patch of lawn, "isn't this great? You're outside. I was, in fact, doing something nice for you, not torturing you."

Mac didn't turn his head toward her. He didn't even twitch an ear. Clearly, she wasn't even close to being forgiven. Well, fine. She wasn't sure she'd forgiven him, either. She took a fast picture of his profile, then held her cell in front of his face so he could see it. "Just so you know, this is what an ungrateful cat looks like." He continued to ignore her.

Deep, cleansing breath, Jamie told herself. Sometimes dealing with Mac required a deep, cleansing breath. She decided not to attempt a walk quite yet. Mac needed some more time to adjust. Instead, she decided to take a few pictures of her bungalow. First a closeup of the front door, she decided. The door set the tone of the whole place. It wasn't a rectangle, for starters. Storybook style definitely wasn't about right angles. The door was shaped like an oval with the bottom cut off, and had huge, wonderfully ridiculously huge, wrought-iron latches and an equally huge round doorknocker.

Jamie made sure she had the ivy growing over the door in the frame, then clicked. She wondered if she could climb up on the roof. She'd love a closeup of the way the shingles had been set in uneven waves. But that could wait. There was plenty she could do from the ground. Ooh! Like the multipaned window over the kitchen sink.

She took a step in that direction. Mac took no steps. She should have gone for a Snugli instead of a harness. Except that would probably have taken an extra hour to get him in. Jamie stayed where she was and used the zoom to get an extreme closeup of one of the door latches.

"Well, hey there, Toots. I haven't seen you around."

Jamie gave a little jump. The voice had come from right behind her. She turned, managing to loop Mac's new leash around her ankles. "I live here," she explained, eyes on the ground as she freed one foot. "I just moved in," she added, as she freed the other.

"Just moved in?" he repeated.

Jamie was finally able to look up. The man who'd been speaking to her was maybe late fifties, with blond hair straight out of the nineties—aggressively gelled and spiked, with frosted tips. He wore khakis, a light blue button-down shirt, and a fishing vest with a dazzling number of pockets. A patch of sheepskin on the front held an assortment of pristine flies. Around his neck, a lanyard strung with wooden beads had several equally pristine tools hanging from it. The only one Jamie recognized was a pair of needle-nose pliers.

"You just moved in?" he asked again. She couldn't see his eyes behind the blue lenses of his round, wire-framed shades, but she had the feeling he hadn't blinked since they'd started talking.

"Uh-huh. That's my place right there. I was just getting some pictures," she told him. "So, you live in Storybook Court, too?"

He pulled down the shades and grinned at her. There was something kind of fake about it, and something really fake about his Southern accent. "I thought I was asking the questions," he said.

"We can't take turns? I ask something, you ask something," Jamie suggested. She was a little relieved when the Defranciscos' door opened and Al ambled out with a broom in one hand.

"Sport!" the man exclaimed. "Toots here says she just moved in. That right?"

Al nodded, then looked at Mac, taking in the leash and harness. "My sympathies," he said to the cat and began to sweep the front steps. Mac gave a long, high yowl in response.

"Saw her skulking around, and I thought I should check it out," the man told Al. He turned to Jamie and held out his hand. "Hud Martin."

"I was hardly skulking," Jamie said as they shook. "I was standing in front of my own home with my own cat taking a picture."

"When you've seen what I've seen . . ." Hud let the words trail off as he sauntered away.

"Wow," Jamie said, watching him go. Al gave one of his grunts.

She took a few more pictures of the latches and the door-knocker, feeling a little jolt of pleasure that for one whole year the magical fairy-tale house was hers. She looked down at her cat. "Okay, MacGyver. Let's move it out." She took four purposeful steps toward the kitchen window she wanted to photograph, then stopped. The leash had reached its limit. She gave it a gentle tug. Mac's tail began to whip back and forth.

Jamie hesitated. The best thing to do was just admit defeat and take Mac back into the house. But how to get him there? She couldn't pick him up right now. She knew what that lashing tail meant. It meant, "You touch, you get scratched."

Maybe if he knew they were going back inside, he'd be willing to walk on the leash. Jamie moved as close to the door as she could. "Come on, Mac-Mac. Come on, pretty boy." Mac didn't move. His tail whipped a little faster. "Okay, I admit it. I made a mistake. You cannot be harnessed. Let's just go back in the house and I'll take it off. And then we'll play with Mousie. That would be fun, right? You love Mousie." Jamie's voice got higher and higher with every word.

She heard the Defranciscos' door click shut. She looked over and saw that Al had disappeared. She didn't blame him. She'd sounded like a demented preschool teacher. Should she try letting Mac off the leash outside? She'd gotten him back in when he'd escaped the other day. But the other day he wasn't pissed off. Maybe she should—

The Defranciscos' door opened again. Without a word, Al threw something to her. Jamie looked at it and gave a relieved smile. It was a can of tuna. "Thanks," she said. Marie appeared behind him holding a can opener. She handed it to Al, and Al tossed it to Jamie. "And another thanks," Jamie added.

She opened the tuna, let Mac get a whiff, and started toward the house, willing him to follow her.

He did.

"I'm gonna have to card you before you eat one of those," David warned Lucy when she picked up one of the cupcakes he had cooling. "There's Jager in the ganache inside, and there will be butterscotch schnapps in the frosting once they're finished."

Lucy just smiled in reply, then took a bite. "Yums."

"They're for the Corner Bar. They want to try selling cupcake shots, so I'm experimenting with combos," David said. He gave her a pipette filled with Jager. "Squirt this on if you want more kick. That's the way the bar will be serving them up."

"You should make some rum and coke ones. With those squishy candy coke bottles on top," Lucy suggested.

"Been done," he told her. "But what hasn't?"

He was sure Lucy had a reason for coming by the bakery while he was working, and he was pretty sure what it was. It had been almost a week since he and Adam had gone out, and they'd decided he needed checking up on. He decided to make it easy for her. "I'm fine," he announced. "You and Adam don't have to worry about me."

Lucy's face flushed. "What? I wasn't—We weren't," she began, then gave it up. "Okay, you're right. I wanted to see if you were okay. Adam said you had kind of a hard night when you guys were out."

"Not really. Just choked a little trying to talk to a woman in the bar," he answered. "Also, I made a complete ass out of myself talking to a woman at the pet store this morning. I'm out of practice."

Lucy looked intrigued. "You talked to a woman at the pet store—without Adam there to egg you on? Do tell."

David shrugged. "She was picking out a leash for her cat, and I showed her which one I got for Diogee. It wasn't like I was trying to pick her up. You know how you just fall into conversations with people in stores."

"You said you were out of practice. Out of practice means out of practice talking to a woman you're interested in, right?" Lucy asked. "Besides, you must have done more than talk pet supplies or you wouldn't feel like you made an ass out of yourself."

Had he been interested? There'd been something about her, standing there talking to herself. Something that had made him decide to talk to her instead of walking by.

Lucy took another bite of cupcake. "This is heaven. I feel like I'm always supposed to be setting a healthy eating example for the kids. I actually scarfed down a Snickers in the closet a couple weeks ago. I felt like a criminal. Anyway, what'd you say to her?"

"Something about making Diogee wear a pink leash so it would be easier for me to be the alpha dog."

"Yeah, you were sort of an ass," Lucy said. "Like, of course, making your dog wear something girly would make him more obedient. But you're cute. And you're charming. You could have turned it around."

"There was nothing to turn around. I wasn't trying to start anything up," David protested.

"The facts indicate otherwise," Lucy said. "I bet she was hot." She took a second cupcake.

David was about to say he hadn't really been paying attention, but he realized he could call up a detailed picture—curly butterscotch-blond hair scooped into a messy bun, brown eyes, dimples, deep ones, and a great voice. Nice body, curvy, not that he was going to tell Lucy that. "She was cute," he admitted.

"Talking to her was good, even if you screwed it up," Lucy told him. "That's how you get back in practice. That's why I think you should do counterpart.com. Practice. You go out with some women. If it doesn't go well, who cares? You don't have to ever see them again. But you get used to being . . ." She hesitated.

"Single," he finished for her.

"Yeah." She touched his arm. "Yeah."

David put together a bakery box and started loading it with the cupcake experiments he'd already finished. "Those better not be for me," Lucy said. "The kids will find them. They're bad enough when they eat sugar. I don't want to see them both drunk and on a sugar high." She grinned. "I'll just have to eat some more here. And while I'm here, I could take some sexy baker man pics for you to use on Counterpart. Adam said he's working on your profile."

She wasn't going to stop pushing. Neither was Adam.

Unless he just told her the truth. Unless he just told her he was barely holding it together. No, it wasn't that bad. Except when it was. And this week it was a lot. "I'm not ready, Luce." She started to protest, and he held up one hand to stop her. "At the bar, I almost lost it. It was like all of a sudden it had been days instead of years since I lost her. And then it happened again a few days later. You know our friend Ruby, I mean *my* friend Ruby." Sometimes he still said "our," when he meant "my."

"With the huge Christmas party," Lucy said.

"Yeah. Her," David answered. "And every year she starts decorating for Christmas in September—September fifteenth. And pretty much since they became friends, Clarissa would spend as much of the day as she could helping her. So I'm walking Diogee, I turn the corner, see that the house is decorated, and—wham, I got that feeling again. I thought I'd gotten past that. It took a long time, but I really haven't had that kind of grief, the kind that sucks the air out of you, for probably more than a year. And now, twice in one week. I can't think of starting up something when I'm still feeling like this."

Lucy broke open the pipette of Jager and squirted it on her tongue. "I'm about to go all therapist," she warned him.

"Okay," David said. Because it wasn't like anything he said would stop her.

"Maybe you've been feeling that intense grief because you *are* ready. And being ready feels like you're really letting Clarissa go." Lucy's eyes flicked over his face as she looked for his reaction.

David struggled not to show how hard he'd been hit by her words, by how true they felt. "It's possible," he answered. He flipped a page in the notebook he used to write down recipe ideas.

"I'll let you get back to work." Lucy snagged one last cupcake. "You know you can talk to me whenever."

"I know. But I'm fine," David said. And he was. He liked his job. He had some good friends. He had a big, stupid dog. He didn't need anything else.

Mac took his secret exit through the rip in the screen door. His skin prickled. He could still feel that harness caging his body. How could Jamie have done that to him? She usually understood him much better than that. She definitely hadn't understood what he was trying to tell her with the sock. She hadn't even tried! He'd been watching her though the window, and she'd shoved it back into the house without giving it a single sniff. Then later she'd thrown it away. He'd dumped over the trash so she'd have to pick it up again, and she'd called him a bad kitty. He'd had to remind himself that she was a human and couldn't be expected to understand everything. When she threw the sock away *again*, he retrieved it. He'd try to get her to actually smell it again later.

He was even more determined to find a way to make her happy, no matter how long it took. He wanted that for her, because she was his person and he loved her. But it could have benefits for Mac, too. If Jamie had a human around and got her happy smell back, maybe she'd stop doing ridiculous things like trying to attach herself to him with a big string. He couldn't stand to think of it as a leash. Everyone knew leashes were for dogs. Did MacGyver look like a dog? Uh, no.

He took several breaths of the cool night air, and the itchy harness sensation and the horror of being on a lea—, on a *string*, faded. He was free. The neighborhood was his. He took off at a lope. He had things to do.

Mac slowed down, then stopped when he spotted something unfamiliar in one of the yards. It looked like an animal was there in the shadows, a large one. But he didn't smell any animal. He crept closer. The animal-thing didn't move. Mac crept even closer.

Okay, he'd seen one of these more than once through the apartment window of his old home. But it had only been out during the coldest months. That's why he didn't recognize it at first. It was a plastic reindeer.

He padded up to it, and took a sniff just to be certain. Definitely nothing that had ever been alive. His ears twitched. Someone was moving through the house. A moment later, the door opened. A woman stepped out. Mac got a faint whiff of Jamie's smell on her. That reassured him. The woman poured water on the plant next to the door. Then she walked across the yard. Mac slid into the shadows under the reindeer. He watched as she hung something in a tree. It smelled familiar, too, like the peanut butter Jamie ate.

Was she a pack leader? She was leaving food for someone.

As she walked back toward the house, he realized that there was a thread of, not loneliness exactly, but something like it, in her mix of smells. He remembered the lonely little one. Maybe this woman had what the girl needed. He decided he would leave a message for her.

But first, he needed to bring something else to Jamie. Something she wouldn't try to throw away.

CHAPTER 4

Mac's loud breakfast-now yowl invaded Jamie's dreams. This morning it was more like a wail, higher and longer than usual. "Mac, come on, is that necessary? We both know you aren't, in fact, starving," she grumbled, still half-asleep. She forced her eyelids up. Mac was sitting on her chest, staring at her. The wail came again, and unless her cat had been practicing ventriloquism in his spare time, it hadn't come from him.

The wail came a third time. Now that she'd reached one-hundred-percent wakefulness, it sounded like it was coming from a little girl! Jamie scrambled out of bed, yanked on yesterday's jeans, and pulled a sweater on over the big T-shirt she used to sleep in, then she rushed outside. Al and Marie already stood in their yard. Jamie hurried over to join them. "What's going on?" Jamie exclaimed.

"I think it's the little Brewer girl," Marie said, frowning.

"Is she—" Jamie was interrupted by another of the wails. This time it sounded like "Paaaaaula." Jamie tried again. "Is she—"

This time she was interrupted by Hud Martin coming around the corner of the Defranciscos' house. "Hey there, friends," he called as he walked toward them. The sun glinted off the white-blond highlights of his freshly gelled hair.

Al gave one of his grunts. This one sounded put-upon.

"I need to talk to you. We've had a burglary," Hud announced, pulling down his sunglasses to look at them. Jamie was pretty sure he looked at her a little longer than the others. "Over at the Brewers'."

"Did he hurt the little girl?" Marie demanded.

"You ever had a toy you loved more than anything?" Hud asked, his fake drawl getting broader and faker. "Me, it was a Stretch Armstrong. For lil' Riley, it's her plastic pony. And that's what was stolen."

"Pauuuuula." The wail came again.

"That's the pony's name, Paula. Riley's going around the neighborhood looking for it. Listening to that cry, I'd say it hurt worse than a bite from a bluefish," Hud answered. "I promised her I'd get it back." He centered the pliers hanging from the lanyard around his neck.

"Anything else taken?" Al asked.

"I'd say that's enough," Hud said. "I'd also say it's not going to be the last burglary. I think the thief was just getting a feel for the water last night, and decided to nab the pony as a practice run." He looked at Jamie again. She forced herself to hold his gaze.

Marie gave an exasperated huff. "All that commotion over a toy. She probably just dropped it somewhere."

"That's a negative." Hud turned toward Marie, allowing his staring contest with Jamie to end. "The older sister, Addison, said Riley won't go to sleep without it. So, she's sure it was tucked in bed with Riley last night. But this morning—it was gone."

"So, it fell under the bed," Marie said.

"I already did a complete search. Not there." Hud gave Marie a wink. "I know you see pretty much everything that goes on around here. You see anything unusual last night, anyone around who doesn't belong?"

Marie crossed her arms. "I have more important things to do than stare out the window."

Jamie knew Marie spent a good amount of time doing exactly that, but she didn't comment.

"That's a no, then?" Hud asked.

Riley gave another wail.

"I'm not listening to that all morning." Marie turned and started for her house. Al gave a grunt of agreement and followed her.

Hud watched them for a moment, then turned back to Jamie. "Not especially cooperative, were they, Toots?"

"I'm sure if either of them had seen anything, they would have told you." Actually, Jamie was sure if Marie had seen anything, she'd have chased the burglar off herself.

"What about you? You have anything to tell me?" He pushed his sunglasses back up.

"I went in pretty much right after I saw you yesterday," Jamie said. "And, anyway, I haven't been here long enough to know who belongs and who doesn't."

"Pretty early when I saw you," Hud commented. "Pretty early for you to go in for the night."

"I still have a lot of stuff to unpack and get organized." She realized she'd sounded sort of defensive. But the way he'd said it, it was almost like she was a suspect, a suspect with a shaky alibi.

"Where'd you move here from?"

"Pennsylvania. Avella."

"Small town?"

"Definitely."

"So, you've just moved here from a Podunk town, and you spend your night *organizing* instead of getting out there and seeing some of the LA nightlife?"

His questions came fast, almost before she'd answered the previous one. It really was starting to feel like an interrogation. And she was feeling annoyed. Except, why *hadn't* she gone out? She should be going out. The Year of Me didn't mean The Year of Hiding in the House.

Not the point. "It's none of your business how I spend my time. I can tell you for sure I wasn't stealing a little girl's toys."

"What did—"

This time Jamie didn't let him finish. "I have to feed my cat," she informed him, then headed for the house, feeling a little pathetic. She did do other things than organize and take care of Mac. Yesterday she'd gone out. She'd gone to the pet store and bought Mac a leash and a harness—wait, that was cat care. But she'd also taken pictures. And she'd worked on her list of stuff she liked. She had nothing to feel even sort of pathetic about.

As she reached for her funky doorknob, she noticed something on the welcome mat. Another sock. A sweat sock this time. She studied it, as if that would give her a clue how it got there. Just a regular tube sock. No goofy decorations, just a couple blue stripes at the top.

"Whatcha got there?" Hud called.

"Nothing," Jamie answered without turning around. She hurried inside. She wasn't going to let herself get sucked into a second interrogation.

"This is getting freaky," she said. She'd put a few empty boxes by the door to take out to the garbage. She grabbed a small one and put the sock inside, then got the hand towel out from under the sink and stuck it inside, too. She didn't know why. It wasn't like someone was going to ask for them back. They weren't anything valuable.

What possible reason could anyone have for leaving those things on the mat? Was it a prank? There were some kids in the neighborhood. But if it was a prank, it was a pretty stupid one. She put the box in the narrow broom closet and shut the door. Maybe it—

Mac pulled her away from her thoughts by uttering a particularly put-upon yowl. "Breakfast, I know, I know. Come on." She walked to the kitchen and opened the cupboard where she kept his food. "What'll it be?" she asked. "Trout? Lamb? Elk?"

There was no answering meow. She looked down—no Mac. Okay, he was a picky eater, but that didn't mean food wasn't way up there on his list of priorities. What was up? She headed back to the porch. Mac was batting the sasquatch sock around like it was made of catnip. He must have gotten into the trash again! Was he acting out because he wasn't happy about the move? He'd never dug around in the trash before, even when he was a crazy kitten.

Mac snatched the sock up in his teeth, then tossed his head, letting the sock fly across the room. As soon as it landed, he pounced on it, then rolled on his back with it clutched between his paws. A few seconds later, he gave a twist-spring to his feet and flung the sock onto one of Jamie's feet. She picked it up and tossed it across the room, expecting him to go bounding after it. Not that Mac would ever deign to play fetch, but he did like to chase.

He didn't chase this time. He walked over to the sock, picked it up, and returned it to Jamie's foot. "Since you're determined to have it, I'll put it in your toy box," she said. She stuck it in the tub that held his Mousie, the laser pointer, the feather stick, and pretty much one of every other cat toy made. The sock had made Mac happier than most of them. "There, now it's nice and safe." She gave the tub a pat and smiled at Mac.

He was giving her The Stare. His tail wasn't whipping like crazy the way it had when she'd forced him into the harness, but The Stare definitely meant he wasn't happy with her. "I thought you were done with it for now. My bad." Jamie took the sock back out of the tub and tossed it to Mac. He didn't even glance at it, just continued administering The Stare.

Jamie gave him a slow blink. She'd read an article that called it a "kitty kiss," because it was a sign of love, an indicator that there was no need for fighting or rivalry. When she gave Mac The Blink, he almost always blinked back. Not this time. It was like he'd decided he would never blink again.

"I don't know what's got your tail in a knot," she told him. He'd cuddled up on her head last night the way he always did, so she didn't think he was still mad about the leash and harness. She'd snapped at him when he'd gotten trash all over the kitchen floor, but he hadn't seemed to care. He never cared when she scolded him.

Why was she even trying to figure it out? He was a cat. He had moods.

Jamie left him sitting there, put the sock in the box with the other stuff that had been left outside her door, then filled his food bowl. After she took a shower and got dressed, Mac was still sitting in the screened-in porch. He'd probably blinked sometime while she was gone, but he was pretending he hadn't.

"I'm heading out to explore," she told him. "I'd bring you along, but you hate the leash and possibly me, so you have to stay home."

Do I talk to Mac too much? she wondered as she stepped outside. *Nah,* she decided. You had a cat, you talked to it. That was normal. Or was it just crazy-cat-lady normal? Wait, was she a crazy cat lady? Nah. Or if she was, then it was too late to do anything about it.

Al was back outside on his front porch, washing a window with what smelled like vinegar. "You ever get a day off?" she asked. It seemed like he was almost always doing some little job outside.

"Secret to a long marriage. Don't spend too much time together," Al answered without turning away from the window. A second later his front door opened and a thin hand held out a cup of coffee. Al took it. The hand retreated and the door shut.

Al turned around and handed the cup to Jamie over the porch railing. "I don't want to take your coffee," she protested.

He nodded his head toward a cup on the little table that sat between two rockers. "That's mine."

"Thanks, Marie," Jamie yelled. She thought she saw the kitchen curtain twitch. She took a sip, so good, then said, "It's gotten quiet over here. Has Paula the Pony been found?' "

Al shrugged. "Maybe. Maybe the girl just wore herself out screaming."

"What's the deal with that Hud Martin guy?" Jamie asked. "He was acting like a real pony had been stolen, and like I might be the thief."

Al picked up his own coffee. "Never gotten over being on that show."

"What show?"

"Something PI." He returned to his window.

The door opened again, and Marie came out. "He was a PI on the show, but the show was called *Catch of the Day*," she told Jamie. "You didn't recognize him?"

Jamie shook her head. "Never heard of the show."

Helen appeared on her porch. "You forgot sugar again," she said, putting a coffee cup on the railing.

"I never forget anything," Marie said. She pointed at Jamie. "She's never heard of *Catch of the Day*."

"Too young," Al commented over his shoulder.

"He played a PI living in Florida. Every episode he started off to go fly fishing somewhere, but then he'd find a dead body or some woman would ask him for help, and he'd have to work on the case," Helen explained.

"It was on about ten years ago. You should remember it," Marie added.

"It was on about thirty years ago," Al corrected.

"It was on when my niece Valerie got married. Remember, Jonathan had his hair the same way Hud wore it on the show. The same way it is now. All the young men were wearing it that way back then. And Valerie got married—" Marie took a moment to do some silent calculations. "In eighty-nine."

"About thirty years ago," Al muttered.

The mail carrier headed over to them. She was probably in her early forties, with her hair in a gray-streaked braid. Her muscular legs showed the amount of walking she did on the job.

"Maybe I've seen him in something else," Jamie said. "What was he in after that?"

"A couple guest spots," Marie answered.

At the same time Al said, "Nothing."

"Who are we talking about?" the mail carrier asked.

"Hud Martin," Helen answered. "We're trying to remember if he was ever in anything after his show."

"He played an agoraphobic on an episode of *Quantum Leap,* a murder suspect on *Murder, She Wrote*—didn't do it—a murder suspect on *Law and Order*—did do it—and friend of the big brother on *Everybody Loves Raymond,*" the woman rattled off, shifting her mailbag higher on her shoulder.

"Wow. I think somebody's a fangirl," Jamie teased.

The woman blushed. Not just her cheeks. The color spread all the way down her throat. Even the tips of her ears went bright red.

"No, not me. I just play a lot of trivia. I'm on a team. The Trivia Newton-Johns," the woman said. She smiled at Jamie. "I'm Sheila, your friendly neighborhood mail gal. And you're the new 185 Glass Slipper Street, right?" Jamie nodded, and Sheila handed Jamie a grocery store circular. "I'm only supposed to put mail in the box, but I'm a rebel." She waved and headed back down the walkway, dozens of colorful keychains bouncing on the strap of her bag.

"She must be the star of her trivia team," Jamie said. "Did you hear how fast she came up with Hud's credits? Not even a second's hesitation." She looked over at Al. "So, when you said Hud never got over the show, you mean that's why he's trying to turn the disappearance of Paula the Pony into the start of a rash of burglaries?" Jamie asked Al.

"Wouldn't be surprised if he didn't take the thing just so he could find it," Al answered. He crumpled up a fresh newspaper and got back to work on the windows.

"What do you think?" Jamie asked Marie.

"I still say it's under her bed or somewhere in the house. I'm sure that place is a wreck. Those two kids are left there alone almost all the time. Mom works till all hours. No dad in sight." Marie tsked. "Addison takes Riley back and forth to preschool. I don't know what they do the rest of the time. Watch TV and eat junk food, probably."

Jamie raised her eyebrows. "Hope it's not too bad." She didn't know what else to say. She took another swallow of coffee.

"I'll send Al over there with some macaroni and a salad tonight," Marie said.

"Paaaula! Paaaula!"

"Got a second wind," Al noted, still working on the windows.

"I hope her sister's trying to help her find it. Or at least trying to distract her," Jamie said. The little girl sounded heartbroken.

"Paaula!"

"I'm going to go put in some earplugs," Marie told Jamie. "Do you want a pair?"

Jamie shook her head. "I think I'm going to take a walk, get to know the neighborhood a little better," Jamie said. "Any suggestions?"

"The Walk of Fame starts a few blocks away from here. Hollywood's not the best at this end, but you'll be fine during the day. It's not a bad walk." She headed inside.

Jamie had seen the part of the Walk of Fame outside Grauman's, but decided it could be fun to walk the whole thing and see all the names. Plus, she got some good ideas when she walked. Maybe she'd come up with some new things for her List of Likes.

It took her about ten minutes to reach the first star—Benny Goodman. She didn't know much about him. Famous Big Band guy . . . And that was about it.

As she continued down the block, there were so many names she didn't recognize at all. Richard Thorpe. Marvin Miller. Genevieve Tobin. The history-loving part of her wanted to start researching each of them immediately. *Had they been happy?* she wondered. They'd definitely been successful in their careers, but did they feel like they were doing what they were supposed to be doing, *meant* to be doing? Or did they even think about that?

There were probably more than 2,500 different answers to those questions. On her tour, she'd found out that's how many stars were on the walk. Forget about the people with names on the stars, what about the people in the cars, working in the stores, restaurants, and offices, dressing up like Wonder Woman farther up Hollywood Boulevard? Were any of them following their dreams?

Jamie suddenly felt silly. These were the thoughts of a college freshman. Who her age mooned around, wondering if people were happy and fulfilled, trying to decide what their own Passion was? But if she never stopped and really thought about it, wouldn't her life just kind of . . . slip by?

Okay, so maybe she was being kind of emo and self-indulgent. But that's what this year was for, and she knew she was so lucky to have it. Her mother's gift had really been the gift of time to stop and think about what was truly important to her and then try to find it.

A sign on an unassuming storefront for a place called Applied

Scholastics caught her eye. VOLUNTEER TUTORS WANTED. Jamie stopped, considering. She'd felt sure she didn't want to teach anymore, but maybe she just didn't want to teach in a classroom. Teaching one-on-one could be a whole different thing. She could really connect in a way that was hard to do with a big group, maybe make a real difference in a kid's life.

Impulsively, she stepped inside. The clean-cut twenty-something guy behind the reception desk greeted her with a friendly smile. "Hi. I saw your sign about looking for tutors, and I wanted to find out a little more," Jamie told him. "I have a teaching certificate," she added.

"Great! I'll get Suze to come out and talk to you. She's the point person for volunteers. Grab a seat." He gestured to the chairs in the empty room and disappeared down the hall. Instead of sitting, Jamie wandered over to one of the glass-front bookcases.

Uh-oh, she thought as she read a few of the titles. *How to Use the Dictionary* by L. Ron Hubbard. *Learning How to Learn* by L. Ron Hubbard. *Study Skills for Life* by L. Ron Hubbard. *Grammar and Communication for Children* by L. Ron Hubbard. Uh. Oh.

She shot a glance at the hallway. No one in sight. She turned and walked out the door, resisting the urge to tiptoe. Deciding she needed to commemorate the moment, Jamie crossed the street, then took a picture of the little tutoring center. She'd so arrived in Hollywood.

And she knew one thing for sure: Her Passion wasn't volunteering for Scientologists.

"Did you eat a sock?" David asked Diogee. Diogee wagged his tail. He wagged his tail anytime anyone said a word related to food.

David had done a load of clothes the night before, and when he'd been putting them away that morning, he'd realized he was short one sasquatch and one tube sock. He wasn't the neat-est guy, but he was usually careful about keeping anything small enough to be swallowed out of the Diogee zone, because if Diogee could swallow something, he probably would. He'd eaten a bar of soap once. Also a mouse pad, a box of crayons from Lucy's purse, a couple squeaky toys, and a sponge. He'd managed to digest or poop out all of it.

David had a vague memory of putting the socks in the bath-room hamper, and he shut the door pretty much automatically to keep Diogee from slurping up toilet water. It didn't seem like Diogee would have gotten at them. But they *were* missing. He looked at Diogee again. "Did you eat two socks?" Diogee wagged his tail harder.

"Damn it." David took out his cell and called the vet. He gave Becky, one of the techs, the rundown.

"Just keep an eye on him. As long as he's eating and drinking and isn't lethargic, you don't need to bring him in," Becky told him. "I'll call you later to see how he's doing," she added.

"You don't have to do that," he told her.

"All part of the service," she said before she hung up.

She'd sounded friendly. She was always friendly. But she'd sounded extra-friendly.

Because you're a good customer, David told himself. Diogee had had more than his share of vet visits, including three for getting sprayed in the face by a skunk. Most dogs would have learned their lesson the first time. Or the second. Not Diogee.

But Becky had sounded maybe even more than friendly. Maybe flirty. Had she always been like that? Could Lucy be right? Was he more ready to—*move on* wasn't the phrase he wanted. Was he more ready to go out with a new woman than he realized? Was that why he was suddenly noticing Becky's flirty tone? Was that why he'd started up that conversation with the cute woman in the pet store? Was that why he was having the sudden grief attacks, because he felt guilty or something?

That was way too many questions. Too much introspection was dangerous.

"You want to go for a walk?" David asked his dog. Diogee bolted toward the box that held all his stuff. He grabbed the leash and raced back. "Not too lethargic," David said as he clipped on the leash. Once Diogee had dragged him outside, David decided to steer him over to Ruby's. He was going to prove to himself that he could look at her house without having a meltdown.

He wasn't surprised to find Ruby outside. She had the ladder out and was adding white flocking to the trees in her yard. Even the palms got treated. Decorating her place was a days-long process.

"Looks good," David called. He didn't feel grief cut into him the way it had when he'd seen the house with Zachary, maybe because this time he was prepared.

"Hey, thanks." Ruby scrambled off the ladder. He heard a soft jingling and realized she wore curly-toed elf shoes with bells on the tips. She liked to decorate herself, too. Clarissa always said she admired how Ruby made everything an event. "Did the kid get off to school all right?" she asked. She walked over and Diogee dropped to the ground and rolled onto his back, legs waving. Ruby sat down next to the dog and started scratching his tummy.

"Yeah, I saw Zachary leave. Nobody will be able to tell he tried to dig a hole through his forehead," David answered.

"That had to hurt. I can't believe he didn't stop before it got that bad," Ruby said, still scratching.

"Any day I'm expecting his mom to ask me to give him The Talk." David shook his head at Diogee, who had entered a blissed-out trance.

Ruby laughed. "Tell her to do what my parents did and leave a copy of *Everything You Always Wanted to Know about Sex* on the bookshelf."

"That's all you got?" David asked.

"It was plenty. In fact, it really was everything I wanted to know, plus some I didn't," Ruby said. "You want to come in? I'm trying out a new recipe for Italian sprinkle cookies."

"I've never made them. They're the ones you have to dip in glaze, then let dry for hours, right?"

"Those are the ones," Ruby said. "They're just now ready to eat."

At the word "eat," Diogee's eyes snapped open and he leapt to his feet. "I thought he might have swallowed at least one sock, but if he did, he's not supposed to be interested in food. So, I'm thinking he's okay."

"He's interested enough to drool." Ruby stood and backed up until her elf slippers weren't in danger of getting splashed with saliva. She led the way up to the house.

"Is the pony a work in progress?" David asked. The small plastic pink-and-purple horse didn't look Christmas-ified.

"It just showed up on my doormat this morning," Ruby answered. She picked the pony up. "I thought maybe somebody left it as a contribution. I'm sure I can think up something to do with it. Maybe I'll create an Island of Misfit Toys." She ran her fingers through the pony's purple nylon mane, which had been cut at different lengths, then tapped the chip in one of its hoofs. "Nah, I can't do it. This isn't a misfit. Somebody just loved it really hard. I'll come up with something special."

"Tootsie Pop, I'm going to need you to put the pony down and take two large steps back."

David knew it was Hud before he looked over at the man. His fake Southern drawl was one of a kind. Diogee's tail began whipping against David's leg. The dog loved everybody, and expected to be loved back, even though Hud always ignored him.

"This?" Ruby asked, holding up the plastic horse.

Hud crossed the small lawn and pulled a piece of paper out of one of the dozens of pockets in his fishing vest. He unfolded it and held it up so Ruby and David could see it. It was a crayon drawing of a couple pink and purple blobs with four lines coming off them. "Are you trying to tell me the pony you're holding isn't the same one in this picture?"

David wrapped Diogee's leash around his hand a few times. The dog was giving a high whine of excitement. David knew Diogee was sure any second Hud would acknowledge him, maybe scratch his head. Hud didn't even give Diogee a glance.

"It could be," Ruby said, looking at the drawing. "But it could be a lot of things."

"So, you're going to do this the hard way." Hud sounded pleased.

"Hud, we don't know what you're talking about," David told him.

"What I'm talking about is a little girl with a broken heart. What I'm talking about is a thief with no heart at all," Hud answered.

David exchanged a "huh" glance with Ruby. "Still don't know what you're talking about, Hud."

"You might not, Sports Fan," Hud said to David. "I'll have to think on that. But your friend here does. She's trying to deny it, but she knows she's holding stolen property. That pony belongs to Miss Riley Brewer of Neverland Way."

"I found it on my doormat this morning," Ruby said. "I thought maybe someone left it for me to use as a Christmas decoration." She handed him the pony.

Hud studied her for a long moment. "I can't prove any different." He let out a sigh. "You've got to hook 'em to cook 'em, and it seems you slipped off the hook. This time." He stuck the pony in the biggest of the vest's pockets, and walked away. Diogee gave a barrage of barks, but Hud didn't look back.

Ruby reached over and gave Diogee's head a consoling rub. "I've known some method actors. But he's the first I've met who is still staying in character years after the part's over."

"I wonder how that toy got all the way over here. The Brewers live over by my place," David said. A connection clicked in his head. "And the pony must be Paula. I heard Riley yelling for Paula this morning."

"Me, too, and I saw her and her big sister. She was crying like she'd lost her best friend. Which I guess she had. I knew the pony had been loved hard. Maybe I'll make a little barn for it. Someplace for her to keep it so it won't get lost again. Or is that too crazy old neighbor lady? I don't know them more than to say hello to."

"She'd love it." David wondered if Ruby regretted not having had kids. Clarissa had said something once that made it sound as if she'd wanted them.

Ruby's like me, he decided. She had good friends. She liked her job. She had her hobbies, like the Christmas decorating. And it seemed like it was working for her. It seemed like it was enough.

Mac sat on the foot of the young one's bed, his chest and belly vibrating as he purred. His message had been understood. He could smell the woman on the toy the girl clutched to her chest as she slept. The connection had been made.

He padded up to the toy and softly batted the bell on the ribbon tied around the plastic pony's neck. The soft jingling made him purr louder, so loudly he could feel it in his entire body now. Mission accomplished.

He watched the girl for another few moments. He would have enjoyed staying there longer, savoring his success, but Jamie needed more help. Or maybe he was wrong about her packmate. Mac understood a lot about his human, but she still baffled him at times. Like the way she slept. She didn't sleep nearly enough, and she slept at night. Why hadn't she figured out that night was the best playtime?

Maybe there was something about the gifts he'd brought her that she didn't like. Something he'd never think of. Maybe there was something in their smell that made her nose burn the way the spray she used in the sink did his. There were other lonely-smelling people around Mac was sure could use a packmate, especially one like Jamie. She really didn't have too many bad habits. Tonight he'd collect smells from several possibilities. He wouldn't stop until he found her one that she understood, the way the woman had understood the smell of the little one's need on the pony Mac had brought her.

He sprang from the bed to the windowsill and shimmied out the window. As soon as he took a breath, he knew the bonehead was outside. Before he got down to the night's mission, he decided to have a little fun. Running up that bonehead's back had been even better than playing with Mousie. Mack wanted to play with him again.

The moon was bright, so Mac kept to the shadows, the soft pads of his feet and his quick reflexes making his movements all but silent. Not that he had to be so careful. The bonehead was a mouth-breather. He probably couldn't hear anything over those slobbery pants.

When Mac reached the fence around the bonehead's yard, he deliberately stepped on a twig to get the dog's attention. Didn't work. The dog had decided to start licking himself. Mac understood. Even he got distracted when he did that.

He jumped up onto the top of the fence and let out a long, low yowl. The bonehead heard that! He lurched to his feet. And Mac was off. He leapt onto the ground and streaked across the yard. The bonehead galumphed after him. Mac led him around the lawn once, twice, slowing his pace a little to be sure the dog thought he had a chance. On the third loop, Mac ran straight for the big tree he used to get up to the second-floor window.

He launched himself at the lowest branch at the last possible moment. The dog couldn't stop fast enough. He rammed into the tree with his big bone head. Score!

That would have to be enough entertainment for now. He had to get to work. He opened his mouth, tasting the air, searching for a scent that matched the loneliness in Jamie's.

CHAPTER 5

Jamie opened her front door and immediately looked down. A pair of boxers with penguins on them, a pair of gray boxer briefs, and a pair of tighty-whities lay on the doormat. She slammed the door shut again and leaned against it. "What is going on?" she cried to Mac. "Who is doing this to me?"

The cat gave the short mew Jamie always interpreted as "uh-huh." Like he wasn't really paying attention, but was acknowledging that she'd said something.

"Not helpful, MacGyver." She could accept that the hand towel had been dropped by the previous tenant. The socks—well, she had no real theory, but socks were always turning up in strange places. Maybe her doormat was a hosiery portal, and socks that went missing from local dryers landed there. But three pairs of men's underwear—

Tentatively she opened the door, took a quick peek, then shut it again. Three pairs of different sizes and styles, all showing up on the same morning. "It's freaky. It's freaky and wrong. It's freaky and wrong and unnatural and bizarre and weird." Mac gave the "uh-huh" mew again.

"Thanks for nothing," she muttered. She marched herself to the broom closet and got the box with the hand towel and socks, then she grabbed a pair of tongs and returned to the door. She couldn't just leave three pairs of men's underwear lying out on the porch for anybody to see. She'd be the talk of Storybook Court—and not in a good way. She opened the door again, and used the tongs to pick up the boxers, briefs, and tighties and place them in the box. She thought about taping the box closed before she put it back in the closet, but she had no reason to think there wouldn't be something else to put in it the next day.

It wasn't just freaky, wrong, unnatural, bizarre, and weird. It was also a little scary. She felt like she'd been targeted, but she didn't know for what. Maybe it wasn't even about her. Maybe it was about whoever had lived here before. Maybe they'd pissed off someone and whoever it was had decided to . . . leave them small, somewhat random items in retaliation.

Or! This made more sense! Maybe they were things the guy who'd lived here before—if it was a guy—had left at his girlfriend's house. Maybe they'd broken up and she was returning things she'd found in his place. Maybe that was even why he'd moved! Maybe she was some kind of psycho stalker chick and he wanted to get away from her!

There were two people who would know the details about the previous tenant. Marie and Helen. They'd known tons of stuff about her before she'd even introduced herself. Jamie would go talk to them. She hated to go over to Marie's empty-handed. But she didn't have much in the house. She'd lived here more than a week, but she hadn't really settled in.

She checked the kitchen. Several flavors of cat food, of course. Coffee, but Marie made much better coffee than she did. Assorted snack foods. She couldn't show up with a bowl full of Goldfish crackers, but maybe a mix. Hurriedly, she mixed the Goldfish with a few handfuls of pretzels and some popcorn, then threw in some Goobers and Raisinettes. It was kind of like trail mix. . . . She really needed to start eating like a regular person. Sometimes it felt like there was no point in cooking, though, if she was the only one who was going to eat. But that was wrong. Her lifestyle shouldn't be determined by whether or not she was in a relationship. Not in The Year of Me!

Jamie picked up the bowl. "I'll be back," she told Mac, doing her not-really-passable Schwarzenegger. She found Al filling a tiny crack in one of the pavers that led from the sidewalk to his house. Had he been there when she'd used the tongs to collect the underwear? *Too late to worry about it now,* she told herself.

"Marie around?" she called.

"Inside with Helen," he answered without looking up from his work.

"Great. I want to talk to them both." She walked up to the front door, taking a moment to admire the flag flying from the turret of their little castle house, wondering if it was the Defrancisco family crest.

She raised her hand to knock, but the door opened before her knuckles could touch it. Marie really did know everything that was going on. Jamie handed her the bowl of snack mix. "For you. To thank you for all the coffee. Also, I wanted to ask you something. You and Helen. Al said she was here."

"Come on in." Marie stepped back.

"Oooh. I love your fireplace," Jamie said. It was huge—at least compared to the size of the living room, commanding most of one wall and reaching almost to the ceiling. It was easy to picture a bunch of knights gathered around it. Or Al and Marie watching TV on the comfy, overstuffed sofa.

"We're in the kitchen." Marie led the way and gestured to a chair at the wooden table. "Jamie has something to ask us," she told Helen.

"I knew you'd change your mind!" Helen exclaimed. "I already told my godson all about you. He wants to meet you. Don't worry about a thing. I'll set it all up. I know the perfect place for you to go."

"I told you, he's too young for her. And he's allergic to cats. That's what they call a deal breaker. Am I right?" Marie asked Jamie.

"Yes! Yes, yes, yes, yes, yes. Big deal breaker. Absolutely." She wasn't going to turn down a ready-made excuse to get out of a fixup with Helen's godson.

Marie gave a satisfied smile as she put the snack mix on the table. Helen stretched her hand toward it, but Marie moved it out of reach. "You don't need that. I'll get you an apple if you're hungry. Nessie still wears a size—"

"I told you not to talk to me about that person. That person can go suck an egg. You, too, Marie." Helen leaned forward and took a handful of the mix. "He can take Benadryl for the allergies," she continued before Jamie could ask who Nessie was. "And women live longer, so it's good that he's younger. Also, he's a teacher, so they have that in—"

"That's not what I wanted to talk to you about," Jamie interrupted. "I wanted to see what you could tell me about whoever lived in my place before me."

"Desmond," Marie said. "He was wonderful. He always separated his recycling."

Did Marie do some kind of trash can inspection? Jamie wondered. "What else?" she asked. "Did he have a girlfriend? Why did he move?"

Neither of the women seemed to find her questions strange, probably because they liked to ferret out everything about their neighbors, too. "He had to relocate. He works for that fancy Harvest grocery store. Almost five dollars for four stalks of asparagus in a jar of water."

"And kale guacamole. Guacamole means avocados," Helen

jumped in. "I don't know how the place stays open. But Dezzy moved to help open up a new store in Austin."

"Well, good for him," Jamie said. "Do you know if he was seeing anyone? Did he maybe have a bad breakup before he left?"

"His boyfriend up and decided to move with him," Helen answered. "Kyle was trying to get into screenwriting. But you know how that is. He managed to line up a job working for some film festival there."

"Did Desmond and Kyle throw a lot of parties?" She didn't know why she'd asked. No matter how wild the parties, people wouldn't still be leaving underwear by the door.

"They had that one party where everyone wanted Al and me to show them how to swing-dance out in the courtyard," Marie said.

"And Dezzy made bananas Foster in his front yard," Helen added.

"It sounds lovely." It did. She wished she could have been there to see Al and Marie do their thing. But nothing she'd heard gave her any explanation for the freaky, wrong, bizarre, strange, and scary happenings at her place. Jamie stood up. "I should get back. I was just curious about who was in the place before me, and I knew you'd know. Thanks!"

"I'll be in touch about my godson," Helen told her.

"He's too young. I still want you to meet my great-nephew," Marie said. "And I know lots of suitable young men, not just him."

"I'm good. I want some time on my own right now. Thanks again."

As Jamie left the kitchen, she heard Helen say, "If you think your great-nephew is a better match, you're wrong. He doesn't—"

"Really. No setups. I'm serious," Jamie called back to them.

"I said my great-nephew is only one possibility," Jamie heard

Marie say before she escaped out the front door. She hurried away from the house.

"Neither of them listens to me," she blurted out as she passed Al. He grunted an *I-hear-you* grunt.

Al, the Grunter, wasn't going to talk her problems over with her. And it was three hours earlier back home. Her friends would be getting ready for work or getting their kids ready for school or both. She took a right at the corner, and saw Ruby's Christmas-ified house. They'd only had that one conversation, but it was a good one.

She walked straight up to the door and knocked. A grin broke across Ruby's face when she answered, and Jamie smiled back. "I would have called first, but I didn't know your number."

"No worries. Come on in. I have sprinkle cookies that a professional baker pronounced 'edible perfection'." Ruby gestured for Jamie to come inside and brought her back to the kitchen.

"What's all this?" The table was covered with fabric, sequins, beads, buttons, lace, and ribbon, mostly in shades of pink and purple. "Oh my gosh. Is that a BeDazzler?" Jamie added, spotting the oversized stapler-looking thing.

"As seen on TV," Ruby answered. "And did you actually say 'oh my gosh'?"

"I did, and I stand by it," Jamie said.

"A woman with convictions. I like it." Ruby unearthed a cardboard box partially covered with fuchsia corduroy. "What I'm making is a barn for a very special pony. She recently had a traumatic experience." She moved a roll of lavender netting so Jamie could sit down.

"The pony's name wouldn't happen to be Paula, would it?" Jamie asked.

"That's the one. Somehow she ended up on my doorstep yesterday," Ruby answered as she cleared some table space for a platter of cookies.

"On your doorstep?" Jamie repeated. "I've been finding stuff on my doormat, too. Today it was three pairs of men's underwear. It's starting to give me the creeps."

"Today? How many other times?" Ruby turned the boxbarn to one of its bare sides and began measuring out a piece of corduroy to cover it.

"This is the fourth. First there was a hand towel, then a sasquatch sock, then a tube sock, and now the underwear," Jamie explained. "I thought maybe they were left for the last person who lived there—not that that makes much sense, either."

"It's hard to think of anything that does make sense. . . . It doesn't sound malicious, exactly. Maybe it's a stupid prank. We have a few teenagers in the complex." Ruby shook her head. "I sound like I'm a hundred years old. 'It must have been those pesky kids.' "

"Do you think they left you the pony, too?" Jamie asked.

"Possible." Ruby cut out a square of the fabric. "I can't think of a reason the little girl would have been at my door. Unless she wanted a closer look at the Christmas decorations and left the pony behind. She's too young to be out by herself, though."

"Okay, for now I'm going to go with the pesky kid theory. Can we move on to my second problem?"

"For sure." Ruby handed her the scissors and corduroy fabric. "Cut me out another piece like this." She handed Jamie the square she'd made.

"Okay, but be warned, you've reached the limit of my craftiness," Jamie told her. "So, my other problem is Marie and Helen. They both want to fix me up with someone, and they've gotten all competitive about it. Even though I've told them, repeatedly, that I'm not interested."

"Marie and Helen. Formidable team. But they can't actually

force you to go out with anyone." Ruby began fashioning a flower out of a scrap of pale pink tulle. "I'm going to put flowers along the side of the barn, like they're growing there," she explained, then switched back to Jamie's problem. "Just because they're old ladies, that doesn't mean you have to be nice and do what they say."

"Yeah, I know. It's just that Marie keeps making me coffee." Jamie finished cutting out the square and compared it to the one Ruby had given her. It was smaller, and now that she looked at it carefully, not exactly square. She groaned, holding it up.

"I'll cut it down for one of the barn doors," Ruby said. "Have a cookie. Cookies always help."

"Especially when you eat them before lunch," Jamie agreed, taking one from the plate. "It feels subversive and decadent."

Ruby laughed. "Maybe it wouldn't be so bad to meet one of the guys. You just moved here. It would give you a chance to—"

"Not you, too!" Jamie cried. "Remember how I told you it's The Year of Me?" Ruby nodded. "Well, if I'm really going to focus on figuring out what I want, I can't have a guy around. Guys, they derail me. I start spending all this time obsessing about whether or not they like me, even before I know if I even like them myself. I get all worried about what they want, and I don't even stop to think about if I want something. Now I want to figure out what I want. Just me. I don't want to think about anybody else."

"Got it." Ruby started fashioning a new flower out of shiny silver ribbon. "How'd your brainstorming session go the other day?"

Jamie groaned. "I wrote down all the stuff I like, but I didn't have an Oprah aha moment." She shook her head. "Like sitting in a coffee shop for an hour should have given me an epiphany."

"You can't have written down all the stuff you like. There have to be a bazillion things you haven't tried, so you don't know whether you like them or not. Like surfing! Have you ever gone surfing?"

"You think I can make a living surfing?"

"That's not the point. The point is finding out whether you like surfing or not." Ruby finished off her flower. She'd created an exquisite little rosebud. "So, have you ever tried it?"

"Nope," Jamie said.

Ruby sprang up from her chair and hurried over to her fridge. It was covered with hundreds of magnets, pictures, drawings, postcards, and business cards. "Where is it? Where is it?" she murmured. "There!" She snatched a card and brought it to Jamie. "You need to have a least one lesson with the Surfer Chick. I won some lessons once in a raffle. It was awesome."

Jamie studied the card. Maybe Ruby was right. Maybe she was limiting herself by only thinking about things she already knew she liked. Maybe there was something out there she'd love, love, love, but had never even thought about trying.

She suspected that surfing wasn't it. But what the heck? The Year of Me was about self-discovery. She slid Surfer Chick's card into her pocket.

"Dude, you better not have eaten my briefs," David told Diogee. Diogee wagged his tail. Never failed. Use any form of the verb "eat" and the tail started up. He did a patrol through the house, Diogee following. He didn't see any scraps of gray cloth. If the beast had eaten his briefs, he would have had to have ripped them up first. Wouldn't he?

David reached under the dog and began palpating his stomach. When Becky, the vet tech, had called to check on Diogee after the possible sock-eating incident, she'd asked if palpating him seemed to cause pain. It hadn't that time. Or now. Diogee had fallen to the ground and rolled onto his back to give David better access. Seemed like it just felt like tummy scratching to him.

Diogee had been drinking water, eating, pooping, and clearly wasn't experiencing stomach tenderness. But if the dog hadn't swallowed the briefs, where were they? David was sure he'd left them on the bathroom floor after he'd taken a shower the night before. His jeans and T-shirt had still been there this morning, but not the briefs.

He couldn't think of any explanation except Diogee grabbing them, even though he'd been almost positive he'd shut the bathroom door. He'd been extra-careful about it since the socks had gone missing. And Diogee wasn't acting like he'd eaten anything other than his usual food, treats, and rawhide chews.

It's not like it's time to open an X-File, he told himself. The briefs had probably just gotten caught in the leg of the pants or something. And the socks—stuck to a shirt with static cling. He'd find everything eventually. Or not. As long as none of them had made it into Diogee's gut, and it looked like none had, what did it matter?

David wandered back into the living room and flopped down on the couch. Clicked on the flat screen. Judge Judy was scolding someone for something. He clicked it off. Afternoon TV sucked. Baker's hours sucked. He had a ton of stuff DVR-ed, plus Netflix and Hulu, but he didn't feel like searching through them. He picked *Infinite Jest* up off the coffee table. He'd been reading it for about a year and a half. He put it back down. All those footnotes—he couldn't deal with them right now. Maybe some music. But the stereo remote was out of reach.

Diogee gave a huge sigh from his dog bed. "That's how I feel," David muttered.

What had he just been telling himself the other day? He had good friends. He had a job he liked. He had a great dog. That was enough.

Today it wasn't feeling like enough. Today his life felt like a tight, itchy suit he was being forced to wear. He was restless, and at the same time, he didn't feel like moving.

He shoved himself up from the couch. He was starting to irritate himself. He'd walked Diogee as soon as he got home, but feel like it or not, what he needed was a run. He needed to turn his muscles into a quivering mass so that when he got home, he'd be grateful to collapse.

"Go get your leash," he told Diogee. Now there'd be no chance he'd change his mind. Once he started the dog up, that was it. A few minutes later they were out the door. David ran with everything he had, until the only thought he could form was *Keep going, keep going, keep going.*

Mac tried the broom closet door. Completely shut. Not a problem. He crouched down, then flung himself at the handle. Missed. He crouched again, muscles bunching, then sprang. Solid connection! Both paws hit the metal bar and it went down, making the *click* Mac knew meant success. He gave the bottom of the door a flick of the paw and it opened.

What he needed was inside. Jamie had put his gifts in a cardboard box. Mac could still smell the loneliness and other scents that gave information about the owners, but he was starting to think that Jamie couldn't. He kept forgetting that a human's nose was pretty much useless. He leapt up onto the box and it began to rock. Mac easily kept his balance, leaning left, leaning right. The box rocked faster—then began to topple. Mac jumped off before it hit the ground with a satisfying *thump.*

The impact had knocked the box open, making the rest of his job simple. He snagged the closest pair of underwear in his teeth, trotted into the bedroom, and vaulted up onto the bed. He walked across Jamie's stomach and dropped the odor-loaded underwear on her chest, just below her nose. Without waking, she turned her head to the side.

Mac batted at the underwear until it was positioned under

her nose again. Jamie rolled over, putting her back to the underwear. Even in her sleep, his human seemed determined not to take in the message he was trying to deliver.

But Mac was determined, too. He returned to the kitchen, picked up the two remaining pairs of underwear in his teeth, and returned to the bed. He dropped one of the pairs under her nose and the other on her chest, surrounding her with scent. He found it so overpowering himself that it blocked all the other odors of the house and the smells coming in through the screened window. As soon as she woke up, Jamie would have to register the scents and what they meant.

Impatient, he used one paw to tap her repeatedly on the cheek, then added in the meow he usually reserved for requesting breakfast. Jamie's eyes fluttered open, then she looked at the alarm clock and groaned. "Mac, it is hours until breakfast. As in *hours.*" She pulled the comforter over her head.

It didn't seem like she'd even noticed the scents he'd arranged for her. Mac scrabbled at the comforter until he managed to pull it off Jamie's face. He flicked the closest pair of underwear on top of her nose. She'd have to get the message now!

But Jamie snatched the underwear off her face before she'd had a chance to take a good whiff. She flung them across the room. Then she noticed the other pairs and hurled them off the bed.

"Ewww. Ewww, ewww, ewww. And I have to say it again—ewww."

Mac let out a growl of frustration. He loved Jamie, but humans could be so dense. It was so easy for him to understand what she needed. Why was it so hard for her?

Jamie scrambled out of bed and hurried to the bathroom. Mac followed. She pulled out a wipe that made the inside of Mac's nose itch and used it to scrub her face. Then she strode to the kitchen and grabbed a pair of tongs from the drawer by the stove. She took the tongs and the box to her bedroom and used the tongs to move the underwear back inside the box.

He reminded himself that in some ways, taking care of Jamie was like taking care of a kitten. Kittens didn't even know how to properly use a litter box. Their mother had to show them that they needed to cover up their poop. He'd have to keep finding ways to show her there were humans nearby who needed packmates as much as she did.

He jumped into the box and flicked the socks out onto the floor. If she handled them enough, the scent would stay with her, even if she put his gifts back in the broom closet again.

Jamie sighed. "MacGyver, come on. It's the middle of the night. The middle of the night is not playtime." She used the tongs to return the socks to the box. "Is there any place I can put this where you won't get into it?" she asked him. "Probably not. But let's try this." She put the box on the top shelf of her bedroom closet and shut the door firmly behind her. "Now, good night." She flung herself back on the bed and burrowed under the covers.

Mac watched her for a few long moments, then padded away and slipped out his secret passageway into the night. He didn't need to taste the air to know where to go. One scent overpowered all the others. It almost burned with loneliness and something stronger, a pain that Mac could feel vibrating in his bones. It was something Mac had smelled before, but he couldn't remember exactly where. The scent made him feel an urgency to act, and he began to run.

The smell came from the house he'd been to several times, the one with the dog. The bonehead wasn't in the yard when Mac got there. On other nights, this would have been disappointing. Tormenting the drool-producer had become his favorite game. But tonight his mission was more important. And it wasn't just about Jamie. Mac felt compelled to help the person who had produced the odor, the one who was in so much pain.

He raced to the tree he always used to get through the bathroom window. He was partway up the trunk when he realized the window was closed. Not a problem. Mac continued to climb. When he was close enough, he leaped onto the roof. He could smell that there was an opening into the house from there, and it took him only seconds to find it—the chimney.

Mac peered into its depths. He could do this. He planted his two front paws on one side of the stone tunnel and his two back feet on the other, then began to inch down. Before he'd gotten halfway, the bonehead began to bark. It didn't matter. Mac could sense that the human wasn't in the house. Let him bark. That would let MacGyver know exactly where he was. Dogs did not understand the tactical benefits of stealth. One of many reasons cats would always triumph over tail waggers.

When Mac had almost reached the bottom of the chimney, he stopped. And waited. Just waited. Because he knew what the dog would do. And, yeah, here he came. Mac knew what he was thinking: *Cat in there. Why cat not coming out?*

Uh, because it was a trap? A cat would always consider that possibility. Not a drooler. No, he stuck his head into the fireplace, and Mac dropped down on his head, claws out. The dog backed up fast. *Whap, whap, whap, whap.* Mac laid down a series of lightning-fast blows with one paw. The bonehead raced around, trying to dislodge him. When he charged past the stairs, Mac jumped off his head and onto the banister. The dog kept going, and Mac ran up the banister to the top floor.

The bathroom door was shut. No lever. A round doorknob. Those were trickier. For some cats. Not him. MacGyver reared up on his back legs and put one paw on each side of the knob. Then he rubbed them back and forth until the knob turned. He dropped back down and batted at the door until it swung open.

Immediately he saw the source of the scent. A T-shirt, still wet with sweat. Humans and their sweat. When he was hot, he sweated a little between his toes, and it felt refreshing. But humans could produce a ridiculous amount of liquid. The shirt looked like it had been rained on. A quiver of distaste ran through Mac's body.

The sweat made the scent of the human's loneliness so powerful even Jamie should be able to recognize it. Mac caught the shirt up in his teeth. The taste of the loneliness and pain saturating the material was almost too much for him, but Mac didn't allow himself to drop it, even when he heard the bonehead coming up the stairs. He didn't need his teeth in order to triumph in Round Two.

Mac saw that the door to the shower was ajar. He hated showers, but this one wasn't spraying water, and he had an idea. . . . He slipped inside and waited for the drooler to find him. The dog charged into the room, then slid to a stop, looking around in confusion. Clearly, he didn't see Mac, even though the shower was made of glass. Pathetic. Mac gave a yowl to get his attention.

The bonehead gave a bray of triumph, and galumphed into the shower. It was a tight fit. Mac darted underneath the dog's belly and out the door, then Mac turned and banged his body against it. The shower door closed with a satisfying *click*.

Mac trotted out of the bathroom, enjoying the howls of frustration coming from the trapped dog. He hadn't intended to take the time to play with him, but it had been fun. Now he had to get the shirt home. If Jamie would just smell it—and she should be able to without even picking it up—she would have to realize that the human who'd worn it needed another human as much as she did.

CHAPTER 6

David's belly churned when he walked into The Roost, even though he was only there to have a drink with Adam. No, that was bullshit. He *would* have a drink with Adam, but that wasn't the reason he was there. He was going to put himself up on counterpart.com, and he needed backup. Not because he couldn't write his own profile and put it up, but after that—

It was just that he'd been with Clarissa practically forever. They met at a dance during orientation week at UCLA. That was back when David thought he'd probably get a degree in accounting or something like that. He'd had no idea what he wanted to do with his life, but for pretty much everyone he knew the next step after high school was college, so that was what he did—for one semester. Then he'd quit and tried a bunch of different, mostly crappy jobs. His eighteen-year-old self would be shocked that he'd ended up a baker, even though he'd always liked messing around in the kitchen, concocting his own recipes.

Clarissa had been totally the opposite. Knew she wanted to be a physical therapist from day one, got the degree, got a job at a nursing home, loved it. She'd been thinking of going out on her own right before—

Now wasn't the time to be thinking about Clarissa. His problem was that he'd been with her his whole adult life, and he felt like he'd forgotten how to even ask someone on a date. He'd done okay talking to that women at the Blue Palm, until he'd brought up his dead wife after about ten seconds. He needed a wingman—a virtual wingman—and that was why he'd asked Adam to meet him here. He snagged a booth and pulled the Counterpart app up on his cell.

He wasn't ready for this. Not without a drink—a real drink, not his usual beer. One of the reasons he'd picked The Roost was their heavy pours. Even though he knew he'd have to listen to Adam complain that the bar wasn't a really a dive bar anymore and how much it sucked that there was no free popcorn.

He'd just gotten his G&T when Adam arrived. "Why do we still come here? Every time I walk in I get depressed. It used to be this great dive bar and now it's like a faux dive. Like a Westworld Hollywood location. Bukowski wouldn't be caught dead in here."

"Even if he wasn't dead already," David managed to comment before Adam continued his rant.

"And there's no more free popcorn. I used to live on the popcorn. It saved my liver by soaking up all the booze."

David laughed. Did he know Adam or what? "The popcorn was stale, we can afford food, and we don't drink a liver-damaging amount of alcohol because we aren't kids anymore. Plus there's AC/DC on the jukebox—and there's still some grime."

"Yeah, okay. But you'll notice it's hipsters playing the jukebox, not middle-aged burnouts who listen to AC/DC unironically," Adam said. He noticed David's drink. "No Corona?"

"Liquid courage," David told him. "I've decided to enter the world of online dating, and I need your advice." Adam gave an air punch. David imitated him. "You know you're a dweeb, right?"

"Don't change the subject. We aren't talking about my dweebiness. Which doesn't exist. We're talking about you getting back out there." The waitress approached and Adam ordered a Rusty Nail. "Lucy told me what you two talked about. I'm surprised that you . . ." He let his words trail off.

"I still mostly feel the way I said I did. But I guess it kind of hit me that I don't want to be alone for the rest of my life," David said. He'd run until he couldn't take another step. He'd even exhausted Diogee. When he dragged himself into the house, he'd collapsed, just the way he'd hoped he would. But his brain wouldn't shut down. He couldn't block out the realization that the life he had wasn't enough. So he'd called Adam and told him to meet him at the bar.

The waitress returned with Adam's drink. "You complain about hipsters, but we both know the only reason you drink Rusty Nails is because you want to think you'd have been part of the Rat Pack."

"You know what Queen Elizabeth's favorite drink was?" Adam shot back. "That's right, gin and tonic." He nodded at David's glass.

"I have nothing but respect for the queen," David said.

"Also, Gerald Ford," Adam told him. "And don't think I don't recognize a pivot when I see one. We weren't talking about drinks. We were talking about dating apps. Did you get an account set up the other night?"

"Not completely," David admitted.

"I knew that. Because I checked. So, I set one up for you. Give me your phone."

David handed it to him. "I signed you up for something, too. The Hair Club for Men. I wanted it to be a surprise."

"I didn't make it go live," Adam said. "I just thought I'd have it ready. That was before you talked to Lucy. Your user name is BakerMan, and your password is Diogee, capital *D*, capital *G*, with a question mark in front."

"BakerMan?" David asked.

Adam shrugged. "Lucy thought it was cute, and Lucy is your target audience. Plus we had a picture of you carrying in that cake you made for Groundhog Day that she said was, quote, adorable. You'll see I kind of went all the way with the baking theme." He handed it over.

David quickly read the profile. "You turned me into a recipe."

"Also Lucy approved. We both looked at a bunch of profiles, and it seemed like they're more like marketing pieces. You're being marketed as sweet and creative, with a little goofiness—as the Groundhog Cake shows," Adam explained. "I don't find you sweet, for the record. But, again, Lucy says you are. I also used a pic of you giving Diogee one of those home-baked dog biscuits." He took a swallow of his drink. "So, you ready? Just hit 'publish'."

David hesitated, staring at the screen for a few seconds, then he did. He didn't exactly feel ready, but he also wasn't ready to keep going the way he'd been going. Not anymore.

"Now that you're on, you can look at profiles. See who's around here. If you see someone you're interested in, you can press the heart or send a message," Adam explained.

"You know way too much about this," David told him.

"Don't you watch my show? We did a few eps where Jess did online dating."

"And some woman broke into his place and made dinner for them both, right?" David asked. "After they'd had coffee once."

"It's TV. It's not like we can show two people going out on a nice, normal first date. If you're not going to look at the profiles, then let me look," Adam added, holding out his hand for the cell.

"I'm doing it," David protested.

"You're doing it too slow," Adam said. "It's all about snap

judgments. Hitting the heart doesn't mean you want to go out with the person. It just means you're saying you're possibly interested. If they are, too, then you exchange messages." Adam began clicking and swiping left or right. "Yep," he muttered. "Yep, yep, uh nope, yep."

"Hold up. That's enough," David protested.

"It's also about volume," Adam told him. "You've got to give yourself lots of possibilities." The phone pinged. "Hey, you already got one who hearted you back! BookMe." He looked at David. "I say yes. You?" He turned the screen toward David. The woman was pretty, sleek brown hair, cat's-eye glasses. "She's marketing herself as kind of a sexy librarian, and who doesn't love one of those?"

"I guess. Yeah. Why not?" David answered.

Adam gave him the phone. "Message her. Your mission is to get her number or set up drinks. Keep it light. Keep it casual. Don't mention—"

"My dead wife," David interrupted.

"I wasn't going to say it like that," Adam protested. "But, yeah. That's something you mention after you've gone out with someone a few times at least."

"Fine." David typed in "hi."

Adam groaned. "You just said 'hi,' didn't you?"

"What's wrong with that?"

"What's wrong with that is she's probably in the middle of conversations with multiple other guys. You want to stand out."

David quickly sent another message and read it aloud. "Want to have a drink? I bake a mean blueberry cabernet cupcake."

Adam gave a satisfied nod. "Nice. Right on brand. Like I'd written it myself."

"She sent back a face with a tongue licking its lips," David reported. "She says, 'If those cupcakes really exist, I want one.'"

"Lock it down. Set a time and place," Adam coached.

Mix It Up Bakery in Los Feliz tomorrow at 6? David sent

back. And got a yes. "She's meeting me at the bakery at six to-morrow," he told Adam. He felt a little stunned. That had hap-pened really fast.

"Excellent work," Adam said. "In the future, I'd meet in a neutral place. You don't want some nutbar hanging around your job. But she didn't look or sound like a nutbar," he added quickly.

"And it's just meeting for cupcakes," David said. "If I don't like how it's going, I can wrap it up fast."

Jamie found a parking spot and checked the time. She had more than an hour to kill. After she'd found that T-shirt—still slightly damp with sweat—on her doormat that morning, she'd wanted to get out of the house immediately. She'd decided to explore Venice before her surf lesson. Her surf lesson! Just thinking about it made her stomach attempt to origami itself. But Ruby was right. Jamie was trying to figure out what her passion was, and only considering things she'd already tried was way too limiting.

She grabbed her backpack, locked the car, and headed out. Her plan was to stroll down Ocean Front Walk to the spot near the Santa Monica Pier where she was meeting up with the Surfer Chick, Kylie. According to all the guidebooks, the Walk wasn't to be missed. As soon as she stepped onto the concrete boardwalk, she pulled out her cell. Everything needed to be photographed. Starting with the guy drinking a smoothie wear-ing only a tiny, shiny gold Speedo and a giant snake draped around his shoulders. Jamie got a shot where the snake's tongue was flicking the cup in the guy's hand.

"A buck a pic," the guy told her.

Jamie stared at him.

The guy smiled. "I don't care, but my snake's a professional model. He doesn't work for free."

Jamie laughed. The guy didn't. Neither did the snake. She

pulled a dollar out of her purse and handed it over. "Thank you kindly," the guy said, and ambled off.

"Hey, wait!" Jamie called impulsively. The guy turned around. "Can I ask you a question?"

"Got another buck?"

Jamie handed one over. "Do you and your buddy make a living doing this?"

"It keeps us in Moon Juice smoothies and a rat a couple times a month," he answered.

"Do you like it? Is this what you want to be doing?" Jamie asked.

"What's not to like? I'm on the beach. No timeclock. Meet new people all the time and have friends up and down the Walk." His face practically glowed as he spoke, and Jamie couldn't resist getting another pic. She handed over a dollar before he could ask, then continued down the boardwalk. Friends, new people, chose his own hours, got to work outside, every day was different. It sounded pretty good, Jamie thought. Except it involved a snake, so it wouldn't be close to her dream job. And what did a guy like that do for retirement? Maybe he wouldn't have to retire, she decided. As an eighty-year-old wearing a teensie gold bathing suit and a snake, he might rack up even more dollars than he did right now.

Everyone working on the Walk looked pretty happy—the woman giving henna tattoos, the man who would write your name on a grain of rice, the b-boys doing their physics-defying flips and spins. Jamie wanted to get pictures of them all and ask them a million questions, but she didn't have enough singles. But when she spotted a bearded man wearing a piece of poster board clipped to his suspenders that said BAD ADVICE $1, she couldn't resist.

She veered over to the bench where he was sitting, and he patted the spot beside him. Jamie handed him a dollar and waited. The man stroked his beard, thinking, then said, "Here's how to get eaten by a shark."

"Oh no. Not today. I'm having my first surfing lesson," Jamie protested.

"Then the advice will be extra-bad. Here's what you do. Go swimming at dawn or dusk. There's an extra chance the shark will confuse you with prey. Swim alone. Wear bright colors— they can look like sunlight on fish scales. And give yourself a couple little cuts. Sharks can smell and taste blood for miles."

"You've now freaked me out completely," Jamie told him. "But I guess I can reverse the advice to get some good not-getting-feasted-on-by-a-shark tips."

He winked at her. "Not what you paid for, but yeah."

"Can I ask you a question that doesn't involve advice?" Jamie asked.

"Sure. No charge," he told her.

Jamie leaned in a little closer. "Do you like doing this? If you could do anything, do you think you'd still want to make a living selling bad advice?"

He laughed. Actually, he guffawed. Jamie didn't think she'd heard a laugh that actually counted as a guffaw before, but his did. And she had to get his picture. "I haven't always been selling crappy advice. I'm an entrepreneur. That's what I love. Finding new ways to get people to pay me a buck—and feel like it was worth it."

"Definitely worth it." Jamie stood up. "Do I owe you for the picture?"

The man shook his head. "All part of the service."

For Bad Advice Man, it seemed like creativity was key. Jamie thought she'd want a job that took creativity, too. She'd felt so stifled in her last job, having to teach to the test. There hadn't been time to find inventive ways to get the kids excited about history. She'd had to focus on cramming the right facts into their heads so they could get the test scores the school needed to get its funding.

Jamie continued down the boardwalk, passing many more opportunities to spend a buck. She could have stuffed one in the pink bikini of a small dog or gotten her picture taken with two plastic aliens. According to a sign shaped like a huge marijuana leaf, she could get a medical evaluation for thirty dollars, and, presumably, use it in the medical marijuana shop attached to the "clinic."

Everyone she passed seemed to have a sunny, happy vibe, until she wandered by a young woman selling her paintings. It had to be hard watching person after person walk past your work without giving it a glance. Jamie backed up so she could really look at the paintings. The girl didn't bother to try to engage her in conversation or even look up at her. Her job was obviously creative, but that wasn't enough.

The paintings were okay, just average beach scenes. Jamie could see why most people didn't bother to stop. That was the thing about passion. Having passion for something didn't mean you were good at it. Which definitely didn't mean you shouldn't do it. If you loved it, you should do it. But it probably couldn't be the "job" part of your "dream job."

Jamie couldn't bring herself to ask the young woman the questions she'd asked the snake guy and the advice man. It seemed too intrusive. And Jamie also didn't think she wanted to hear the answers the woman would give about the level of her job satisfaction. She hurried off, feeling a little guilty that she hadn't bought something.

She was starting to feel overstimulated. A man in a turban whizzed by her on roller skates, playing a guitar as he went, and she didn't marvel at him or at the teenager dressed as a mermaid blowing bubbles within bubbles. She picked up her pace, and reached the pier where she was supposed to meet Kylie, her surfing teacher, about ten minutes later.

Even though Jamie was early, Kylie was already waiting. Her fuchsia Surfer Chick T-shirt made her easy to spot. She was maybe thirty, with muscular Michelle Obama arms. Jamie took a deep breath and walked over to her. "Hi. I'm Jamie. Here for my surfing lesson." Hearing herself say those words was slightly surreal.

"Ready to have some fun?" Kylie asked. "Because fun is at the top of my list of what I want you to accomplish today. I don't care if you don't do one successful popup. I want you to leave the lesson feeling surf stoked."

" 'Surf stoked'?" Jamie repeated.

"It's this high you get," Kylie explained. "Surfing gets your dopamine and adrenaline going, and the breaking waves are surrounded by charged ions. The combo leaves you euphoric, as long as you don't spoil it by expecting yourself to be perfect on day one."

"I'm definitely not expecting that," Jamie said. "Fun would be great."

"Okay, let's get you into a wettie. This way." Kylie gestured for Jamie to follow her.

"As in wetsuit?" Jamie asked. "It's still so warm. Do I need one?"

"The water's in the sixties, so you'll want it," Kylie answered as they walked. She led the way into a small surf shop and pulled a wetsuit and two plastic bags out from behind the counter. She handed them to Jamie. "Put the bags on your feet. That will help you slide your legs in. Then switch them to your hands when you're ready to pull on the arms." She pulled back a palm-tree printed curtain, revealing a tiny dressing room. "Call if you need help."

Jamie went into the dressing room and shut the curtain. She stripped down to her bathing suit and slipped her feet into the plastic bags. "Oh, here." Kylie tossed a Lycra shirt into the room. "Wear this under the suit. That way you won't get surf rash."

"'Surf rash'?" Jamie was starting to feel like she should have done some pre-lesson research.

"It's a rash you can get from the friction between the suit and your skin," Kylie answered.

Jamie pulled on the tight lime-green shirt. Then she tried to get one foot into a leg of the wetsuit. She wriggled. Not much happened. She tugged. Then yanked. And managed to get the suit up to her calf. "Um, I think it's the wrong size."

"Just take it slow," Kylie advised. "It'll loosen up in the water."

Jamie tried again. Arm muscles straining, she got the suit over her knee. Then it clamped down on her thigh. "Can these things ever cut off the circulation?" she called, hopping on her free foot.

"Well . . . I've never seen it, but—"

The hesitation and that "but" were enough for Jamie. "I don't think I can feel my toes!" she cried. "You might have to cut this thing off me."

The curtain was jerked back, letting Kylie, the counter dude, and two other guys get a good look at her in her surf shirt, bikini bottoms, and part of the Wettie of Death.

"Is she wearing the—" the counter guy began, but couldn't finish. He was laughing too hard. The other guys were laughing, too. Even Kylie's lips were twitching.

"No worries, Kooky. You've just been trying to get your leg through the sleeve," Kylie explained. Her lips kept twitching, but she didn't laugh.

"Oh. Okay. That explains it." Jamie felt like an idiot. "I must be more nervous than I thought." Her stomach felt like it had origami-ed itself into a porcupine, all sharp spikes.

"Let's start again." Kylie guided Jamie onto the small stool in the corner of the dressing room and pulled the curtain shut.

She worked Jamie's leg out of the neoprene vise, adjusted the plastic bag, and began gently working her foot into the correct opening of the wetsuit. Compared to the sleeve, the leg of the suit felt almost roomy.

About five minutes later, Kylie was zipping up the suit. "Are we having fun yet?" she teased.

"Well, I've completely given up any tiny expectation of perfection I'd been holding on to," Jamie answered. "I guess that means I should be having fun any second now."

Kylie slapped her on the back. "That's the spirit, Kooky."

"What's with the 'Kooky'?" It was the second time Kylie had called her that.

"It's what we call new surfers," Kylie explained. "You ready?" She nodded at the curtain.

"As I'll ever be," Jamie replied and Kylie whipped the curtain back, getting snickers from the guys.

"Take a bow," Kylie whispered in Jamie's ear. So she did, and the guys gave her a round of applause as she waddled toward the door.

Once they were outside, Kylie handed her a soft, bright yellow board. Jamie had been expecting one more like the one Kylie held—narrow and sleek, something that didn't look like it was made of the same stuff as pool noodles. Maybe she kinda had been expecting perfection from herself. She'd had a few daydreams where she was riding through a wave tunnel looking extremely cool.

Kylie must have caught Jamie's disappointed expression. "I always have beginners start with a foamy. It's a lot easier to keep your balance on a soft board. And if—let's make that when—you fall off, it won't hurt so much if it smacks you on the head. You'll have it attached to your ankle with a leash." Kylie held up a length of turquoise cord with a Velcro strap at each end.

"We're going to start off in the whitewater," Kylie said as they headed down to the beach.

"Whitewater? Am I ready for that? Isn't that the most dangerous part?" Jamie asked.

"You're thinking of a river. In the ocean, whitewater is the part where the waves break near the shore. The only dangerous part is that once you catch your first wave, you'll be gone. You'll never want to do anything else," Kylie answered. "The waves near the shore are the best place to let you get the feel of the water under the board, and we can stay out of the way of the serious surfers. They can be obnoxious, act like the entire beach is their property."

They reached the edge of the surf. "We're going to get right into the water. Like I said, I'm all about the fun, and I don't think practicing moves on the sand is the way to get introduced to surfing. We're going to walk out a ways. What you're going to do is hold your board out to one side, one hand on each rail. That's each side," she translated. "Keep it an arm's length away from you. You don't want it to pop up and smack you in the face."

"No. No, I do not," Jamie agreed as they began wading into the ocean. *Click,* she thought. She'd started doing that. When she didn't have her cell in her hand and she wanted to save a moment, she'd just think the word "click." And she definitely wanted to hold on to the memory of her first time in the Pacific Ocean—with a surfboard.

"Okay, now turn around and point the nose of the board toward the shore," Kylie called. "Look over your shoulder, and watch for a good wave, one that's big enough to carry you in. Don't go for one that's already breaking."

Jamie studied the waves rolling in. She had no idea which one would carry her. "How big is big enough?"

"Doesn't have to be that big with the soft board you're using," Kylie answered. "When you see one you want to try, get on your stomach on the board and start paddling. Keep paddling until you feel the wave lift you. And remember—fun!"

Jamie nodded. It was hard to focus on picking a wave and fun at the same time. "That one? The second one back?"

"Looks great!" Kylie answered.

Jamie pulled herself onto the board, wiggling around to get herself centered, then she started to paddle. The wave took her—and carried her all the way in. She tumbled off at the last moment, but came up laughing. "That was awesome!" she yelled. "Awesome! Let's do it again!"

By the end of the lesson, Jamie had successfully popped up to her feet three times and was completely surf stoked. She felt like she'd been drinking champagne, champagne and sunlight, her body all fizzy inside. She couldn't stop grinning as she headed back down the Walk to her car.

It wasn't like she saw herself finding a way to turn surfing into a career, but she definitely had something new for her list of likes. Not likes. Loves! Today definitely belonged in The Year of Me.

Mac purred, kneading his claws into Jamie's hair. Tonight his person smelled happy, and new scents that Mac couldn't identify clung to her. He could have stayed right there the whole night, but he knew Jamie still needed a packmate. It was a dog and human thing. She couldn't help it. And there were other people out there who needed Mac. They didn't belong to him, but he couldn't ignore their loneliness, especially since they all seemed too stupid to know what to do about it. Maybe it wasn't stupidity. Maybe it was just that they had extremely weak noses.

He stood and stretched, then leapt off the bed. Time to get to work. He slipped into the night, and darted through the shadows to the house of the young one, feeling the need to check on her again. He squeezed through a partially open window and padded back to her bedroom. The plastic pony was tucked into a box that smelled like the woman. There was contentment in that smell, and happiness in the scent of the young one. Satisfied, he started to leave, but paused near the sofa. The other girl was on the sofa again, reeking of anger and hurt. She wasn't a young one, but she wasn't fully grown. He remembered when he was that age. Sometimes it was like madness ran through him, making him want to run in circles and climb up the curtains. Mac opened his mouth and tasted the scent, taking in all the flavors. He'd see what he could do for her.

But first, some fun. Tail up, whiskers twitching, Mac trotted to the bonehead's house. He wasn't in the yard, but he was close. Mac stuck his head through the dog door, took a quick look, then crawled through. A second later, he heard the bonehead's bellowing bark. Mac trotted to the kitchen and leapt up onto the counter. He pawed a container close to the edge, and when the big mutt raced by, Mac gave it one last push. The barks turned to a howl as the container bonked down on the dog's butt. Something white and powdery that Mac couldn't identify spilled out, coating a patch of the dog's fur.

Mac started pawing at another container. "Diogee, what are you doing?" the dog's packmate yelled. And Mac heard footsteps coming down the stairs.

The bonehead finally noticed Mac—just in time for Mac to send the second container off the counter. The dog leapt back with a yowl. Mac's bomb missed, but hit the ground with a satisfying *thump* and sprayed coffee everywhere. Mac knew coffee when he saw, and smelled it. It was Jamie's catnip.

The man burst into the kitchen. "Have you gone rabid?" he yelled, and the dog rolled over and showed the man his belly. Pathetic. But it gave Mac the perfect opportunity to escape. He started for the dog door, then turned and raced up the stairs instead. He'd get a little something for Jamie. He knew she'd gotten a good whiff of the man's smell from that shirt he'd given her, but she hadn't *done* anything. She might need reminders.

Sometimes he still had to remind her about breakfast, and she knew he always wanted breakfast as soon as he woke up.

Mac decided to keep giving Jamie other choices, too, even though he liked this man's smell the most and thought the man needed a human packmate as much as Jamie did, maybe even more. He'd keep bringing her smells, and eventually he knew she'd figure out what she was supposed to do.

CHAPTER 7

Jamie groaned as she reached for a can of cat food. Yesterday's surf lesson had been mind-blowing. She hadn't realized until she got out of bed this morning that it had wrecked her body. Her ribs hurt, her arms hurt, even her toes hurt. Paddling didn't sound like something that would take much exertion, but Jamie now knew how Kylie had gotten those biceps. She figured she must have been gripping the board with her toes, but she had no idea why her ribs were aching. She'd taken a few spills, but nothing too bad.

"I'm addicted now, though," she told Mac, who was twining himself around her ankles. "I already signed up for another lesson. Maybe I should start a conditioning routine. A little weightlifting." Playfully, she scooped Mac up and raised him over her head. He gave a yowl of disapproval, and she gave a groan of pain. "That was not a good idea," she said as she put Mac down. He glared at her, but she knew how to get his forgiveness. She quickly filled his bowl with food that mixed venison with salmon.

Now that he was taken care of, she turned her attention to herself. What she wanted to do was soak in a tub of Epsom salts. Not that she had any. Would regular salt work? She'd just use bubble bath, she decided. She'd found a new kind in a little shop nearby, lavender and basil. Absolutely delicious. The woman who owned the place had given Jamie a tour of the back room and let her take some pictures. Jamie had loved the intensity of the woman's expression when she talked about the properties of various plants.

Jamie started to fill the tub with the hottest water she could stand, then turned off the taps. She had to check the porch. If she didn't, she would spend the whole time she was in the bath wondering if something had been left on the doormat.

Jamie hobbled to the door and opened it, then forced herself to look down. There was a man's sandal that looked like it had a lot of wear left in it, a hairbrush, a Red Sox baseball cap, and a crumpled, moist-looking tissue. Who was doing this? What was it supposed to mean? Maybe she should put a note on the door saying that Desmond didn't live here anymore. The stuff had to be for him. Or was it from kids goofing around? She should ask Ruby if she'd gotten anything other than the pony left on her doorstep.

What if it wasn't kids? Could all the stuff be from the same guy? Could some guy be obsessed with her? Why? The town was full of models and actresses to stalk. The idea that someone had specifically targeted her was creepy. She tried to shove the thought away. Way, way too creepy. And the underwear was different sizes, so that meant—

"Morning, Toots."

Jamie jerked her head up and saw Hud Martin heading up the walkway to her house. She rushed down the steps to meet him. If he saw the random pile of stuff on her porch, she knew he'd have questions, lots of questions. She wasn't in the mood.

She was in the mood for a bath and a book that would make her forget the creepiness for a while.

"Good morning," she said, forcing a smile. "Going fishing?" He had on the vest again.

"That's always the plan, but somehow something always comes along that requires my attention," he answered. "Today it's a missing shoe." He pulled a little notebook out from one of the vest's pockets. "Teva sandal. Size ten. Mosaic pattern. You wouldn't know anything about that, would you?"

Jamie's heart started beating a little faster. She felt guilty, even though she had no reason to. Should she tell Hud that the shoe had shown up on her porch? She'd definitely be questioned. But if he saw the shoe, and she hadn't said anything . . .

"In fact, I do," she answered. Maybe he'd actually help and find out what was going on. From what Al said, he was always looking for a mystery to solve. "A shoe like that showed up on my doorstep this morning." She stepped back and pointed. "That brush and baseball hat, too. Oh, and that tissue."

" 'Showed up,' you say."

" 'Showed up,' I said." Jamie agreed. Hud made a note in his little book. "Do you think you could give the shoe back? Or tell me who to give it back to?" she asked.

"You're saying this morning was the first time you saw it or the other items?"

"That's what I'm saying."

He stared at her. She stared back.

If Ruby hadn't shown up, who knew how long the stare-off would have lasted. Hud turned his attention to her. "Is there a reason you're here this morning?"

"Do I need a reason?" Ruby asked. Hud gave her The Stare. He was almost as good at it as Mac was. Ruby sighed. "It seems like you really think I need a reason to be in my own neighborhood. I came over to visit my friend"—she nodded at Jamie— "and find out how her surfing lesson went."

Hud turned his attention back to Jamie. "Surfing lesson. Kind of a pricey hobby, isn't it?"

Jamie was getting tired of his intimations. "If I was financing it by selling stolen goods, don't you think I would have taken both shoes?"

"Put some thought into what would be the most profitable, have you?" Hud asked.

"Help me," Jamie said to Ruby. "Please just help me."

"Interesting that the two of you are friends," Hud said before Ruby could jump in. "Seeing as Tootsie Pop here also had a stolen object appear on her porch and claimed to have no knowledge of how it came to be there."

"And you know what? I felt bad for the little girl, Riley, so I made her a barn for the pony. She loved it," Ruby told Hud.

"Made you feel good, didn't it?" Hud unclipped a small pair of scissors from the lanyard around his neck and began using one of the blades to clean his fingernails.

"Made me feel great. I've never seen anybody smile so wide," Ruby answered.

"The criminal mind is a fascinating thing," Hud commented. "We think of profit as a motive. We think of revenge. And many times, those are reasons a crime is committed. But for some, the brain's wiring is stranger, more twisted. A criminal could, for instance, steal so that they could be seen as a hero by returning what they took."

"So, you think I stole the pony so I could get gratitude from a little girl by bringing it back to her, and then making it a barn?" Ruby demanded.

"Did I say that?" Hud asked, all wide-eyed innocence. No wonder he'd never starred in another show, Jamie thought. His acting sucked.

"You pretty much did, yeah," Ruby told him.

"And I'm supposed to get a thrill from the used tissue?"

Jamie asked. "Do you really think anyone would be grateful to get a used tissue back?"

Hud continued working on his nails. "A clever criminal understands the value of misdirection."

Jamie shook her head. "I'm going in. You coming?" she asked Ruby.

"Of course. We have a crime spree to plan," Ruby said.

"There are times when criminals with a shared psychosis team up. It always ends badly," Hud called after them.

"He's very subtle, very Sherlock." Jamie opened the door for Ruby.

"I almost confessed. I almost admitted we are the Thelma and Louise of Storybook Court," Ruby said.

"I must have coffee. Do you want coffee?" Jamie asked, heading for the kitchen.

"Of course." Ruby sat down at the kitchen table and Mac immediately leapt into her lap.

"Wow. Mac usually takes his time before he honors someone with his presence," Jamie said. "Do you mind?"

"How could I mind?" Ruby tickled Mac under the chin, and his eyes drifted most of the way closed as he entered a pleasure trance.

"Have you gotten anything else on your porch?" Jamie asked as she poured two big mugs of coffee and set them on the table.

"Nope. Obviously you have."

"Yeah. Since last time we talked, I've received a sweaty T-shirt, plus the stuff from this morning. I'm really struggling not to have a complete freak-out." Jamie added two big spoonfuls of sugar to her coffee, then took a slug.

"It's definitely weird. But it's not necessarily malicious." Ruby continued to work on Mac's chin.

"What about the ex–TV detective? Is he going to turn us in?" Jamie asked.

Ruby laughed. "To who? Besides, he's enjoying the mystery too much to want it to end. So how was the surfing?"

"I'm so glad you suggested it. It was amazing. I'm already hooked. I'm also ridiculously sore," Jamie answered.

"I thought you'd go for it. And Kylie's great."

"Yeah, I loved how important it was to her to make it fun. And it really seemed like she was having fun, too. Look at these pics I took of her." Jamie got her cell, brought up the photo gallery, and handed it to Ruby. "I think that's something I want as part of my dream job. I want it to be fun—at least some of the time."

"These are really great," Ruby said, clicking through the pictures. "You caught her personality. I love the one of Bad Advice Guy, too."

"Thanks."

"Jamie! Marie says to come to dinner tomorrow tonight," Al hollered.

"What does he do in the winter when people close their windows?" Jamie whispered to Ruby, then she yelled an answer. "That sounds great. What should I bring?"

"Nothing. But Marie says to wear a dress. Come at seven."

"Uh-oh," Ruby said.

"Dinner won't be so bad. I actually like them," Jamie answered.

"Me, too. I've gone to dinner there myself. But Marie has never made Al tell me what to wear." Ruby took a sip of coffee and smiled. "My friend, I think tomorrow night you're getting set up."

"I told Marie and Helen I didn't want that. I told them both!" Jamie exclaimed.

"You haven't known Marie that long, but I bet you've already found out that she does whatever she wants to do."

"If you're right, she's probably going to have her great-nephew over there. She keeps bringing him up. And then Helen brings up her godson. Can I just not go? Can I say I'm sick?" Jamie asked.

"Marie will be over here with ginger ale, soda crackers, and chicken soup, checking on you and your alibi," Ruby predicted. "It's going to happen. I say just get it over with."

Jamie sighed. "You're right. And it's just dinner with Al and Marie there. How bad can it be?"

It'll only be about a half an hour, David told himself. He'd expected to be a little nervous. It had been a long time—a long, long time—since he'd been on a date. He hadn't expected sweat to be popping up between his fingers.

This wasn't a date, anyway. They were going to meet quickly so they'd both have the chance to confirm who they were dealing with. He'd told Madison, the high school girl who worked behind the counter part-time, that a friend was dropping by. She didn't need to know more than that, and she should be busy with customers. A lot of people stopped at the bakery on the way home. Next time, he'd choose a place where he didn't know anyone.

He checked his watch. A couple minutes until six. He brought a plate with a couple of his boozy cupcakes on it over to a table by the window and sat down. He used a napkin to wipe between his fingers, while he mentally reviewed the possible conversation starters he'd come up with. Well, he'd come up with them with the help of some online articles. "What's your dream job?" "Are you a dog or a cat person?" And the classic: "How was your day?" He was thinking of borrowing Ruby's favorite getting-to-know-somebody question: "What would be the title of the movie of your life?" He didn't usually have trouble talking to people, but this wasn't usual.

He resisted the temptation to check Sabrina's picture again, even though it wasn't as if he'd forgotten what she looked like. They'd exchanged a few texts during the day, and he'd liked how she came across. She had a quick sense of humor, although she hadn't picked up on his *Pulp Fiction* reference, and you had to be a little suspicious of people who didn't appreciate *Pulp Fiction.*

The string of bells on the front door jangled, the door swung open, and there she was. She looked like her picture. Adam had warned him that she might not. But she really did—until she walked past the back of the booth by the door and he could see her from the waist down.

She was pregnant. Preg-nant. Eight months? More? He didn't know. But *really* pregnant, possibly even rush-to-the-hospital pregnant. David's brain started sending out instructions. *Smile. Don't stare at the belly. Introduce yourself.*

He smiled. He stood. "Sabrina?"

She smiled back. A nice smile. "David?"

He nodded, gestured to the seat across from him. "Cocktail cupcakes, as promised."

"Fabulous." She sat down, took one of the cupcakes, and bit into it. "My boyfriend would have a fit if he saw me eating this. He was so worried about me gaining weight."

"Boyfriend," David repeated. Was his first counterpart.com meet-up actually a pregnant woman with a boyfriend?

"*Ex*-boyfriend," she amended. "He acted like he didn't want me to eat junk because he cared about my health and the baby's. But, come on, he didn't want me to get fat. He probably expects—expected—me to be in a bikini on the way home from the hospital." She took another bite of the cupcake. "Amazing."

It sounded to David like the guy hadn't been her ex-boyfriend for long. What the hell was he supposed to do here? "Do you want some coffee or tea or anything?" he asked. Clearly what the hell he was supposed to do was act normal, have a coffee with her, say it had been great to meet her, and go on with his life.

"Coffee, please," she said. "Another thing my boyfriend—ex-boyfriend—didn't want me having. The doctor said a little caffeine was fine, but that wasn't enough for Patrick. He didn't want me to have coffee for nine whole months. Not that he was willing to give up his two-shot-of-espresso Black Eyes as moral support. He kept saying he wasn't pregnant and there was no way what he ingested would hurt the baby and that I was being unreasonable to expect him to give up anything."

"Right back," David said. He took his time getting coffee, cream, and sugar from behind the counter and returning to her.

"I guess I should have asked before," Sabrina said when he sat back down. "There's not too much alcohol in the cupcakes, right?"

"You'd probably have to eat about a dozen to get as much alcohol as in a beer," David told her. "As long as you don't squirt on anything from the pipettes."

Sabrina swiped one finger across the top of a cupcake and licked off the icing. "I'm not asking how many calories. It's been a long eight and a half months."

"I bet," David said. He wanted to look at the clock, but he didn't let himself. He'd let her drink her coffee, and hopefully that wouldn't take long, then he'd make an excuse for why he had to go.

Sabrina snorted. "Men always try to act sympathetic and understanding. But there's no way any of you can understand, no possible way, so you shouldn't even try." Her voice had turned shrill, and her eyes had brightened with mania. Or maybe it was just a sugar high. She was already starting on a second cupcake.

"Okay, yeah, you're right," David answered, keeping his voice low and calm. "No man can know what it's really like to be pregnant."

She started chewing so hard he could hear her teeth clicking together. "And now you're doing that thing where you make your voice all soothing, like I'm a rabid animal about to bite you."

Got that right, David thought. It seemed like any reaction he gave would be the wrong one, so he turned his attention to stirring some sugar into his coffee.

"See? You expect me to give up sugar, but there you go, using it yourself, and right in front of me," Sabrina accused.

"Hold up," David said. "We've never even met before. I don't expect anything."

"So, you don't care about the baby." Sabrina finished the second cupcake and took the half-eaten one off his plate.

"Look, clearly this isn't a good time to be starting up something new. I hope everything goes—"

Sabrina didn't let him finish. "You're disgusted by me. You can't have a baby without getting fat. It's impossible."

"Not gonna argue with you. Let me get you a few cupcakes for the road." David stood up so quickly, he almost knocked over his chair. He returned behind the counter, mind racing as he boxed up a half dozen of the cupcakes. Was he going to be able to get her out of there without her having a complete meltdown? Could she get so upset she could bring on premature labor? Was that a possibility?

He glanced over at Madison. She goggled back at him. She wasn't going to be any help.

"Here you go," David said when he returned to the table. He set the cupcake box down in front of her without sitting back down. "There are two more of the cabernet ones. The rest are alcohol-free."

"I can make my own choices, you know," Sabrina cried. "I read four hundred books on being pregnant. I know what's okay and what's not."

"Sure. Of course." David took a step back, holding his hands up in surrender. A dog, friends, a job he liked, it was sounding pretty good. It was sounding very good.

The bells on the door tinkled, and a tall man with thinning red hair rushed in. "Sabrina! What the hell?" he shouted.

She jerked her chin up. "You caught me. I'm eating cupcakes—with booze in them. And I'm drinking coffee. If you cared about the baby, you wouldn't be yelling. You're always saying how bad stress is for her."

"I'm not talking about the damn cupcakes," the man whisper-yelled. "I'm talking about you being here on a date."

"Why shouldn't I?" Sabrina asked. She opened the cupcake box, grabbed a cupcake, and shoved half of it into her mouth without even peeling away the paper. "You obviously don't want to be with me. I'm way too fat and selfish and stupid to be with you."

David took a few more steps back. Madison leaned forward, mouth falling open.

"You know that's not true, sweetheart," the man crooned. He knelt next to Sabrina and wrapped his arms around her. "You're perfect. Absolutely perfect."

Madison shot David an *are-you-hearing-this* look. The man looked at David, too, his face hardening. "Nice move, hitting on a woman when she's hormonal and vulnerable."

"I didn't even—" David didn't finish the sentence. Anything he said could make the guy, Sabrina, or both of them lose it. "I'm sorry." That was absolutely true. He was extremely, massively, colossally sorry.

"Let's go home," the man said to Sabrina, running his hand tenderly over her belly.

Sabrina shoved herself to her feet. She smiled at David as if she hadn't been ready to stab him with a fork a few minutes before. "You seem like a nice guy. I'm sure you'll meet someone who's right for you. I'm just not that person. I put up that profile when I was sort of upset."

"Not a problem," David told her. He watched Sabrina and the non-ex-boyfriend walk out of the bakery. He kept watching until they were out of sight. Then he let himself take a breath.

"I'm thinking reactive attachment disorder, her. Dependent personality disorder, him." Madison said. She was thinking of studying psychology when she started college, and she had a diagnosis for everyone who came in.

"I'd diagnose both as Coo-Coo for Cocoa Puffs." David answered. "I'm going home."

His plan was to walk the beast, get a beer, then find sports of some kind, didn't matter what, on TV and not have another thought until at least the next morning. But when he got home, he saw Zachary sitting on his front steps, Diogee leaning against him. The kid clearly had something on his mind.

"What's the up, my man?" he asked as he took a seat next to Zachary. Diogee got up and presented David with his butt. David began scratching it.

Zachary held up a small book with a fuzzy purple zebra-print cover. "I found this outside the front door this morning."

David took it and flipped it open. The first page had a warning written in all caps with a black felt-tip pen: "ANYONE WHO READS THIS WILL BE DISMEMBERED."

"It's Addison Brewer's diary," Zachary said.

"You read it?" David asked, handing it back.

"No. Well, only a little. To see whose it was," Zachary admitted. "Now I don't know what to do. If I give it back to her, she'll probably kill me, because she'll think I read it."

"Which you did," David reminded him.

"Not all of it," Zachary protested. "I thought of sneaking it back onto her porch, but what if she caught me? She'd kill me. But there's really personal stuff in here—"

"Which you didn't read," David commented.

"Not all of it," Zachary said again. "It would probably make her nuts not to know where it was. Nuts-er. I was thinking maybe you could—"

"No way. I'd do a lot of things for you, kid, but I'm not risking dismemberment," David told him.

"Maybe we could let Diogee chew it up?" Zachary sounded hopeful.

Diogee's tail whipped into action at the sound of his name connected with something that involved eating. "I'm sure he'd be happy to," David answered. "But no. You have any idea how much a vet bill would be for sewing all his legs back on?" He thought for a minute. "How about mailing it back? We could print out a label and wear rubber gloves. No handwriting to analyze, no fingerprints."

"Genius." Zachary leaned back, propping his elbows on the step above where he was sitting. "You know, in the pages I read—"

"The pages with writing on them," David said.

"I didn't read it all!" Zachary protested. "But I saw some stuff that made it sound like her boyfriend is kind of a jerk."

"You didn't need to read any of it to know that." David's fingers were starting to cramp, but when he stopped scratching Diogee, the dog gave him such a beseeching look that David started up again. "Everyone in the neighborhood has heard her reaming him out on the phone. Although maybe it's a combination of him being a jerk and Addison having unreasonable expectations."

"I don't think it's that unreasonable to expect him to acknowledge her in front of her friends, show up when he says he'll meet her, or remember her birthday. Even I remember her birthday," Zachary said.

He has a crush on her, David realized. He'd suspected the red-golf-ball-looking-mark-on-the-face incident had to do with a girl, but never in a billion years would he have thought that girl was Addison Brewer. Not that Addison wasn't pretty. But as Zachary himself said, she acted like a shrew. At least she had over the last year or so. But maybe it was because her boyfriend was making her crazy.

He looked at Zachary. Did Zachary realize he had a crush on her yet?

"Do I put a note with the diary or anything?" Zachary asked. He straightened up. "I just realized—don't you think it'll freak her out to get it the mail when her address wasn't even in it? She might think she has a stalker."

"Okay, I've got it," David said. "Ruby has been working on some kind of dream barn for Riley's toy pony. I'll give the diary to Ruby, and the next time she goes over there, she can just stick it under the sofa or something. That way Addison will never know anyone saw it."

"Genius." Zachary leaned back again. "Thanks."

"Not a problem," David said. "Feel like walking Diogee with me?" At the word "walk" Diogee bolted through the dog door, which was perfectly round to match his perfectly round Hobbit house front door.

"Yeah."

As Diogee barreled back through the dog door with his leash in his mouth, David's phone vibrated. He checked it. Adam. He knew his friend wouldn't give up until he let him know how it had gone with Sabrina.

"I have to answer this," David told Zachary. "You and Diogee go ahead and go. I'll catch up with you."

Zachary nodded. He took the leash from Diogee and snapped it on his collar, then Diogee dragged him across the lawn. David noted that Diogee didn't let Zachary go out the gate first.

David answered the phone. He didn't bother with a "hello." "She was pregnant. And she had a boyfriend," he announced.

"You can't let this stop you," Adam said when he stopped laughing. David heard Lucy's voice in the background, and then he heard Adam relaying what David had told him. "Lucy says that she wants to pick the next woman because you and I clearly suck at it."

"I need a little recovery time," David said. "I feel like I just stepped out of a soap opera."

"Screw that," Adam answered. "A little time would turn into a year. Lucy's going to go through the profiles. She'll find you someone good." He hung up before David could tell him no.

CHAPTER 8

Jamie stretched out on her belly so she could get a picture of Ruby and Riley looking at Paula's dream barn. Ruby had decided it needed to have one side open, like a dollhouse. Their expressions were so similar—excitement mixed with deep concentration as they discussed what should be in Paula's stall. Should she have a bed, or the softest hay of shining gold, or maybe something made of pink clouds?

"How about this?" Ruby asked. "A canopy bed, but with the gold hay on top of the mattress part."

"And a pink cloud pillow!" Riley clapped her hands, then made Paula clap her front hooves.

Ruby grabbed her duffel bag off of Riley's bed and pulled it down next to them on the floor. "I brought some different kinds of material. Let's see what we can find for the canopy."

Smiling, Jamie took more pictures of the two of them examining a filmy flowered scarf. Purple on pink, of course. *This is probably how Ruby is with directors,* she thought. *Listening to their vision and finding the best possible way to make it reality.*

She definitely had found her passion and was using it to make a living. And to make a little girl insanely happy.

The door to Riley's room banged open, and Jamie, Ruby, and Riley all jerked their heads toward the sound. Addison, Riley's big sister, stood there, holding her diary. Jamie knew it was her diary, because on their way over, Ruby had confided that a neighbor boy had found it on his porch and Ruby was sneaking it back into the house so Addison wouldn't realize anyone else had seen it.

"Riley, you said you hadn't touched this." Addison waved the diary at her sister.

"I didn't," Riley whined.

"Then how did it get in the corner behind the chair, along with your Princess Sofia coloring book and your fairy wand?" Addison demanded.

"I didn't," Riley repeated.

"I'm always finding things in places I don't remember putting them," Ruby said quickly. "The other day I found a bag of frozen peas, *formerly* frozen peas, in my sock drawer. Seriously, my sock drawer."

"I find things in weird places, too," Jamie added. "Maybe you set it on the chair and it just fell off."

"I guess," Addison muttered. "Just don't touch it, no matter where it is, Riley," she added, then left.

"I didn't." Riley held the scarf up against her cheek, then ran it over her pony's back. "Paula likes this one."

"Great choice," Ruby said. "Jamie and I have to go. I have to help her get ready for a big date."

"It's not really a date," Jamie said to Riley, then felt silly for feeling the need to clarify that to a four-year-old.

"I say, keep an open mind," Ruby told Jamie. She picked up her duffel, then ruffled Riley's hair and gave Paula a pat. "I'll get to work on the canopy. If it's okay with your mom, you can come over tomorrow and pick out what you want for clouds and hay."

"It'll be fine. I'll bring her over after school," Addison called from the living room. "She just needs to be back by seven. That's when Mom gets home and she insists we eat dinner together on the nights she gets home in time." The girl actually sounded cheerful. It had to be hard being responsible for a little sister, even one as adorable as Riley, so much of the time. The addition of Ruby to the mix was perfect for all three of them. Addison got some free time. Riley got some attention. And Ruby got to enjoy the company of a kid. Jamie remembered the wistful tone Ruby'd had when she'd talked about losing the chance to have children.

"We have a plan, then," Ruby said. "Bye-bye, cutie."

"'Bye. Thanks for letting me visit," Jamie added.

"'Bye," Riley answered, staring into the dream barn as if she was already imagining the canopy bed inside.

Jamie and Ruby had just left the house when they heard a scream. They rushed back inside. "What's wrong? What happened?" Ruby cried, looking from Addison to Riley.

Addison threw her cell onto the floor. "What happened is that my boyfriend is an—" She glanced at her little sister. "He's not very nice, okay? He just sent me a picture of him at McDonald's with his buddies, and this girl who works there, Olivia, she goes to our school, she's practically sitting on his lap. And he's loving it. He sent it out to a bunch of people. I don't even know if he meant to send it to me. Doesn't matter. Either way makes him an—Makes him not very nice."

"How long have you been going out with him?" Jamie asked, while Ruby went over to Riley and took her back to her room.

"Two years. Unless you don't count the times when we

were broken up," Addison answered. "I count them, because we always get back together."

"I guess that makes sense," Jamie said.

"Just so you know, Riley says the scream scared Paula, but that the pony's okay," Ruby said, returning to the living room. "I've gotta admit, that scream made my heart stop for a second, Addison. It sounded more like an I'm-being-stabbed scream than a my-boyfriend-is-not-very-nice-scream."

Addison picked up her cell. "I'm texting him that breathing in a combination of zit cream and hamburger grease can cause cancer," she announced.

"We have to go," Ruby said. "Remember to bring Riley over after school tomorrow."

"Yeah," Addison said, eyes locked on her phone.

"I was trying to come up with a way to tell her to stop wasting her time with that guy," Jamie said once they were back outside. "But everything I thought of sounded too preachy, even though I have actual experience staying with the wrong guy for way too long."

"Don't we all?" Ruby asked as they started for Jamie's. "I should have figured out my ex and I didn't want the same things before we got married. Except, now he has kids, so I guess he *did* want the same things, just not with me." She gave one hand a flick. "That way lies madness. I'm not thinking about it. I'm going to think about Paula's barn instead. I think I can whittle some posts for the bed."

Jamie understood that there were some things it was better not to dwell on. She didn't feel like thinking about Mr. Cling-Wrap or Mr. Forgot-to-Mention-I-Was-Married or any of her other relationship mistakes. "Whittle? You are the definition of multitalented," she said.

"I whittled some little animals for a movie I worked on. That's one thing I love about my job. I'm always learning how to do new stuff," Ruby told her. "I'm addicted to the learning curve."

"I want that, too. Teaching the same thing over and over got hard. Thanks again for suggesting the surfing," she added. "Got any other ideas for me and my search for personal fulfilment. And a living wage?" That was what she wanted to focus on. The future, not the past.

"I don't know about the living wage, but I took an improv class once. The Groundlings have some. That's where Melissa McCarthy got started. Cheri Oteri, Lisa Kudrow, Julia Sweeney, Kristen Wiig, Jennifer Coolidge, too. So many amazing women. And guys. The class was a hoot," Ruby answered.

"It sounds somewhat terrifying," Jamie said.

"What doesn't kill you makes you stronger," Ruby sang. "Is it okay if I go through your closet?" she asked when they went into Jamie's place. She was already heading toward the bedroom, Mac trotting along behind her.

"Sure. There's not much there in the way of dresses. I'm actually in this stage where most of my clothes don't feel like me. You ever get like that?" Jamie asked.

"My closet looks like it belongs to someone with multiple personality disorder. But I like having options." She opened the doors to Jamie's closet and began flipping through the hangers. "Ah, the little black dress," she said. "Nice, but not exactly dinner at the neighbors'." She continued flipping. "Looks like the only other choice is what looks like funeral wear."

"That's the last time I wore it. My mom's funeral," Jamie admitted, reaching out to touch the sleeve of the navy-blue sheath dress.

"Sorry," Ruby murmured.

"It's okay. Do you think a skirt would satisfy Marie?" Jamie pulled out a beige-and-brown plaid pencil skirt she used to wear to parent-teacher night. "It's nothing special, but that's the only other option."

"I need to take you shopping," Ruby said. "We'll go to The Way We Wore, for starters. Great vintage stuff. But, yes, that skirt will do. With this." She selected a casual chambray shirt. "Under this." She pulled out a green-and-white-striped pullover. "And these shoes, which I want." She grabbed Jamie's favorite peep-toe ankle boots, a big splurge from a few years ago.

"Never would have thought of those together," Jamie said. "You've definitely got an artist's eye. You have any idea who Marie might spring on me tonight? She mentioned a great-nephew. Ever met him?"

Ruby shook her head. "I don't envy you, getting tangled up in one of Marie and Helen's competitions. The one over whose soda bread was better was epic, lasted for more than a year. Nessie, Helen's sister, got involved in that one. Not that they ever said a word to each other. It all went through Marie."

"I've heard Marie mention Nessie, but I didn't know who she was," Jamie said.

"Helen's twin. They grew up in Storybook Court. Their parents got divorced when they were eleven. Dad moved to a house on the other side of the Court. Mom stayed in the one next to the Defranciscos. Nessie—Clyemnestra, if you can believe that—went with Dad. Helen stayed with Mom. Helen and Nessie never spoke to each other again."

"Sad," Jamie said.

"Yeah. Sad. I can't imagine not talking to my sis. I wish she lived closer. She's in New Orleans," Ruby answered.

"I wish I had a sister. Or a brother. With my mom gone, I have no family. Well, you know, some relatives I exchange Christmas cards with." Jamie noticed that Mac had gotten into her closet and was staring up at the box of stuff that had been left outside the door. She picked him up, set him on the bed, then quickly shut the closet door so he couldn't get back in. He gave a little growl of annoyance, but she ignored him. There were times when MacGyver had to be ignored.

"What about your dad?" Ruby asked.

"Car accident. When I was about Riley's age. I honestly can hardly remember him," Jamie answered.

"That's so hard," Ruby said, giving Jamie's shoulder a squeeze. Jamie did a subject change. She didn't want to get all emotional before what was probably going to be a blind date at Al and Marie's.

"The frustrating thing is, I tried to stop Marie from setting me up. I said no. I think I actually said, 'No, no, no. No.' So maybe this dinner is just a dinner," Jamie said.

"Signs point to no," Ruby told her. "Marie hasn't ever even mentioned her great-nephew to me, so I've got no intel for you. Helen's godson, I met once. I've got nothing there, either. He was on the bland side. Whatever he said, it wasn't memorable."

Mac began to purr loudly, and Jamie saw that he'd curled up on the outfit they'd just picked out. "No need for accessories. I've got cat hair." She gave him a nudge. He jumped off the bed and stalked out of the room in a huff, tail high. "Does Marie try to fix up everyone? Or am I special?"

"She attempted to matchmake for me years ago, but you're the first new blood she's had in a while."

"What about Helen? Has Marie ever tried to find someone for her?" Jamie asked.

"Not as far as I know," Ruby said. "But Helen, unlike you and the rest of us, can actually go toe to toe with Marie and occasionally win."

"Ah."

"I need to head out. I don't want to fall behind on my holiday baking," Ruby announced.

"Yeah, it's getting on toward the end of September. Time's a wastin'," Jamie teased.

"I expect details tomorrow! Or later tonight. Come over if you want." Ruby started for the door.

Jamie caught her by the elbow. "How about if you come to dinner, too? I promise I'll help you with holiday baking. I'll bake a million cookies if you come. Marie won't mind. I'm sure she's made enough food for a dozen people."

"At least. Probably Al will be sent out to deliver leftovers later," Ruby agreed. "But I'm not going over there uninvited. Marie would just order me to go home."

She was probably right. Jamie had already learned that Marie never had a problem saying what she thought, politeness be damned.

"Think positive," Ruby told her. "Whoever it is might be great. And a guy doesn't have to derail your Year of Me. You could just use him for sex."

Think positive, like Ruby said, Jamie reminded herself as she knocked on the Defranciscos' door a few hours later. Marie answered. She shook her head as she ushered Jamie inside. "Well, you wore a skirt. But plaid doesn't go with stripes. You look a little like a hobo."

Boho, Jamie wanted to correct her. She loved the funky outfit Ruby had created for her, but there was no point in getting into that with Marie. Instead, she handed Marie the bouquet of flowers she'd chosen as a hostess present. This time she got an approving nod. "Al, get a vase," Marie called.

Al appeared from down the hall, took the flowers with a grunt, and disappeared into the kitchen. Marie gestured to the sofa in the—empty!—living room, and, relieved, Jamie sat down. The relief only lasted for another few seconds, then the doorbell rang.

"Our tax man broke his wrist. He's been living on canned food, so I invited him over for dinner when I ran into him at the grocery earlier today," Marie told Jamie, then she went to get the door.

Earlier today. Right, Jamie thought. That was why *yesterday* Marie, via Al, had told Jamie to wear a dress when she came over. She wondered how well Marie knew the tax man, and what, if anything, made her think he and Jamie would be a good match. Maybe she thought at Jamie's advanced age of thirty-four, all that was needed was a pulse.

But the man Marie led into the living room had more than a heartbeat. He was what Jamie's mother would have called "nice looking." Average build. Average height. Had put some effort into his appearance, wearing a sports coat and tie with pressed khakis. She wondered if Marie had told him how to dress, too. Jamie noted that he didn't seem surprised to see her there.

"This is Jamie Snyder. She just moved in next door. She's from Pennsylvania. She teaches high school history," Marie said.

"Actually, I'm not currently teaching, but I *have* had all my shots," Jamie joked. Marie frowned at her, but the man smiled. He had one of those smiles that transformed him, turning his face from your basic nice to really attractive.

"This is Scott Reid. He's been Al's and my tax adviser for eight years, since his father retired," Marie continued.

"Nice to meet you," Scott told Jamie, then turned to Marie. "I brought you this. Thanks for inviting me." He handed her a box of See's candy.

Nice manners, Jamie noted. But she shouldn't have expected less from someone Marie-approved.

Marie set the candy on the coffee table. "I'm going to help Al with the cocktails," she announced, then left Jamie alone with Scott.

"How'd you break your arm? Or are you tired of answering that?"

"Not tired, but kind of embarrassed," Scott said. "I fell off my boogieboard."

"That's not embarrassing," Jamie told him. "Everybody falls off sometimes. I just took a surfing lesson and I fell off a ton of times, sometimes before I even tried to pop up."

"Surfing? You know we're supposed to be mortal enemies, right?" Scott asked.

"How come?"

"Surfers like to think surfing's the sport of kings and that you have to earn the right to join the lineup," Scott explained. "Which, I can sort of see. It takes a lot of practice to ride standing up, and then some boogieboarder comes along and is getting a tube almost on the first time out—while lying down on basically a sponge."

"The board I used was actually kind of spongy. My instructor said it was more forgiving of balance mistakes. And yet, I still fell, so it wasn't completely forgiving. It was great, though. I loved it," Jamie said.

Marie returned, followed by Al, who carried a tray of martini glasses filled with a golden liquid. "What are those? Pear martinis?" Jamie asked.

"Heathen. Those are sidecars," Scott joked. "You even sugared the rim," he said as Al handed him one of the drinks. Al gave a pleased grunt.

Jamie took a sip of hers. "Mmm. I feel like I'm at one of Gatsby's parties."

"It definitely would have been served on East Egg," Scott agreed.

Maybe Ruby had called it. Scott did seem to have at least the potential for being great. He knew surfing and literature and he had a good smile. She didn't want anything serious right now. She definitely didn't want a relationship. But maybe she could use him for sex—and a little conversation, maybe a few trips to the beach—during her Year of Me. Nothing serious. Nothing that would distract her from her goals.

*   *   *

"You had fun," Ruby said when she opened the door to Jamie several hours later.

"I did," Jamie admitted.

"Was it the great-nephew?" Ruby asked as they headed to the kitchen. Ruby was one of those people whose kitchen was their living room.

"Nope. Al and Marie's tax guy." She handed Ruby a large paper bag. "Leftovers. I told Al I'd do delivery duty."

"Did you get cocktails? I'm sure you did. Al is Mr. Mixologist. Once I got grasshoppers complete with chocolate shavings, and once French 75s with a perfect long lemon spiral. The man believes in presentation."

"Sidecars for us. I didn't recognize them. I now know my cocktail education is woeful," Jamie said.

"But why are we talking about the drinks? You had fun. That means the accountant had to have been at least decent company." Ruby opened the bag, took a sniff, and smiled. "Marie's chicken Kiev?"

"You got it. And this cake called the Tunnel of Fudge."

"Bundt pan, right?" Jamie nodded. "But why are we talking about the food? Give me the details on the man." Ruby rolled the top of the bag closed.

"I think he might actually be great. Smart, lots of interests, good manners, excellent smile," Jamie answered.

"I told you to stay positive!" Ruby exclaimed. "Did you exchange numbers?"

"We did." Jamie felt a grin spreading across her face and tried to dial it back to a regular smile. "But I'm not going to get all crazy. I have more important things on my agenda than romance."

"Are you telling me that or yourself?" Ruby asked. She

opened the bag again and took out a Tupperware container. "I already ate, but I have to have some. Do you care?"

"Of course not," Jamie told her.

"He doesn't have to get in the way of you figuring out your life. He can be just a fun addition. Like surfing." Ruby leaned back in her chair and managed to snag a fork out of a drawer without standing up.

"Well, we'll see if he calls," Jamie said.

"He'll call," Ruby assured her.

"Oh my gosh. Just when you said that, my cell vibrated." Jamie pulled her phone out of her pocket.

"I still can't believe I'm friends with someone who says 'oh my gosh' unironically," Ruby said.

"It's a text from him," Jamie announced.

"He's not playing the game where he acts like he's not too interested. Good for him." Ruby took a bite of chicken.

Jamie read the text. Read it again. Read it again. Read it one more time.

"So? What does it say?" Ruby asked. She took another bite of chicken as Jamie handed her the cell. She couldn't bring herself to read the text aloud.

Ruby read the message, choked, grabbed a napkin, and spit the chicken out. "Marie would—I don't even know what Marie would do if she read this."

"She's not going to. I'm getting rid of it right now." Jamie took the cell back. Deleted the message. But she didn't think she'd be able to delete it from her mind: *Not up to all my usual moves with my cast and don't want you to miss any pleasure. Have a hot friend who could join us? I'm free later tonight.*

Mac wasn't sure how to interpret Jamie's smell that night. He opened his mouth and breathed in so he could pick up extra information, but he still wasn't sure. So he wasn't sure what kind of gift to get her.

He felt restless, though. He wasn't ready to go to sleep. He'd patrol the neighborhood. He knew there were others out there who needed help.

And the bonehead needed another lesson in humility.

CHAPTER 9

"Okay, this one sounds good," Lucy said. "She says she's addicted to stupid online quizzes. I love that. It's so annoying when people are all 'I like learning about new cultures and rereading Proust'. Not that she seems shallow. She said one of her fave movies is *Eternal Sunshine of the Spotless Mind*. And she didn't give a list of things she doesn't want in a guy. Or a list of a billion things she thinks the guy has to have."

"Did she not hear that I need time to recover from the pregnant lady who confused me with her boyfriend? I did mention she had a boyfriend, right?" David asked Adam. The three of them were out on Adam and Lucy's deck with the baby monitor on. Lucy was worried that their youngest, three-year-old Maya, would have a nightmare and they wouldn't hear her, even though when she had one of her nightmares she screamed loud enough to wake the dead.

"That was days ago," Lucy said, still scrolling through profiles. "If we let you wait too long, we'll never get you out on another date."

"There are times when you make me feel like your third child," David said.

"Our big, somewhat dim child," Adam said. "That's exactly how we feel about you."

"And we want you to be happy," Lucy added. "Here's another good one. She says she's eaten foie gras ice cream at a molecular gastronomy restaurant. She likes to try new things because it can start up new neural pathways. But that her absolute favorite food is McDonald's French fries. She sounds smart, and adventurous, and down to earth."

"Let's see the picture." Adam held out his hand for the phone.

Lucy didn't give it to him. "The picture shouldn't matter. Is what you love about me the way I look?" she asked her husband.

"Is there actually a right way to answer that?" David asked.

"Of course." Adam looked at Lucy. "I love everything about you."

"Ah." David took a swallow of his Corona.

"And anyway, she's really pretty. I just don't think that should be the most important thing." She turned the cell toward Adam, and he leaned forward. "She is male approved," he told David.

"So, what should I say to her from him?" Lucy asked Adam.

"I can come up with my own responses," David protested.

"Okay, so what do you want to say to her?" Lucy asked David.

"I mean I could come up with my own response if I wanted to, but I don't want to," David said, suddenly feeling very tired. They'd spent at least an hour going over profiles.

"What didn't you like? I'll find someone else," Lucy told him.

David ran his fingers through his hair. The only way to end this was to go out with someone. Anyone. And he probably shouldn't base his opinion of Internet dating on one bizarre encounter. And the woman's profile was decent. And he really didn't want to be alone for the rest of his life. "Give me the phone."

Lucy handed it over with a little squeal of delight. David read the profile, looked at the pics, then sent a short message that said he was hoping to improve his neural pathways by trying Internet dating and creating new cupcakes, none of which included meat products.

"If you decide to get together, maybe you should take her to the Silent Movie Theatre," Lucy suggested. "That would make a memorable first date."

"Memorable for the level of boredom," Adam said. "You know I love movies, but those faces they made." He pursed his lips and batted his eyelashes in an extreme version of someone in love. "Movies need real dialogue."

"Says the writer," David pointed out.

"Come on, even Clarissa wouldn't go with you," Adam shot back.

For a moment, the only sound was Maya breathing over the baby monitor. David caught Lucy shooting Adam an *I-can't-believe-you-said-that* look. "I'm not taking anyone to the Silent Movie Theatre," David said, breaking the silence. "What if she loves it there, but we hate each other? Then I might keep running into her whenever I go. I don't want to have to start avoiding one of my favorite places in LA."

"Way to be positive." Adam slapped him on the shoulder. "You've had one bad date, but that doesn't mean they're all going to suck."

Adam was right. If he ended up getting together with this woman, it had to go better than his last meet-up. Didn't it?

Jamie took a seat in the small theater on the Los Angeles Community College campus. The next Groundlings improv class didn't start for a few months, but she'd found a drama class at the community college that was just starting up, so she decided to go for it. New things! Woo!

Except her stomach wasn't quite sure about the idea of attempting to act. In front of people. *Stomach, you weren't sure about surfing, either,* she told it.

It didn't seem like she was the only nervous one. The woman a few rows ahead of her was nibbling on her thumbnail, and the seventy-ish man a few seats down was frantically tapping one heel against the floor. Jamie smiled at him. "What made you decide to take this class?"

He gave a little start, then smiled back. "I actually moved out here to be an actor."

"How long ago?" Jamie asked, trying to hide her surprise. "I just moved out to LA myself."

The man laughed. "About fifty-two years ago," he answered. "Back when I had a full head of hair and thought I had a face made for the movies."

"What happened?" Jamie asked.

"I went on a lot of auditions. I even got an agent. A lot of people said they loved me. It took me a while to realize that's pretty much what every casting director says to every agent." He laughed again. "I got a commercial. Well, an infomercial. Usually it came on from four to five a.m. I have the videotape to prove it. Eventually I realized that my Hollywood dreams weren't going to come true. I got a job as a pharmacist." As he spoke, his words came out faster and faster, until they'd almost matched the pace of his tapping heel. "Fortunately, I'd listened to my parents when they said I needed some kind of backup degree. But now that I'm retired, I figured I'd take a class, just for fun. And to get a little time out of the house in order to keep my wife from divorcing me. I'm halfway thinking maybe I should have taken the watercolor painting class instead, but it's not as though anyone's going to care if I'm no good." He finally had to stop to pull in a breath.

"It's everybody's first class," Jamie said. "I think we're all pretty nervous. I know I am."

He reached over and shook her hand. "Clifton," he told her.

"Jamie. Good to meet you."

The door opened and a short woman with long light brown hair came in. "Welcome to Introduction to Acting," she called. "I'm excited to see you all here. Why don't we dive right in? Let's all introduce ourselves and say why we're here. I'll go first. I'm Ann Purcell. I'm here to share my enthusiasm for acting. I'm one of the founding members of LA's Journey Theater Ensemble, where I've both acted and directed. That's me. Okay, who's next?"

Jamie decided she'd rather go first than sit there agonizing, and so she told everyone she was taking the class because she wanted to do something she'd never tried before. The nail-biting woman said she was a TV writer and thought an acting class would help her pitch projects in a more engaging way. Clifton told the group pretty much what he'd told Jamie—speaking even faster. His infomercial was the closest anyone in the class had gotten to acting professionally.

"Great, everyone. Just great," Ann said when they were done. "I love the way you all have such a spirt of adventure. We're going to start out with an improv exercise that I've found really effective in bringing up emotion. I think you'll be surprised how deep you can go with the right starting point. Jamie, would you like to kick us off again?"

"Uh, sure," Jamie said, ignoring her stomach's protest.

"Great. Come on up here."

Jamie joined Ann on the small stage. The class hadn't seemed that big when she introduced herself, but suddenly standing on the stage, it felt like hundreds of people were looking at her. "Okay, what you're going to do is pretend you're at a cemetery and you're visiting a grave. It'll be easier if you use your own life as a starting place for now. You can talk or not talk. Just imagine yourself there—and go!" Ann backed into the wings, leaving Jamie alone.

Of course, the first grave she thought of was her mother's. She pretended to put some flowers down on top of it, then stared at the wooden floor, waiting for something to come to her. "Hi, Mom," she said, and found that her voice was shaking, not just with nerves, but with emotion. Just saying "Mom" aloud made her eyes sting and the inside of her nose prickle. She hadn't been expecting that.

"So here I am in LA! Surprise! Thanks to you. The inheritance. I'm taking a year off to . . . sort of figure things out. To figure out what I want to do with myself. I know you'd say I can do anything I set my mind to, but we both know that's not exactly true. But guess what? I went surfing. And I loved it. So, I'm looking for other things that I never thought about doing before. Like this. An acting class. So, thanks. Thanks, Mom."

To her shock, tears started running down her cheeks. She used the heels of her hands to brush them away, then looked over at Ann. "I'm done, I guess." The class burst into applause.

"Excellent," Ann said. "You really put yourself there, and you let what happened happen. You surprised yourself, didn't you?"

"I wasn't expecting to start crying," Jamie admitted.

"That's part of acting. Letting the feelings come up. Okay, next?"

Jamie hurried back to her seat. Clifton gave her a thumbs-up, and Jamie managed to nod back. Putting herself there, as Ann called it, had been easy. Getting herself back from there wasn't as easy. All that emotion was still roiling around inside her. "Um, I . . . I'll be back." She got up, stumbled down the row to the aisle, and hurried out.

She leaned back against the wall of the theater and sucked in a couple long breaths. Even though she'd only done one acting exercise, she was already almost positive the class wasn't for her. She liked her feelings squashed down, until she released them in an appropriate place, like in a dark theater while watching a sad movie that was nothing like her life, or while drinking wine in the bathtub. She decided to head home. She'd e-mail the teacher later.

About half an hour later, she was heading up her walkway, looking forward to some cat-cuddling time. Mac didn't always want to be cuddled, but he seemed to know when she really needed to hug him and would deign to allow it.

She was just sliding her key into the lock when someone called her name. She looked over and saw Helen glaring at her from the sidewalk. "You let Marie fix you up!"

"Not on purpose," Jamie protested. "She asked me over for dinner. She didn't tell me she'd invited anyone else."

"Well, now I get a turn," Helen said.

"No. Really, Helen. No," Jamie said as firmly as she could. "I would have told Marie no if she'd asked me. Actually, I *did* tell her no. You heard me. I told both of you no at the same time."

Marie came out on her porch. "Scott told me he texted you and you didn't answer," she accused.

Yeah, well, he's a pervert, Jamie thought, but didn't say. "I didn't want to hurt his feelings," she lied. "I'm bad at telling someone I'm not interested. I figured not answering would give him the signal without me actually saying it." *That and blocking his number,* she silently added.

"What possible reason can you have for not wanting to at least speak to him again?" Marie demanded.

"Marie, I told you I wasn't interested in meeting anyone right now," Jamie said, struggling to keep her voice calm.

"You have to give my godson a chance or it's not fair," Helen said, walking across the lawn toward Jamie.

"Helen, if she didn't like Scott, she definitely won't like

your godson," Marie said. "I know. I've met them both." She pointed her finger at Jamie. "You have to get over yourself. You think there's any one person who's exactly what you're looking for? There isn't."

It was like she hadn't heard anything Jamie said. "Good to know. I guess that's my problem. You heard her, Helen. I'm too picky. It's pointless to set me up with your godson. I'll see you both later." She whirled back to the door, unlocked it as fast as she could, and ducked inside.

Before she could close the door, she heard Helen say, "I think my godson is exactly what she's looking for. She just doesn't know it, because she hasn't met him yet."

"Yet!" Jamie cried after she slammed the door. "She said 'yet'! I'm doomed, Mac. Doomed."

Mac trotted over, and Jamie scooped him up. He butted her chin with his head and began to purr. "You're the only guy I need, MacGyver."

But even so, three nights later there she was, walking into Sorella, a little Italian restaurant a few blocks from her house, looking around for a guy who matched the picture of Helen's godson that Helen had told Jamie to keep. Helen just refused to stop insisting that it wasn't fair that Marie had gotten a turn matching Jamie up with someone and Helen hadn't, and Jamie had caved. After tonight, Marie and Helen would be even, and Jamie would be free to go on with her life.

Jamie saw two men sitting at tables by themselves. One dark-haired and athletic looking; one blond with what she always thought of as aristocratic features, aquiline nose, thin lips. The blond was Helen's godson. The other guy looked more approachable. For starters, he wasn't studying the menu as if he had to take an exam the next day, and he'd smiled when he'd seen her, a good smile that made the laugh lines at the corners of his eyes crinkle.

Wait. She knew him! Not *knew him*, knew him. But she'd

talked to him that day she'd been trying to pick out a leash for Mac at the pet store. She had the crazy desire to walk over and sit at his table. He'd seemed nice that day, funny. But Scott, Marie's pick, had seemed nice and funny, too, and look how he'd turned out.

The hostess approached, and Jamie told her she was with the guy at the table in the back. Helen's godson didn't look up from the menu even when she was standing a foot away. "Charles?"

Finally, he raised his head, but didn't say anything. "Hi, I'm Jamie. You're Helen's godson, right?"

"Yes. Hi," he said.

Very welcoming, Jamie thought. But maybe Helen's godson hadn't wanted to be fixed up, either. She could totally see Helen hounding him until he'd agreed to have dinner with Jamie. Or maybe he was just on the shy side.

Jamie sat down. "Helen told me you're a teacher. I used to teach, too." She was sure Helen had already passed that along to him, but it was a reasonable conversation starter.

"But now you're taking a year off to find yourself." He didn't put actual air quotes around the words "find yourself," but he might as well have, and he made the phrase sound faintly ridiculous.

"Yep. I was feeling burned out by teaching, and I got the chance to spend a year out here," Jamie answered. "I'm planning to look for a job, but right now, I'm trying out some new things. I actually took a surfing lesson the other day."

"Most of us don't have that luxury," Charles commented. He sounded kind of bitter about it.

"True, completely true. I know how lucky I am," Jamie answered. "My mom left me a little inheritance, and that's what's given me the chance."

"Well, you know what teachers' salaries are," Charles said. "Since you're a lady of leisure"—another phrase that felt like it could have had air quotes. He made this one sound contemptible—"I thought tonight could be your treat."

"Um, sure. Of course." Jamie hadn't been able to come up with anything else to say, or at least nothing she'd want repeated back to Helen.

A young waitress in a peasant blouse and flouncy skirt came over. "What can I get you to drink?"

Before Jamie could answer, Charles jumped in. "I'll have the white truffle and prime strip steak appetizer, and I think a bottle of the Vega Sicilia Unico."

He hadn't bothered to ask if there was an appetizer she'd wanted to share, and Jamie was pretty sure he'd ordered wine that was way out of her price range. Classy. Jamie's eyes drifted over to the man from the pet store. His date had just arrived, and he'd stood to greet her, saying something Jamie imagined was about how nice the woman looked.

"And what would you like to drink?" the waitress asked. "I love those earrings, by the way." Jamie smiled. The waitress was being friendlier—and more complimentary—than her date.

"Thanks, I—"

"I think I'll also have the bruschetta," Charles interrupted.

"You two decided?" the waitress asked.

David and Annabelle looked at each other and laughed. "We *still* haven't decided," Annabelle admitted.

"Possibly because we still haven't looked at the menu," David added. "Sorry."

"Not a problem. I'll check back in a few," the waitress told them, then left.

David couldn't believe how easily the conversation had been flowing. They'd been keeping it light, going from movies, to running, to graphic novels. She was a fan of Sakai, and she admitted it was partly just because she loved how rabbit ears made such a perfect samurai top knot.

"Just one more thing before we look at the menu," Annabelle said. "Even you have to admit that *Finder* isn't something you can read every day. Me, I can't handle endnotes on a Monday."

"Okay, good point. There are some days when all I want is my *Calvin and Hobbes,*" David answered.

"The cartoon equivalent of comfort food," Annabelle agreed, and they smiled at each other. "Now, menu, or we'll get kicked out."

They decided to split an appetizer, because they both loved grilled mussels. When it arrived, Annabelle took out a small vial. "I'm just going to put MirMin on some. Is that okay?" She raised her dark eyebrows. David liked the way they peaked. They made her look a little devilish, in a good way.

He'd noticed her eyebrows. He was *admiring* her eyebrows. He couldn't remember the last time he'd looked at a woman so closely.

"Sure," David answered. "What's MirMin?"

"You haven't heard of it? It's awesome. It's actually called Miracle Minerals. I've been using it for about a year, and, okay, I know people say this all the time when it's not really true, but really, for me, it's true. MirMin changed my life. I used to have horrible food allergies. Going out to eat? Nightmare. But now I can eat whatever I'm in the mood for."

"Great. What does it taste like?" He picked up his fork and pried out a piece of mussel flesh from the shell.

"Try a little." She shook some on the mussel on his fork without waiting for him to reply. "It doesn't really have much of a flavor. And it has so many benefits. Not just curing food allergies. It strips fat out of the liver. It's great for controlling blood sugar. It gets rid of all kinds of toxins, which means clear skin, and more importantly, reducing headaches, preventing benign tumors and even cancer, and stopping cellular degeneration."

"Wow." Annabelle had sounded more animated talking about that MirMin than she had about anything else. He took the bite of mussel—and had to force himself to swallow. The MirMin tasted salty, bitter, and metallic, plus a flavor that he couldn't describe in words, although he knew for sure he didn't want ever want it on his tongue again. He took a long drink of water.

"See, you hardly know it's there," Annabelle said. David nodded, then drained the rest of his water glass.

"It's so important to eliminate as many toxins in the body as possible," Annabelle said. "There are actually three types of toxins. Did you know that?" She continued without waiting for him to reply. "Two of them are internal, called ama and amavisha, and one is environmental, which is called garavisha. Ama is from poor digestion, when you eat things like fried food, or cold food, or leftover foods." She leaned forward and placed one hand over his. "I eat all of that. You know how happy I am that I can eat ice cream? Insanely happy. And I can because MirMin got rid of my allergies, and it nullifies the ama. Amavisha is—"

She was still talking, but David couldn't focus. He felt like he'd slipped into another dimension. Who was this woman going on and on and on about the miraculous benefits of this mineral combination? He tuned in for a second. Now she was talking about how flatulence was caused by amavisha, whatever that was, and how you'd never get gas if you used the supplement.

He told himself to give her more of a chance. She was the same person he'd just had that amazing conversation with less than fifteen minutes ago. She still had those devilish eyebrows, that thick dark brown hair, and that fit body. So, she got a little carried away when she talked about something that had really helped her, so what? He took a mussel that hadn't been doused with the MirMin and began prying out a bite. Annabelle leaned over and coated the bite with MirMin before he could bring it to his mouth.

"Just wait. Tomorrow you're going to be feeling the effects. You might be a little nauseous or even have to spend some extra time in the bathroom," Annabelle told him. "But after that, you're going to feel sooo good. I love telling people about MirMin. I even started selling it to make it easier for my friends to buy it. And then some of them started selling it. We weren't doing it for the money, but"—she leaned closer, and gave his hand a squeeze—"we've all made a crazy amount. I'm even thinking of quitting my job. And one of my friends already did. It's working out great for her. She's making almost twice as much as she was as a hairstylist, and I'm talking about a stylist at a super trendy salon, where she got fabulous tips."

This isn't a date, David realized. *It's a pyramid scheme pitch.*

He did everything he could to wrap things up quickly so he could get out of there. He ate quickly without talking much. Annabelle was talking plenty for both of them, telling story after story about how friends of hers had benefited health-wise and finance-wise through MirMin. He refused dessert and coffee, telling Annabelle that he had to get to the bakery early, which was true, but nothing he would have cared about if the date had continued the way it had started.

At least they'd met at the restaurant. He didn't have to worry about getting her home and turning down an invitation to come in. Her place was probably filled with Miracle Mineral brochures she'd be eager to go over with him. He just walked her to her car, where she kissed his cheek and told him she couldn't wait to see him again. He'd murmured something noncommittal, and started for home. He'd walked, since the restaurant was only a few blocks away.

He paused outside the Thirsty Goat, then decided to go in. He could use a drink. He found a spot at the bar and ordered a loaded Corona. No better way to get a fast buzz, and that was what he wanted.

"I haven't had a bomb shot since college," a woman said as she slid onto the just-vacated stool beside his. "Any chance you have a Skittles bomb?" she asked the bartender.

Curious, David looked over at her. Brown eyes, curly blond hair. She looked vaguely familiar.

"I know, I know. I should be ashamed to order anything with candy in the name at my age. You know what they call it in France?"

"A Royale with Cheese?"

The woman gave an appreciative snort of laugher. "Close. A *retreau*. Hold the cheese," she added. "I know what I'm doing here, but what are you doing here? I mean, alone. You looked like you were having a great time back at the restaurant."

David stared at her.

"Sorry. That was a completely inappropriate question. Sometimes I am completely inappropriate. But not as inappropriate as the guy I was on a blind date with back at the restaurant where you obviously didn't notice me," she continued. "About two seconds after I got there, he pretty much forced me to say I'd pay, and then he ordered two appetizers, one with white truffles, which he didn't offer to share, and a bottle of ridiculously pricey wine, no sharing of that, either, and the most expensive entrée on the menu. And yet he was surprised when I wanted to go home as soon as dinner was over."

"My date, also of the blind variety, tried to sign me on to a multilevel marketing scam," David told her. "At first she seemed so great. She seemed to be into everything I liked. Although now that I'm thinking about it, it was all stuff she knew I liked from my dating profile. I didn't think of that at the time. I just thought we were really hitting it off. And then it all took a horrible turn."

"And so we both ended up here, ordering drinks designed to

get us quickly drunk," she said. She stuck out her hand. "Jamie. Sorry you had suck a sucky night."

"David," he told her.

"The restaurant wasn't the first place we saw each other," Jamie said. "Well, I saw you there. You clearly didn't see me."

"The pet store! You were talking to yourself!" he burst out.

Jamie smiled. "And you were bragging about making your dog wear a pink collar."

"I apologized for the whole pink thing," David reminded her. "What did your cat think of the leash?"

"Hated it. Hated me for putting it on him," Jamie answered. "Hey, if you're tired of conversation after your date from hell, I'm happy just to have my drink and leave you in peace," Jamie told him.

"No, I'm feeling like I just met an old war buddy," David answered. "So, you go on lot of blind dates?"

"Two, recently. Because I'm a wimp and couldn't tell my two old lady neighbors no. But now they've each had a turn fixing me up, so I'm free," Jamie answered. "You?" she asked as the bartender set down their drinks.

"I've got these," David told her. "You've paid for enough for one night."

"Thanks. That's so nice. But if we get a second round, it's on me," Jamie said. "Although I'm not sure two of these is a good idea." She took a sip of her drink. "Mmm. Tastes like the vodka-infused gummy bears I used to eat in college."

"Sounds like you had a good college experience," David commented.

Jamie laughed. "I did. Surprisingly, I also learned a few things. How about you?"

"I didn't go to college. Well, I did, but only for a semester," David said, wondering if she was one of those people who'd assume he was stupid because he didn't have a degree. "I'm a baker. I basically learned on the job, plus helping my mom make Christmas cookies every year."

"Do you like it?" She sounded genuinely interested.

"I do. I can't imagine doing anything else."

"See? That's what I want. Something like that, where I want to go to work. You want to go to work, don't you?"

"Most of the time." David took a swallow of his drink. "But not if I go crazy with these. What do you do that you don't like doing?"

"I was teaching high school history," she told him. "I liked some of it, especially at the beginning. But I got to hate going in. I'd have to have cookies every day at lunch as a little reward, just to get me through."

"It was bad enough to start a cookie habit? Good thing you got out," David commented.

"Seriously. And now I'm trying to find myself. Which I know sounds stupid and self-indulgent. My date made that clear. I need to come up with a better way to describe it. But basically, I got an opportunity to have a year to do what I want, and what I most want is to figure out if there's something I can do that makes me feel like how you said you feel about baking." She took a sip of her drink. "So, back up. What about you and blind dates? Do you go on a lot of them?"

David shook his head. "That was my second in, well, ever. The first was about a week ago. She turned out to be pregnant, very pregnant, with a boyfriend, a boyfriend who showed up while we were having coffee."

Jamie groaned. "Oh, man. That might be worse than the first one I had. He seemed great. Really great. I hadn't wanted to meet him, because this is supposed to be the—never mind. Anyway, I thought we really hit it off. I was looking forward to seeing him again. He texted me about an hour later. I was thinking he felt the same way I did. But nope. He wanted me to find a friend to join us in, let's say, a romantic capacity."

The bartender shot Jamie an interested look. David turned on his stool to block her from the guy's gaze. "I have nothing to say to that," David admitted. "Actually, I have too many things to say to that, and I'm having trouble picking one. I'm going to go with, what an asshole."

"Okay, to be fair, he had a cast on his arm and he was worried that he couldn't give me enough 'pleasure'." She drew out the word, turning it into "pleaaaashaaare."

"Yeah, I was right. Asshole," David said. He finished his drink.

"Want another one?" Jamie asked. "I would be happy to buy you a drink. You've earned it."

"Tempting, but no. I go to work at five. And drunk baking doesn't always get the best results. Although I've ended up with a few genius new recipes. Which usually I couldn't remember."

"I'm going to go, too. But first—" She nodded to the ladies' room. "Thanks for the drink. You may have at least begun to restore my faith in men."

"And you, mine. In women, I mean," David told her. As he left the bar, he wondered if he should have waited for her, maybe asked for her number. But she'd thanked him for the drink, which pretty much ended the conversation.

Anyway, after his blind date—both his blind dates—he was ready for some time with only Diogee for company.

Mac sat on Jamie's chest, staring down at her. The mix of scents coming from her tonight was confusing. She seemed to be feeling many things at once. And she almost always put on new clothes when she went to bed. Tonight she'd just fallen down on top of the covers. Something wasn't right. He'd just to have to work harder to complete his mission and find her a packmate. Humans were strange. Sometimes it took another of their own kind to completely understand them.

He headed out. Tonight there was a scent similar to Jamie's in the air, a mix of loneliness, and anger, and something else. It was like there was invitation in the scent. He followed it, and ended up at a place he'd been to many times. The house with the bonehead and the lonely man. Maybe that invitation he was pumping out meant he'd realized he needed a human packmate. Since Jamie had that same smell, maybe she'd finally understand that Mac had found her a human he knew would be a good mate for her. He'd bring her things from a few other potential packmates, too, just in case she didn't agree with him. There were times she didn't. Mac had never been able to convince her that his food should be provided every time he asked.

Jamie and the man were at the top of his list. But he also had some work to do for the adolescent girl pumping out anger and sadness and frustration. Humans—so many of them needed help.

CHAPTER 10

Jamie opened the door the next morning to get the paper, still in the rumpled clothes from the night before. How could one drink have knocked her out? Maybe she'd just fallen asleep so fast to escape the memory of her horrible date. Although meeting that guy, David, at the bar had made up for it, at least a little.

It took her a second to realize that Hud Martin sat on the front steps, working on knotting a fishing fly. He turned and smiled at her, his eyes hidden behind sunglasses as usual, even though the day was overcast. "Hello, Sunshine," he said. "Have anything you want to tell me about these?" He patted the pile of stuff that sat next to him. She hadn't registered it, either.

Jamie leaned down so she could study the pile—another pair of boxers; two T-shirts, one much larger than the other; a neon-orange Speedo; a nose-hair trimmer; one sock, purple with tacos; a well-worn toothbrush; and a leather belt with a silver KISS belt buckle. "I have never seen any of that before."

Hud didn't reply. Just raised his eyebrows.

Jamie rolled her eyes. "If I stole it, why would I leave it on my front porch? You don't need to be an evil genius to know you should hide your stolen goods."

Hud didn't answer. He kept working on the fly.

"If you want to investigate this, that would be great. I mean it. Like I told you, ever since I moved here, weird things have been appearing on my doormat," Jamie blurted out to fill the silence. "My theories are: someone who has something against Desmond, who used to live here, maybe an angry ex-boyfriend. Or that I've picked up some freak stalker, which seems unlikely." She had to pause to take a breath. "Honestly, it's starting to scare me. If you could figure it out, I'd be grateful. I truly would."

Hud attached the finished fly to his vest, then stood and propped one foot up on the top step. "Interesting that you never brought up these theories before."

"Why would I?" Jamie snapped. "You've made it clear you suspected me from day one. Or me in cahoots with Ruby."

"I keep an open mind until I catch the criminal. Which I always do. But I also don't ignore the evidence. And you seem to be in possession of many items that don't belong to you, as you yourself have admitted."

"I'm not 'in possession' of them. They're just sitting there," Jamie burst out.

"On your property," Hud answered.

"Yes, my property. Where you're standing without my invitation," Jamie shot back. She knew she shouldn't let him get to her. He was just an aging actor trying to relive his glory days. But he made her nuts with his insinuations and his stupid fishing vest. The thing looked like the closest it had gotten to a body of water was a swimming pool.

Hud nodded. "I'll be off. But I won't be far." Jamie watched him until he turned the corner at the end of her block. She'd half-expected him to set up a surveillance station on the sidewalk in front of her house.

It was time for her to get to the bottom of this herself. Tonight, she'd keep watch on the front porch. By tomorrow morning, she'd know exactly who kept leaving all this crap.

Jamie woke up with a start. James Corden was on the TV, but the last thing she remembered was watching Colbert. Clearly, she'd fallen asleep on the job. She stood and stretched to try to get the cramps out of her back. Her sofa was great for lounging, but not for sleeping.

She hurried over to the door and cracked it open. Nothing on the mat. Good, she hadn't slept through that night's delivery. She went to the fridge and got out a big bottle of Dr Pepper, not bothering with a glass, then pulled a chair up near one of the front windows where she had a good view of the walkway leading to the house.

Before she'd even had the chance to sit down, she saw something moving across the lawn. "What?" She dropped the soda bottle on her toe, but ignored the jab of pain. That was Mac out there! Outside! She'd figure out how he managed to escape later. First, she was going to find out what he was doing.

Jamie slipped outside and followed her cat though the quiet neighborhood. He trotted up to a house that made Jamie think of hobbits. Without hesitation, he raced to the dog door. He didn't use it to go in. Instead he positioned himself to one side. A few seconds later, Jamie heard wild barking and a dog's head—a very large dog's head—poked out. Mac gave his snout four fast whaps with the paw, which got the dog crying and jerking his head back into the house.

My cat is a little bully, Jamie thought, mesmerized as Mac immediately darted over to a large tree, climbed up to a window that was partway open, and disappeared inside. Less than a minute later, he reappeared—with something in his mouth.

"Oh no," Jamie whispered. "Oh no. Mac is the thief. He's a cat burglar."

Mac trotted across the lawn, jumped to the top of the fence, then down to the ground. He walked over to Jamie and dropped the object at her feet. It was a jockstrap. It felt moist. Her cat had just brought her some strange man's recently worn jock.

"We are not taking this home," Jamie told him sternly. "You're a bad kitty. Bad." Mac began to purr loudly. He'd never had a problem with being called bad. Sometimes, like now, he even seemed to enjoy it.

She looked down at the jock. What should she do with it? Just throw it back into the yard? That should be okay.

She gingerly picked it up, but before she could launch it, she was caught by an eye-searing beam of light. She squinted into it, and saw Hud pointing a flashlight at her, the biggest flashlight she'd ever seen. "This is what you mean by knowing nothing about the stolen items, Toots?" he asked.

"I didn't do it!" Jamie cried. "It was him!" She pointed down—but Mac had disappeared.

"Are you going for an insanity defense?" Hud asked. "That rarely works, doll baby. And I'll testify that you and I have had several lucid chats."

"My cat. He must have run off. But that's what I meant," Jamie exclaimed. "My cat took this." She waved the jockstrap. "He dropped it in front of me, and I picked it up. Then you came at me with the Flashlight of Doom." He still had it trained on her. She shielded her eyes with one hand. "Does it have a lower setting?"

"I think I should be asking the questions here," Hud told her. "Exactly how many—"

The door to the house swung open, spilling soft yellow light from inside. "What's going on out here?"

The man's voice sounded familiar. Jamie turned and squinted at him, but couldn't make out his features. Her eyes might be permanently damaged by the industrial-strength flashlight.

"I've got absolute proof of the identity of the Storybook Court thief," Hud said, his voice ringing with triumph. "I caught her. Just like I'd catch a fish if this danged job ever let me get to the creek."

The man snorted. "Aren't you tired of saying that yet? How many episodes was it?" He opened the gate and stepped into the circle of light thrown by the flashlight.

"David?" Jamie exclaimed.

"Jamie?" David—it *was* David—sounded as surprised as she was. "What are you doing here?"

"I live here. Not right here, obviously. But in the complex," Jamie answered. "I moved in a few weeks ago."

"You know Toots here?" Hud asked. "And she lied to you about where she resides?"

"I didn't lie. It just didn't come up," Jamie protested. "He didn't tell me he lived here, either."

The dog door clinked, and a huge dog wearing a pink collar slunk through. He cautiously moved over to the man's side. David pushed him back into the yard and closed the gate. "You've got to stay there, dude," he said. Then he looked from Hud to Jamie. "Can one of you tell me what's going on?"

"Take a look at the item in her hand," Hud suggested. "I believe it's stolen, and most likely it was stolen from you. I caught her with it right here."

Jamie realized she was still holding the jockstrap. She hurled it to the ground. "My cat went through your bathroom window and got it."

"Clearly, you've trained the cat to be your accomplice,"

Hud accused. He turned to David. "I think PETA needs to be notified, along with the police. She also managed to involve Ruby Shaffer in her crimes, someone who has never shown criminal tendencies before."

"Wait. A cat?" David said, looking around.

"He ran off. He shouldn't have been outside in the first place. He's an indoor cat," Jamie explained in a rush. "He's obviously found an escape route. I'll have to check the house."

"I'll handle this from here," Hud said to David. He took Jamie by the elbow and she shook him off.

"There's nothing to handle," she snapped.

"Then you wouldn't object to a search of your abode for other items you've stolen—with or without the assistance of your cat or Ms. Shaffer?"

David bent down, grabbed the jock, and shoved it in his pocket. "No matter what exactly happened, it's hardly grand larceny. I'm not planning to press charges, so like Jamie said, there's nothing for you to handle," he told Hud.

"You're clearly thinking with the wrong part of your anatomy," Hud said. "I'll be tracking down the other victims to see if they feel the same way." He walked off, whistling.

Jamie and David stared at each other in the dim light coming from his house. "Thank you for that," Jamie said. "I swear, my cat . . ." She shook her head. "It sounds too ridiculous to repeat."

"You want to come in and have some coffee or something?" David asked.

"I wouldn't mind sitting down for this conversation," Jamie admitted.

"Come on." He opened the gate. Jamie stepped through, and immediately staggered backward under the weight of two saucer-sized paws.

"Diogee, down!" David ordered. The dog kept his paws

planted on Jamie and gave her a lick that went from chin to hairline. "Sorry," he said. He grabbed the dog's collar and yanked him off.

"Not a problem. I'm not one of those cat people who dislikes dogs." She gave the dog a pat on the head and was almost taken out by the frantic tail wagging that followed. "You go first, Diogee," she said, then said, "Diogee? What kind of name is that?"

"*D. O. G.*," David explained.

"Ah," Jamie said as they walked inside. "Clever, and yet unimaginative at the same time," she teased.

"What brilliant name did you come up with for your cat?" he asked.

"Fluffy," Jamie answered, trying, and failing, to keep a straight face. "No, actually, his name is MacGyver. But it's looking like I should have named him Robie. After the—"

"Cat burglar Cary Grant played in *To Catch a Thief,*" David finished for her.

"Exactly!" Jamie said. "I love that movie, especially all the rich colors. That green in the night scenes." She smiled. "I'm gushing. I love pretty much all Hitchcock, black-and-white or color."

"If you love movies, you gotta love Hitchcock," David answered. "He influenced so many of the next generation of directors. Tarantino wouldn't be Tarantino without him."

"The suitcase in *Pulp Fiction*—classic McGuffin," Jamie agreed. "McGuffin could be a great cat name. I could have a McGuffin and a MacGyver. Except I don't think MacGyver would tolerate another cat in the house. Too used to having things his own way." Jamie ran out of words, remembering that she was standing in David's house because her cat had been stealing from him.

David shoved one hand through his hair. "I guess it's kind of late for coffee. Or are you one of the continuous coffee drinkers?"

"I don't need anything. Except another chance to apologize and thank you for not letting Hud take me away," Jamie told him. David dropped down on the sofa and was immediately joined by Diogee. Jamie took one of the armchairs. "Since you let me in, I guess you don't think I'm some kind of deranged stalker. That's something," she added.

"Considering I didn't tell you my last name and you had no way of knowing where I lived, I think I'm safe," David answered.

"I thought maybe I had a psycho stalker," Jamie admitted. "Random stuff kept showing on my doormat. I guess Mac, my cat, brought it all. So if you're missing anything else—socks, a T-shirt, a shoe, a Speedo. What else? Nose-hair clippers. Basically, if you're missing any smallish items, let me know and I'll search through the stuff that's been left. Or you can come by and take a look."

"No to the Speedo, but some of the other stuff is probably mine," David told her. "I thought Diogee might have eaten some of them. I even called the vet."

Jamie winced. "I'm sorry. I didn't realize Mac had found a way out. I still can't believe he's been doing this. He used to bring me the occasional dead bug as a present, but—" She lifted her hands, then let them fall in a gesture of helplessness. "I should go. It's late. You've been really great about this. Thanks again. Just come by whenever to look at my cat's ill-gotten goods. I live in the house that looks like Snow White's cottage, next door to the Defranciscos."

"Okay. I will." He walked her to the door. "I need to meet this cat burglar of yours."

The next afternoon, as soon as he got home from work, he let Diogee drag him around a few blocks, then took a shower. "Guess I'll go get my stuff back," he told the dog, who began to wag frantically at the word "go." Diogee wasn't the smartest dog on the block, but there were a few words that seemed to be directly hardwired to his tail. "Sorry. I didn't mean you." The wagging slowed, but kept up a hopeful back-and-forth swing.

David grabbed a biscuit from the enormous plastic jar on the kitchen counter and tossed it to Diogee. "I'll be right back." The tail drooped, and David heard one long, extremely pathetic howl as he left the house. But he knew Diogee would be snoozing on his king-size dog bed before he got to Jamie's.

He noticed a flier on bright blue paper attached to a tree near the corner, something that wasn't allowed in Storybook Court. He was surprised Hud hadn't dealt with it already. He diligently enforced even the most inconsequential rule.

When David got close enough to read the flier, he realized that no one but Hud himself could have put it up. He must have had them made this morning. The flier said: "Storybrook Crime Spree! If something of yours has been stolen, come to the fountain. If you've found any items you don't recognize on your property, bring them to the fountain. Statements will be taken. The thief and all accomplices will be caught and not released for two to four years."

That made no sense. Why would a thief leave the stolen goods on other people's property? Although that pony of Riley's had ended up in front of Ruby's house. And Zachary had found Addison's diary outside his. Weird. But definitely not some kind of crime ring, the way Hud was spinning it. None of the things that had been taken from him would sell for enough to buy a drink at the Blue Palm.

He passed seven more trees with fliers before he reached Jamie's street. Hud had gone all out. David didn't think Hud had any other speed but all out. He was sitting over by the fountain right now, tying a fly and waiting for subjects to interrogate.

He shoved his sunglasses down on his nose when he saw

David approach. "Sports Fan! Good to see ya. Decided you should do your part for our community and make a statement against the thief?"

"No. I'm good. It was just a jock, Hud. And I'm not going to bring charges against a cat," David answered.

"A cat trained by a thief," Hud countered.

David gave him a wave and kept walking. He grinned as he turned up Jamie's walkway. A tan-and-brown tabby cat sat in the front window, staring at Hud. It turned its attention to David, gave a meow of greeting, then leapt down. When Jamie opened the door, she held the cat under one arm. "I don't trust him not to try to make a run for it," she explained as she stepped back to let David inside. "I found his escape route, a rip in the screen around the porch. I fixed it so he won't be able to bother you again. Or Diogee. I didn't tell you this, but I saw Mac whack Diogee on the nose a few times last night." She paused for a second. "Am I talking a lot? And really fast? I am," she said, answering her own question.

"No problem," David said. "And Diogee's fine. No signs of being cat-slapped."

"Good." Jamie drew in a deep breath. "It's been a strange day having all those fliers around. They don't say my name, but I know they're about me."

"No one takes Hud seriously," David told her.

"That's something. Here's the stuff that Mac has left on my doormat." Jamie led him over to a cardboard box sitting on the coffee table. He sat down and opened it. Jamie stayed on her feet, watching him. Mac jumped up on the arm of the couch and watched, too, purring loudly.

David pulled out one of his sasquatch socks, one of his tube socks, his A's T-shirt, and a pair of boxer briefs. "These are mine." He took out a white hand towel. "This, too, I'm pretty sure." He looked over at Mac. "You've been busy."

"I'll buy you another hand towel. I actually used that as a dust rag. It was the first thing that showed up, and I didn't think it belonged to anyone. I mean, I knew it didn't belong to me. I just thought it got left behind by the previous tenant or something. And I'm talking too much again."

She'd gotten so flustered that her cheeks had flushed and her eyes were extra bright. Agitation looked good on her. David scratched the cat under his chin, and Mac's purring went up to eleven. "You said he's never done anything like this before?" David asked Jamie.

"Never. But I used to live in an apartment, and he never got out. I still can't believe he did this," she answered.

"Can you sit down? It's making me nervous just looking at you," David told her, and Jamie sat. "It's really no big thing." He took another look in the box. "Seems like at least half the stuff was mine. I wonder how he picked his victims."

"I can't possibly explain the mind of a cat," Jamie answered. "Especially MacGyver's."

"It's easy to explain Diogee's. He has a few things he loves, like walks and treats, and he wants them all the time. Except when he's snoozing."

"So, kind of like a guy." Jamie slapped her hand over her mouth and rounded her eyes in exaggerated horror. "Did I say that?" she mumbled through her fingers.

David laughed. "Yeah, you did. But I'm not offended. Cats, and women, might be more complicated, but that doesn't make them superior."

Jamie lowered her hand and smiled at him. "True. In fact, there are times when I wish I thought a little less." She gave a sigh. "What am I supposed to do with the rest of the stuff Mac brought home?" Jamie asked. "Should I bring it out to the fountain? I want whoever it belongs to to get it back. But if

Hud tries to interrogate me again, I might end up doing something that I'll regret. Probably regret."

"I'm intrigued. Like what?" David asked.

"Like . . . push him in the fountain," Jamie answered. "I can't actually think of anything worse. See? I'm not really an evil genius, slowly robbing all my neighbors with the help of my cat. If I was, I'd be able to think of a whole bunch of things to do to him."

"I'll go with you," David offered. "But I'm not going to try to restrain you if you decide to shove Hud in the fountain. I'd enjoy watching too much."

"Thanks." Jamie picked up the box. "Let's get this over with." She led the way out to the courtyard.

"You're one of the good ones, Sports Fan!" Hud called to David. "Not many would be as forgiving as you. Socializing with the thief who stole from you. I guess it doesn't hurt that Toots here is easy on the eyes."

"Hud, Toots—I mean, Jamie—didn't even know what her cat was doing until last night." He glanced back at Jamie's house. Mac was back in the window, watching.

"Are you planning on showing me what's in the box?" Hud asked Jamie.

Jamie silently unpacked the box, laying the boxers, tighty-whities, orange Speedo, and the rest of the stuff on the edge of the fountain.

"I hope these get back to whoever my cat took them from," Jamie said.

"Hey, Sugar Baby. What did you have stolen?" Hud asked Addison as she came up.

"Don't call me that," Addison growled. "And, nothing. This was on our doorstep." She dropped a Great Mushroom War T-shirt next to the stuff Jamie had laid out.

"That's Zachary's shirt," David said. He was about to offer

to take it back to him, but thought Zachary would much rather have Addison do that.

Addison eyed the shirt. "That's Zachary's? He doesn't seem like an *Adventure Time* kind of guy."

"When's the last time you two actually talked to each other? Back when you were seven or something like that?" David asked. "He grew up, too, you know."

"Whatever," she muttered, then left with the shirt. Marie took her place next to David.

"I heard that you and Helen's godson didn't hit it off," Marie said to Jamie. "Helen said he said you were sour, the way some women get if they haven't gotten married by your age."

Jamie's mouth opened and shut like she was trying to answer but unable to find the right words. "He said what?" she finally got out.

"He's a little weasel, always has been," Marie answered. "Don't worry about it. I found out that my great-nephew is dating someone, but our dentist just got divorced. I'll set something up."

"No! Marie, no! I told you I don't want to meet anyone. No guys. This year is The Year of Me," Jamie blurted out.

Marie sniffed. "That's ridiculous."

"Many criminals aren't able to form normal relationships," Hud jumped in. "They're able to steal and worse because they don't have the same emotions as the rest of us."

"My emotions are fine," Jamie told Hud. "If I get a cavity, I'll see your dentist. Otherwise, forget it," Jamie told Marie. She turned and stalked away.

David followed her. " 'The Year of Me'?" he asked.

Jamie groaned. "I keep saying things out loud that I mean to keep inside my head." She sat down on one of her porch steps, and David sat next to her. "I have been calling this The Year of Me, but only to myself," she admitted. "When my mom died, she left me enough money to take a year off. And, like I told you the other night, I want to try to figure out if there's something else I want to be doing with my life. I just don't want to start up a relationship right now, even though Marie and Helen seem to think that's all I should be thinking about."

"I'm sorry—about your mother," David told her.

"Thanks," Jamie answered. "It's been a little more than a year. I . . . the pain of it was so intense, and now that it's fading, it's almost worse. Because the . . . the specifics of her are fading, too, getting just a little fuzzy, and I hate that."

"I know," David answered.

"Are your parents still with you?"

"Yeah. They live in Northern California. I drive up there a couple times a year. I have a brother up there, too. But my wife, she's been . . . she died almost three years ago. Sometimes I can't remember things as clearly as I used to, like her laugh. Sometimes I can still hear it in my head, but sometimes it just won't come."

Jamie nodded. "Exactly. Exactly."

Adam would be shaking his head right now. Here was David, bringing up Clarissa when he was sitting next to an attractive woman. But this wasn't like that night when he and Adam had been at the Blue Palm. He wasn't trying to start something up with Jamie. They were just talking, like friends. He liked talking to her.

Mac opened his mouth and pulled in a long breath, enjoying the way Jamie's scent changed when she was sitting with the man. His changed, too. The lonely smell was lessening, and something else was taking its place, something warm, something inviting.

Still, the desire to search wouldn't leave him. In stealth mode, he crept to the screened-in porch, forgetting that Jamie had blocked his secret passageway. *Pffft.* As if that could stop him. He'd gone down a chimney. Going up shouldn't be too much harder.

Although his body was thrumming with the need to act, he decided to wait until Jamie went to bed. Then he would make his move.

CHAPTER 11

"Well, I haven't been to a puppet show since I saw one at the library when I was about six," Jamie told Ruby. "So, I guess this will almost count as something new."

"It absolutely will," Ruby said as she maneuvered her Bug into a space on the street between an SUV and a fire hydrant. "Almighty Opp isn't just a puppet show. The guys who created it call it a service. I'm not going to even attempt to describe it to you. It's something you have to experience."

They got out of the car and crossed the street. "Holy cripes, is that a giant bucket of chicken?" Jamie asked.

"Oh my gosh, yes, it is." Ruby teased. "They don't have ten-story, bucket-shaped KFCs in Pennsylvania?"

"Not in Avella, or any other place I've ever been," Jamie answered.

Ruby came to a stop by a bus stop across from a dollar store and a few apartment buildings. A couple teenage guys had set up lawn chairs on the sidewalk and were drinking PBRs. Ruby smiled at them, and they waved to her. "Is the theater near here?" Jamie asked.

"The theater is here. Or it will be," Ruby said. "They perform on the sidewalk."

"Do they do this full-time, do you think? Like, as a job?" Jamie saw a hipster couple toting folding chairs heading their way.

"They only do a performance once a month, so doubtful. They get donations, but I'm not even sure they'd cover the costs. The guys are always adding new stuff," Ruby answered. "I think the main reason they do it is because it makes them happy. I think they might actually want to change the world, or at least the people who show up."

"Thanks so much for bringing me." Jamie couldn't wait to see what the show—or the service—turned out to be like. From what Ruby had said, the guys who'd created the Almighty Opp had found their passion.

Ruby wrapped her arm around Jamie and gave her a squeeze. "I've been neglecting your LA education. But I'm going to get you out to see the sights."

"Isn't it supposed to start at nine?" There was no sign of the performers.

"Punctuality isn't an Opp thing," Ruby answered. "But they'll be here."

"I wonder if anything will go missing tonight. It's been two days since I fixed the rip in the screen Mac was using to get out, but stuff is still getting stolen. There were a bunch of new things dropped off at the fountain. Mac can't be responsible for them—not the new ones. I didn't bother telling Hud that. He can twist anything I say so it fits his theory that I'm a criminal mastermind. Like, he's sure that I left things on other people's doorsteps to throw suspicion off me. He thinks I put the stuff I really wanted on my own doorstep and am using the rest as a smokescreen. Because you know how much I've been wanting a neon-orange Speedo."

"I don't think it would have made any difference if you dragged him into your porch and showed him the spot in the screen you fixed," Ruby said. "He doesn't think Mac is your only accomplice, remember? He'd probably think I stole the new stuff—if you actually convinced him Mac couldn't get out of the house. He gives me the side-eye every time he sees me. He's sure I'm one of your goons."

"The craziest part is that Mac did steal some stuff. I saw him take David's jockstrap. It's bizarre that someone else happened to be nabbing things at the same time Mac was."

"Maybe Mac has a copycat," Ruby suggested. She elbowed Jamie in the ribs. "Get it? Copy*cat*."

"I actually don't. Do you think you could explain it to me? I'm but a naïve, small-town girl." Jamie fluttered her eyelashes. "But, come on, it's weird."

"Yeah," Ruby admitted. "You haven't gotten anything else left at your place, have you?"

"No. I would have told you right away. I hope you don't mind that you've become my go-to to calm me down, give me advice, and feed me cookies," Jamie said.

"It's all my pleasure," Ruby answered. "When I'm working on a project, those people become almost like my family. When the movie wraps, we all say we'll keep in touch. But we don't, unless we end up working together again. I can use a friend who isn't in the business, especially because my next movie doesn't start production for a few months."

Jamie did another street check. "They'll come. Don't worry," Ruby told her. "In your fountain watching, have you seen David again?"

"Nope," Jamie answered. "He must not have gotten anything else taken since I gave him back the stuff Mac brought me. I think he'd have checked with me if he did, since I had all the other things."

"It seemed kind of like the universe was trying to throw you two together, with you seeing each other at the pet shop, then being at the same restaurants for your dates, which both sucked, then running into each other at the bar," Ruby told her. "And then, to top it off, your cat was stealing from him."

"I could deal with you decorating for Christmas in September," Jamie answered. "In fact, I thought it was charming. But if you're going to start talking about the universe's intentions for me, that I won't be able to take."

Ruby held up both hands. "Okay, okay. But David's a great guy. And you're great, too. And I don't want to be like Marie and Helen, but—"

"Then don't," Jamie pleaded. "Just believe me when I tell you I don't want to get anything going with anybody right now. Even somebody great. Because I agree, David seems like a great guy. He's funny, nice, didn't suggest anything obscene within a few hours of meeting me, even bought me a drink after my night with the complete user."

"And nice butt," Ruby said.

"Okay, yes, he's also good-looking, from all angles," Jamie admitted. "But, seriously, I'm not interested."

"I know. And I get it, I do. But I've known David for years. I'd like to see him happy. He's had a hard bunch of years. And even though I've only known you for weeks, I'd like to see you happy, too. I can see you two together. David's not someone who could get in the way of you figuring out what you want to do with your life. I think he'd encourage you."

Jamie wanted off this topic. "I talked to the administration office at the college today, and they're letting me apply the fee for the drama class to a special-effects makeup one," Jamie said. "I'm continuing on with your advice to try new things. Plus, I'll be able to create an awesome Halloween costume."

"Here they come!" Ruby exclaimed. She pointed down the street at two men in clown makeup riding bikes toward them. Both bikes towed carts that looked like mini covered wagons.

Maybe the universe is on my side, Jamie thought. *Now Ruby won't have the chance to turn the conversation back around to*

David. The two men pulled up next to the bus stop and began to unload, silently urging Jamie and Ruby to help.

She felt a tingle of excitement as she saw the stage coming together, complete with two big tops, a confetti cannon, and a collection of wonderfully strange puppets. If you did this, come out to a quiet neighborhood, almost unannounced, to put on a show that probably wouldn't pay for itself, you had to do it out of love. If these guys had found something they loved to do, so could she. And that was where she wanted to keep her focus. So, no guys for now, for this gift of a year. Especially no David, because he seemed like he could be a distraction, a way-too-enjoyable distraction.

"Addison brought me back my *Adventure Time* T-shirt," Zachary told David as they set out for a walk with Diogee. "She said it ended up in front of her door, and that you told her it was mine."

It had been a few days since Addison had brought the shirt to the fountain. She'd taken her time giving the shirt back. Not that David was going to tell Zachary that. David could see Zachary was struggling to keep his voice casual, but the kid couldn't stop smiling. "How is the shrew?" He couldn't resist teasing Zachary a little.

"She's not a shrew," Zachary protested. And David didn't remind him that it was Zachary who had called Addison a shrew in the first place. "In her diary—"

"Which you didn't read," David said. Diogee stopped to *I-was-here* a clump of hydrangeas.

"I just flipped through it. Anyway, on some pages she sounded really pissed off, and I could see why with some of the crap her boyfriend pulled. But on some pages she sounded kind of funny. And there were a couple poems that were really insightful."

The crush was more serious than David had thought. "It

seemed like she was an *Adventure Time* fan, too. She recognized that Mushroom War shirt right off. Did you guys end up talking about the show?"

"Yeah, actually," Zachary said. "She has this theory that the mushroom bomb created mutations, and the slime monster you see around Simon and Marcy are actually human mutations. Which I'm not sure I agree with, but it makes sense."

"I still need to get caught up," David told him.

"You have to." Usually Zachary would have gone on for the rest of the walk about all the reasons David needed to read every issue, but instead he said, "We talked about Ms. Marvel, too. I think she was a little surprised I read it. There are all these Reddit posts from guys who think diversity is being shoved down their throats, and that Ms. Marvel just panders to a few small groups. Like women! Which is not a small group. We both think Kamala is kind of a Peter Parker–type character, and that her characterization is really complex."

David jumped in. He knew Zachary could go on about comics forever, and usually he was happy to hear it. He read some of the same rants on different comic sites. But today he was too curious about what was happening between Zachary and Addison. It sounded like his boy had scored some points by defending Ms. Marvel. "Have you seen her at school since then?" he asked.

Zachary's smile faltered. "In English. But we hardly have any time to get from one class to another, so there's no time to talk to anyone. And at lunch . . . You know how it is, everyone sits with the same people they always sit with. Addison's always with her boyfriend."

"It sounded like she was kicking him to the curb that day she threw her phone out the window," David commented.

"Yeah, well . . ." Zachary shrugged. "I thought she did. And her diary made it sound like she wanted to." David didn't tease him about reading the diary this time. "But today she spent half of lunch sitting on his lap feeding him French fries, so I guess if they ever did break up, they're back together now."

"Things change. You gotta remember MJ had a boyfriend when Peter Parker first met her," David reminded him.

"What's that supposed to mean?" he yelped, and Diogee stopped sniffing and looked around to see what was the matter. "I don't—It doesn't matter to me if she has a boyfriend or not. Except that she made him sound like such a jerk, and I don't see why she'd want to be with someone who doesn't treat her better."

"Nobody should be with somebody who treats them badly," David agreed.

"Yeah. That's why it bugged me to see her all over him at school," Zachary said.

"Right," David said. He wondered if Zachary had actually managed to convince himself that was true.

Mac batted Mousie around, but even though Mousie smelled as wonderful as usual, Mac just didn't feel the usual delirium. It was the humans' fault. They were just all so stupid. At first he'd blamed it on their noses, which were so bad they shouldn't be called noses at all. They should be called something like face blobs.

But now he knew he couldn't only blame their horrible sense of smell. He'd gotten Jamie and the human who had the drooler as a packmate together. They'd sat right outside the house, and Mac had been able to smell the loneliness leaving both of them. He'd been able to smell the pull between them. He'd been sure he'd completed his mission.

Then—nothing! They hadn't been together since then. Why? It was incomprehensible. Something makes you feel good, you want more of it. Like tuna. Tuna made Mac feel good, so he wanted more. He wanted tuna anytime tuna was available. Or like Mousie. Mousie made Mac feel good—well, almost always it did. He would play with Mousie every minute of the day, except that sometimes Jamie hid Mousie in a box with a latch, a latch Mac was still working on learning to open.

The two young ones, the ones who weren't quite as helpless as kittens, but not like grown cats, either, were just as bad. The same thing had happened with them. Mac had managed to get them near each other. He knew that. He could smell it on them both. And he could smell that they'd made each other happier. But did that make them get near each other again? No. Because they were humans and they barely knew how to keep themselves alive without help.

At least the littlest girl and the nurturer didn't need more pushing from Mac. Somehow one or both of them managed to realize that they were better together.

Mac gave a huff of aggravation. He'd have go out tonight and work on fixing things. He wouldn't be able to enjoy Mousie time until he did.

He trotted into Jamie's room, where she was peacefully asleep, clearly unaware of what a mess she'd made of things. He picked something up from the floor, something with an odor that should be able to penetrate a face blob. Then he returned to the living room, stepped into the fireplace, and began to slowly work his way up the chimney. The ones who weren't full-grown should be grateful he felt sorry for them. And Jamie should be grateful she was Mac's person. If he had to go out every night for the rest of her life, he'd make her realize what she needed to be happy.

He went directly to the man's place. Mac's usual window was closed. It didn't matter. He'd use the bonehead's door. He waited a moment, until he was sure the dog wasn't right on the other side, then he slipped through.

No drooler in sight. Good. Mac wasn't in the mood to play. Not tonight. He dashed up the stairs and into the room where the man slept. The dog was sleeping in there, too, curled up, nose to tail, on an enormous fluffy pillow. Mac could use a pillow like that. He'd work on a way to get it home later. Tonight was for work.

He leapt onto the bed. He was going to make sure the man didn't miss the gift Mac had for him. He crept forward and laid it on the man's chest. Then—mayhem.

The man jerked upright. The bonehead started to bray.

Mac needed to get out of there. He scrambled off the bed and darted into the bathroom. He remembered a second too late that the window was closed. Didn't matter. Mac was a master at opening things. He bounded to the windowsill and began pawing at the latch.

Too slow. The man was on him. He caught Mac up in his arms. Mac struggled, but the man held tight, even when Mac gave him a warning scratch.

"Knock it off," the man said. "I caught you fair and square, MacGyver."

CHAPTER 12

Jamie woke to the sound of someone knocking. She checked her alarm clock. A little after one. It felt as if she'd been asleep for hours, but she'd actually just gone to bed about a half an hour ago. Still, it was waaay too late for someone to be knocking.

But whoever was out there didn't think so. The knocking kept coming, even louder now. Jamie jerked the jeans she'd worn to the puppet show on under the T-shirt she was using as a nightgown. She started for the door, then turned around and grabbed her cell from the nightstand. She punched in 91—. If there was some crazed, as opposed to sane, maniac out there, all she'd have to do was punch another 1 and wait for the police to show up.

"Who is it?" Jamie yelled, trying to sound like she was seven feet tall. Her cute door didn't have a peephole.

"It's David," he called back. "Sorry to wake you up. I have your cat."

"Mac?" He hadn't been on her head, his usual spot in the middle of the night. She opened the door and saw David, who looked disheveled; Mac, who looked furious; and Diogee, who looked ecstatic.

She reached out her arms for her cat, and David took a half step back.

"You might want me just to put him down inside," he said. "He's . . . agitated."

"Come on in." She opened the door wide. David stepped inside, waiting until Jamie had the door shut to release Mac, who streaked into Jamie's room. "I can't believe he got out. I didn't try to fix the screen with duct tape or anything. I bought a spline. I bought a spline roller. I'd never heard of either of them before, but I figured out how to use them." She hurried to the porch and checked the spot where the rip had been. "See. It's still good," she said, running her fingers over it.

She looked up, and that's when she saw the long red scratch on David's forearm. "He scratched you!"

"Don't worry about it," David told her.

Diogee whined and strained at the leash. Clearly he wanted some love. Jamie crouched down in front of him and began petting him. "I'm sorry I ignored you. Yes, I am. Yes, I am." Diogee flopped onto his back, and Jamie obediently began scratching his belly. "I'm going to get you something for that scratch. You don't want it to get infected," she told David, and stood up. Diogee pawed at her leg, not ready for her to stop.

"Diogee, knock it off," David said.

"Do you want to let him off the leash?" Jamie asked.

"It's okay?"

"Sure. There's nothing he can hurt."

After David unclipped the leash, Jamie led the way to the bathroom. "Wash the cut while I get the Neosporin."

"It's not—" David began to protest.

"Just do it," Jamie said. And he did. She leaned around him and started rooting through the medicine cabinet. She was standing so close that she was breathing in his scent. He smelled good, like soap and man and maybe a little vanilla. "So, um, where did you find Mac?" she asked, trying to distract herself. "I still have to figure out how he escaped."

"He was in my bedroom," Mac answered.

"Oh my gosh. I don't know what's gotten into him. He's going to get me kicked out of Storybook Court." Jamie found the Neosporin and shut the cabinet door, then stepped away from David.

"Don't worry. I won't be reporting you to Hud." David turned off the water, and Jamie reached for a towel, her chest brushing against his warm, solid back. That's when she realized she wasn't wearing a bra. Because she'd just pulled her jeans on under the Pulp Minion tee she used as a nightgown. The bathroom was too damn small. She gave him the towel and sat down on the edge of the tub.

"Did he manage to grab anything of yours?" she asked.

"Uh, no. But he brought me something I'm assuming it's yours." David reached into the front pocket of his jeans and pulled out a pair of hot pink bikini panties covered with little green aliens.

"Yeah, mine." Jamie jumped up, grabbed them, and stuck them in the pocket of her jeans. She felt her cheeks get hot and knew she had to be blushing. She hated blushing. She twisted off the top of the little Neosporin tube and squirted some of the gel onto David's arm, then wondered why she hadn't just given the tube to him, because now it sort of seemed like she should rub it in. But was that weird? Before she could decide, David did it himself.

"Want a Band-Aid?" Jamie asked.

"I'm good," David told her. He headed out of the bathroom, but stopped when he got to the living room. Jamie stepped up beside him and stifled a laugh. Diogee was lying on her sofa. So was Mac. They were almost nose to nose, eyes locked, both motionless.

"I can't believe Diogee isn't trying to dig his way out your front door," David said softly. "He's usually a big wimp."

"I can't believe Mac hasn't brought out the claws," Jamie admitted. "Clearly they're working on some kind of negotiation. Let's leave them to it."

David didn't move. "My grandma used to read me this poem about two stuffed animals who had a fight. When it was over, all that was left was scraps."

"The gingham dog and the calico cat! It was in this book my mom found at a garage sale," Jamie answered. "I think if they were going to tear each other to shreds, they'd have started already. Come on." When they reached the kitchen, she opened the fridge. "What can I get you? I'm having a beer."

"Sounds good."

Jamie handed him a Corona and they both sat down at the table. She resisted the urge to cross her arms over her chest. It was too late now. He'd seen whatever he'd seen. Shouldn't be much. The T-shirt wasn't especially thin. "You must have to be at work in a few hours. You don't have to stay. You can take the beer for the road, since you're walking and not driving."

"You're throwing me out? When I'm recovering from cat scratch fever?" David asked. He smiled. "I had an early night. I got some sleep already."

"Stay as long as you want," Jamie said. She took a swig of her beer. "Sorry again about Mac sneaking into your house. I was sure I'd made my place escape-proof. It makes more sense that he's found another way out than that someone else is also stealing and redistributing things around the Court."

"His thieving might have actually done my neighbor Zachary a favor. He's goes to high school with Addison and has a big crush on her. You know her, right? Riley's big sister?"

"I've met her," Jamie said. "Has the kid who has the crush, in fact, met her?"

David laughed. "Yeah, they've known each other practically since birth. And he's aware of her temper. But hormones are strong in that one. And who knows, maybe if she had a boyfriend who wasn't a jerk, she wouldn't be so furious all the time. At least that seems to be Zachary's theory."

Jamie raised her eyebrows. "It's possible. Does Zachary know her boyfriend?"

"He's seen Addison and him together at school, and he read a little of her diary," David said.

"Her diary? Wait, he must be the one who found the diary on his doorstep. I was there when Ruby sneaked it back into her house."

"Yeah, I asked her to do that. Zachary thought if he gave it back to her himself, she'd be upset because she'd think he read it. Which he did," David answered.

"Is that what you meant about Mac doing him a favor? You think Mac took the diary?" Jamie groaned. "He must have taken it. And Riley's pony. I don't even want to think about how many houses he's snuck into."

"I wasn't thinking about the diary. I was thinking about the *Adventure Time* shirt of Zachary's that went missing. Remember, Addison brought it to the fountain when we were there?" David said. "I told her it was Zachary's and she returned it to him. They got into a big conversation about it and other graphic novels. I think it's the first time they've really spoken in years. Zachary definitely won't be registering a complaint against Mac."

"What do you think I should do? Do you think I need to go door to door and confess I'm the owner of a cat burglar and apologize?"

"I think you should just find Mac's new exit and seal it up,"

David said. "Then the whole thing will just blow over. Nobody but Hud seems that worried about it. I can help you go over the place to figure out how he's getting out if you want."

"That would be great. I could use another set of eyes."

"I'll come by tomorrow after work, around three thirty, if that's good for you." David finished his beer. "Let's go check for scraps. I can't believe you knew that poem."

"It doesn't look like either of them have moved a muscle," Jamie said when they returned to the living room. "Props to Diogee. I've never won a staring contest with Mac, but he's hanging in there. You should bring him tomorrow."

"Great. See you then." David snapped the leash back on the dog. He had to half-haul Diogee to the front door. He kept trying to look back at Mac.

"Thanks for bringing Mac home," Jamie said. "I hope you get a little sleep before work."

"I will. Nice T-shirt," he said as she was swinging the door closed.

She hoped he was really talking about the shirt, and not her braless state. Vinnie and Jules as Minions were pretty funny. That had to be all he meant.

Jamie flopped down on the couch next to Mac. "You are a lot of trouble," she told him. "But I love you." She rubbed her cheek against the top of his head, and he started to purr.

"Let's go back to bed. Well, back for me, not you." She picked him up and carried him to the bedroom. "Please be good and stay put, or I'm going to start making you sleep with your leash on. I'll tie it to myself if I have to."

Mac curled up in the exact center of the bed. Jamie sighed, pulled off her jeans, and arranged herself around him, but she felt wide awake. "You had a whole houseful of things to choose from, and you had to go with panties. Thanks a lot, Mac-Gyver."

Well, it wasn't like she hadn't seen David's underwear. His had turned out to be the boxer briefs. She bet he looked good in them.

She gave a moan and rolled over onto her side, pulling her pillow over her head. She didn't want to be thinking about how David looked in his briefs. She wanted—and needed—to be thinking about how to keep Mac where he belonged. That and what her next step in figuring out what her dream should be.

"I hope when I said 'nice shirt', she knew I meant nice shirt," David told Diogee as they walked home. He'd realized right after the words came out of his mouth that they could have seemed like some kind of skeevy innuendo about her going braless. Which had been impossible not to notice. At least for him.

"And you. I'm proud of you for standing up to that cat—and not getting mauled," David continued. Sometimes he thought he talked to the dog too much. But if you had a dog, you talked to it. He bet Jamie talked to MacGyver.

When he and the dog reached home, David went straight back to bed. He'd need to get up in a few hours. He heard Diogee flop down on his gigantic pillow with a sigh of contentment. A few moments later, the dog was snoring, loudly.

But it felt like all the lights were on in David's brain. He couldn't stop thinking. It was interesting—weird, freaky, uncanny?—how MacGyver had given something of Zachary's to Addison and vice versa. What were the odds? There were twenty-three houses in Storybook Court.

Jamie had looked damn good in that T-shirt. The thought just popped into his head. He pushed it away.

Why had Mac taken so many of his things? From what David could tell by what had been left by the fountain, the cat had stolen more from him than anyone else.

Jamie had looked damn good in that T-shirt.

He'd managed to stop thinking about it for about fifteen seconds. That shirt had been pretty funny. The Jules and Vinnie Minions holding bananas instead of guns. "Ba-nah-na," he said aloud, in a decent Minion impression. He'd seen all the movies with Minions in them way too many times, because Lucy and Adam's youngest, Maya, who was David's goddaughter, loved them. At least she had decent taste in movies. She'd absolutely refused to watch more than the first half hour of *Norm of the North*.

Jamie had looked damn good in that T-shirt.

Clearly, he had no control over his own brain. He bet Jamie'd look damn good in those tiny alien panties, too. His mind started flashing him the visuals, and he groaned and pulled his pillow over his head. He was never going to fall asleep now.

The next afternoon, Jamie couldn't sit still. She picked up her notebook. She had a few things to add to her List of Likes, including creating a fake scar, which she'd done in her class that morning, and Almighty Opp, although she was still trying to figure out exactly how to describe what she'd seen. Puppet therapy? Puppet enlightenment? The two guys who put on the spectacle, Jeffrey and Kranko, seemed to want to assist people in connecting, and to create . . . jubilation. *Jubilation* was the only word that came close. How cool would it be to do something like that? Not creating a street theater art piece—although she hadn't tried that yet, so maybe she shouldn't be counting it out. But something where the purpose was connecting people and making them happy?

She tossed the notebook aside. She had lots of thoughts, but not the patience to write them down. Instead, she hurried into the screened porch and checked her repair job again. Mac really couldn't have gotten out that way.

She wandered into the kitchen and opened the fridge, shut it, then opened it again, and took out a pickle and ate it, even though she wasn't really hungry. Then she had a cracker to take away the pickle-y taste, then she decided she had to brush her teeth.

As she brushed, she studied herself in the mirror. Should she change? She had on a basic pink V-neck T-shirt and khakis. Nothing special. Wait. Why was she even thinking about changing? Why did it matter if her clothes weren't anything special? Her neighbor was coming over to help her figure out how her cat was escaping. She looked fine. She was wearing a bra. She was presentable. That was all that mattered.

Still, she went into the bedroom, opened the closet door, and flicked a few hangers, then she shut the door firmly. She was *not* changing. See, this was one of the reasons The Year of Me shouldn't include men. An attractive guy was coming over to do her a favor, all friendly and neighborly and not date-y, and she couldn't focus on anything important, like her list.

She scooped up Mac from the spot of sunlight where he was snoozing and cuddled him. He endured it for about two seconds, then squirmed away. Mac liked to be petted and fussed over—but only when *he* was in the mood. Or if he was feeling sorry for her.

Jamie picked up her cell and looked up the gingham dog and calico cat poem. It was called "The Duel." She'd forgotten that. She wondered if David knew the title. And she was doing it again. Not thinking about clothes, but still thinking about him. This was ridiculous.

She took a deep breath and walked outside. She'd start looking for Mac's escape route by herself. It had been nice, very nice, of David to offer, but she could do it on her own. But before she'd even started her inspection, Marie appeared on her porch. "Check your e-mail," she told Jamie.

"Why?" Jamie asked. She didn't like the way Marie was looking at her. There was an eager gleam in her eye.

"Because Fred Hernandez, that's our dentist, just e-mailed me and said he'd just e-mailed you," Marie said.

Jamie closed her eyes, counted to three, then opened them. "Marie, please don't give my e-mail address to anyone without checking with me. I told you, I told you very clearly, that I'm not interested in meeting your dentist or anyone else. Please e-mail him back and tell him that you were wrong."

"It's okay to tell her, Jam."

Jamie looked over her shoulder and saw David coming toward her. He gave her a quick wink, then wrapped his arm around her shoulders and pulled her up against him. "Jamie and I have gone out a couple times. We didn't want to say anything to people in the Court in case it didn't work out. But I don't think we have to worry about that anymore."

Marie narrowed her eyes at them. "You went out a couple of times," she repeated. "Where did you go?" She sounded a little like Hud Martin.

"Universal Studios. I know it's completely touristy, but Jamie just moved here. Plus she had to see the Bates Motel. She's a Hitchcock fan," David said.

"Make that a fanatic. Love him," Jamie added quickly, feeling a little dazed. She didn't want to go out with Marie's dentist, but she wasn't sure she liked David swooping in and taking charge. "We also went for drinks at this place a few blocks from here. What was it called?" His body heat was soaking into her shoulders and side, distracting her.

"The Thirsty Goat," David said. "Jamie, if you can believe it, had a Skittles Bomb. She said it reminded her of the vodka-infused gummy bears she used to sneak in her college dorm room."

"Busted," Jamie said.

Marie tilted her head and studied them a moment longer, then nodded. "I'll tell Fred that you've started seeing someone," she told Jamie. "But if it doesn't work out with you two, you're going out with him. You're thirty-four. You have to think about that." She returned to the house.

Jamie started to move away. "Stay close for a minute," David said. "Marie sees everything."

"True." Jamie turned a little so she could look at him. "Did you call me Jam before?"

"I thought I'd be more convincing. I figured if we were going out, I'd have a cute nickname for you," David said. "I didn't have much time to think. Jam is sweet. And it starts with the first letters of your name. Seemed okay."

A smile tugged at Jamie's lips, but she forced herself to say, "I didn't really need rescuing."

David winced. "That was presumptuous of me. I guess it's because I've been in the same position, with my friends pushing me to go out. I thought I'd give you an assist, that's all."

"You did help me out," Jamie admitted. "Lucky we ran into each other at that bar. That gave us lots of good details. I'm not sure we'd have convinced her without them, even though the Hitchcock was a nice touch. If she'd quizzed me about his movies, I would have been able to answer." She looked up at him and smiled, in case Marie was still keeping an eye on them, then said, "Think we can move on to figuring out how Mac's getting out now?"

David nodded, kissed her temple, then slowly slid his arm away. Even though he was no longer touching her, Jamie felt like she could still feel his warmth soaking into her body. "Hey, you didn't bring Diogee." She wanted to say something, and that was the first thing she thought of.

"I decided to let him go for a walk with Zachary," David said.

"Okay, but I meant it when I said he could come," Jamie answered. "I was going to start looking for the escape route by walking around the house."

"Sounds good." They started walking. "Maybe I'll tell Adam and Lucy, that's my oldest friend and his wife, we're going out, if it's okay with you. Every time I see them, they're trying to show me new profiles on counterpart.com. They're relentless. And you know how my first two encounters went."

Jamie shrugged. "Why not? You might as well benefit from the lie, too."

"I got some, actually a lot, of texts today from one of the Counterpart women Lucy picked for me," David said. "I sent her one text, and she sent me like ten, with no response from me in between. I wasn't ignoring her. It's just that I was at work."

"Ten is a lot, when you're not having any back-and-forth," Jamie said.

"Yeah. It's not that there was anything wrong with what she said in any of them. But the number kind of freaked me out. I'm thinking I don't want to meet her now."

"Yeah, I get that," Jamie said. "But maybe she just thinks you sound great and is excited to get to know you." She wanted to be fair to this unknown woman. It wasn't like she and David were really going out. There was no reason for her to be feeling little pricks of jealousy.

"Maybe," David agreed.

"All these windows look okay to me. You?" Jamie asked.

"Yeah, I'm not seeing anything, either. Although . . . See those California lilac bushes?" David gestured to the shrub that grew under her bedroom window. "The tops are a little bent, like something fell on them. Or like if a cat jumped down from the roof."

"But we're left with the same problem. How would he get outside to get to the roof?" Jamie asked.

They made a complete circuit of the house without seeing anything else that suggested a way Mac was escaping. "Let's check from the inside," Jamie suggested.

They started with the living room. Mac decided to be sociable and followed them as they searched, purring with contentment.

David's cell buzzed. "Sorry. I should check it. I fill in for the bakery manager when he's out of town—like now." He flipped open his phone, then shut it a moment later.

"Everything okay?" Jamie asked.

"It was her. MsRight347. She said she just realized my profile didn't say whether I wanted kids or not and she was curious if I did."

"Oh. Well, I guess not wanting kids is a deal breaker," Jamie said, still wanting to keep an open mind about the woman, even though she sort of disliked her. No, *disliked* was too strong. But the woman had to be boring. MsRigh347? Couldn't she come up with anything more interesting than that?

Jamie didn't share her screen name analysis. Instead she asked, "Is it typical to want to get all that addressed right up front? I've never done online dating. In Avella you pretty much know everyone around. Or it feels like it." They continued to search the house as they talked.

"I don't know. Not with the first two. It would have been nice if the pregnant one had asked how I felt about having kids, but otherwise—what's wrong with waiting until you know you're getting at least somewhat serious before you start talking about what kind of family you want?"

"There's nothing wrong with it," Jamie told him. "It's just that sperm doesn't have a sell-by date. I guess if you know you absolutely want kids, you might not want to even go out with someone who definitely doesn't. Seems like she would have put it in her profile, though." There. That was very fair. And it was true that women had to think about things that men didn't.

"Maybe she did. I read it pretty fast," David admitted. "I messaged her, because if I didn't I'd still be listening to Adam and Lucy try to choose someone for me, and I couldn't take it. So it's really okay that I tell them we're going out?"

Jamie forced herself to continue being fair. "It's fine. But if you change your mind and want them to keep helping you look at profiles, just tell them we're not seeing each other anymore. I mean, you signed up. You must want to meet someone."

"I did. I was recently really gut-punched by the idea of spending the rest of my life alone," David admitted. "But the online thing isn't me. I want to just meet someone when I meet someone. If you end up meeting someone, just tell me and we can fake break up."

"The whole reason I want to fake date is so I won't have to meet someone," Jamie reminded him. "I'm not seeing any place Mac could have gotten out."

"Me either," David answered. "Maybe you should read the e-mail from Marie's dentist, just to be sure he's not actually someone you think you want to meet."

Jamie studied his face. Had he already changed his mind? Was he trying to get out of pretending to be going out with her? "Fine. Let me look." She took out her phone, opened her e-mail, and found one that had to be from the dentist. "The subject line is 'My Needs.' Sounds promising, no?"

David's cell buzzed. He checked it. "Another message from MsRight347. She wants to know if I do want kids, how many I want and if I have a preference about boys or girls."

"I can top that. The dentist's e-mail? It's a list of qualities the women he goes out with has to have. Must have a job. Must have a car."

"He's trying to weed out sugar-baby types," David said. "That's not so horrible."

Jamie held up one finger. "Shorter than five-foot-seven. Hair to mid-back, although he says he knows mine is shorter but we can 'fix that'." She shut the cell. "I've read enough. I haven't even met him and he's already deciding there are things about me that need to be fixed."

David's cell buzzed again. "Oh, come on." He checked it. "She wants to know how I feel about the name Charlotte for a girl, possibly with the nickname Charley, and Ethan for a boy." He looked at Jamie. "Still think she's asking reasonable questions?"

"Uh, have to say no." Jamie felt a little jolt of pleasure that now David would never agree to go out with the woman. She tried to shove the feeling away. It was none of her business. Except they were becoming friends, and friends didn't let friends date crazies.

"I'm going to tell her I just started to date a neighbor, and I want to see how that goes." He smiled at her. "You're coming in handy."

Jamie smiled back. "So are you. The dentist should be grateful. I probably would have stabbed him through the heart with my fork if we attempted to meet for dinner."

"You know, since we're pretending to be dating, we should probably actually go somewhere together," David said. "Because Marie sees all. And my friends will want details."

"I'm up for going somewhere. Where?"

"I know you like old movies, but do you like really old movies?" David asked. "Because if you do, I know the perfect place. It's one of my favorites."

Jamie's pulse sped up, like he was asking her out for real. "If it's one of your favorites, I want to see it."

"It's the Silent Movie Theatre. They only have shows on Fridays and Saturdays. Does Friday work for you?"

"Sure," Jamie answered. "I love old movies, but I've never seen a silent one, well, just a few little bits on TV, and I'm on a mission to try new things. It sounds perfect."

"I'll pick you up at seven. Let me give you my number, in case you want to send me any psycho texts before then," David said.

Jamie handed him her cell. "Put it in. If I'm your fake girl-friend, I should definitely have your number."

Mac stretched, lazy and content that night. Jamie and the man, David, had spent more time together, and they'd both smelled happy. And David hadn't brought the bonehead this time. The other night, Mac had to use all his self-control to keep the claws in when the dog was in his house. He hadn't wanted to disturb Jamie and David by making the bonehead cry.

He wouldn't mind staying in tonight, but he'd planned to continue working on the not-quite-adult ones before he'd gotten caught yesterday. Caught! He still couldn't believe a human had been fast enough to catch him. At least it got David and Jamie together. It was almost as if he'd planned it.

He also needed to pay a visit to the bonehead. The mutt needed to know that just because Mac had shown him mercy for a few hours, it didn't mean Mac was even close to tolerating the dog. If Mac, Diogee, Jamie, and David were going to be together in Mac's territory, Diogee needed to understand his place in the pack order—the bottom.

CHAPTER 13

"How about this one?" Ruby held out a buttercup-yellow A-line dress. The placket had large scallops and tied at the neck. "Demure, but sexy. Like something Megan Draper would have worn back when she was Don's secretary."

"Adorable. But yellow isn't a great color for me," Jamie said. "Do you think it'll seem silly wearing something obviously vintage to the Silent Movie Theatre? I don't want to look like I'm wearing a costume."

"You won't. It'll be perfect. The crowd at that theater will absolutely appreciate it. There will be other people there in vintage." Ruby kept flipping through the hangers in the boutique. "Oooh. Look at this one!" She held up a short skater skirt that was covered with hot dogs and hamburgers, like the cover of a fifties diner.

"I think that one's more you than me," Jamie said.

"You could be right. I'll try it on." Ruby kept searching the rack. "This. Is. It." She held up a full, pleated midi skirt the color of pine needles. It was embellished with fans of flocked black velvet, but the pattern wasn't at all busy, nothing like the hectic jumble of hot dogs and hamburgers on the other skirt.

"I love it," Jamie breathed.

"And with this—" Ruby pulled out a simple black boatneck shirt. It looked like something Audrey Hepburn would have worn in *Sabrina.*

"I love it," Jamie said again.

"But?" Ruby asked.

"Part of The Year of Me is wearing what I want, without caring what anybody thinks. But that combo is an outfit with a capital *O*. I'm not sure I can pull it off. It needs the right hair. The right lipstick. It won't work unless I go all the way with it."

"I agree. So, go all the way. It'll be fun. I can help you with the hair and makeup. I think you'd look killer with a Veronica Lake swoop and seriously red lipstick. I have the perfect color," Ruby said.

"I don't know . . ." Jamie said.

"Yes, you do. I can see the clothes-lust all over your face," Ruby answered.

"But I'm not going on a real date. It's just an act. Won't it seem strange that I'm getting so dressed up?"

"I'm telling you, you'll have every woman in the theater wishing they'd gone retro," Ruby told her. "And you'll look gorgeous."

"You don't think David will wonder why I put in so much effort?" Jamie asked.

"You're forgetting, guys don't analyze. At least not the secret meaning of a lipstick shade. David will think you look great, but he's not going to be trying to decode your outfit."

"I'm going to go try it on."

"I'll come. I want to try on the diner skirt," Ruby said.

The shop's two little dressing rooms were side by side, so they were able to continue talking as they changed. "Did you see that little girl's dress with the fauns on it and the red tulle underskirt?" Ruby asked. "That's such a Riley dress. Although I guess it would be even more Riley if it had ponies instead of fauns. I bet I could find the perfect material and make a pony version. But I don't know how her mother would feel."

"Maybe as a Christmas present?" Jamie suggested as she pulled off her pants. "Her mom probably wouldn't mind you giving her a gift. Do you know her mother at all?"

"I know her by sight, but that's it," Ruby answered. "From Riley and Addison, I know she works two jobs. I should make a point of introducing myself, since Riley's been spending time at my place. Addison knows where she is, but I need to make sure her mom is okay with it."

"Yeah, but I'm sure she will be. You have lots of people in the complex who will vouch for you. Including me," Jamie said. "Just don't let her talk to Hud."

"Hud's loving his life right now," Ruby commented. "He has a mission."

"With the fountain as mission control," Jamie agreed. She stepped into the skirt and zipped it. It fit perfectly, hitting her just below the knee. "I saw the guy who the Speedo belonged to picking them up. Maybe midforties. Balding. Little belly."

"Brett Morris," Ruby said. "He lives in the place with the moat. Good guy. Bad taste in swimwear. He's going through a nasty divorce right now."

"It looked like Hud was taking down his life story. He must have asked him questions for a solid hour," Jamie said. She pulled on the top. It was form-fitting and made a good combo with the full skirt. She smoothed her hands over it, then turned and looked over her shoulder to see the outfit from the back.

"My skirt is just a little too short," Ruby said. "How are you doing?"

"I'm getting both," Jamie said. There was no way she could leave the store without them, now that she'd tried them on.

"*Brava*," Ruby called.

Just as Jamie was replacing the skirt on the hanger, her cell buzzed. She opened the text and started to laugh.

"What's so funny?" Ruby asked.

"David just texted me. He wants to know if I have tats, because he is unable to spend time with a woman who doesn't care enough about her body to adorn it. He does say that if I don't have any, but am willing to get a minimum of three in the near future, he might still consider going to the movies with me." Jamie was laughing too hard to continue. She sucked in a few breaths, then managed to go on. "He very generously says that if he thinks we're well suited, he might consider paying a portion of the cost of the tattoos, because he wants to make sure they're quality."

"And this was from David? *David* David?" Ruby demanded.

"He's just messing around," Jamie explained as she got dressed again. "I read him part of an e-mail from Marie's dentist, the one David rescued me from. The guy had a whole list of requirements. There were some, like hair length, that he said we 'could fix'."

"Did you tell Marie that?"

"Uh-uh. I didn't want to get into a conversation where she tried to convince me I was being too picky and that the dentist was some great catch. Right now, she thinks David and I are going out, and that's the way I want to keep it," Jamie said, as she stepped out of the dressing room.

"Don't get mad," Rudy said, joining her, "but what if, just what if, you and David have amazing chemistry and have an amazing time? Are you going to at least consider going out with him for real?"

Jamie groaned. "Please don't turn into a Marie or a Helen. Please believe me when I say I want time to myself."

"I believe you. And I get it. But there might not be someone as great as David around when you decide you have the rest of your life figured out. He's special. It's just something to think about," Ruby added quickly.

"I have one year when the only thing I have to do is explore and try to figure out what I want my life to be like. One year. That's special, too," Jamie said.

When Diogee stopped to pee, David grabbed the chance to read the latest text message from Jamie. They'd been exchanging texts since he sent her the one about the tattoos that morning. Jamie said she'd like him to bring the last five years of his tax returns when he picked her up. She'd feel more secure if she knew he could pay his own way when they went out. He grinned, trying to decide what to answer. Maybe he'd tell her he'd need to see her driver's license, because he believed the man should be at least ten years older than the woman he was dating and he'd need proof of her birthdate.

"David, hold up!"

Diogee gave a bellow of greeting as Zachary trotted across the street. David was pretty sure he was wearing a new shirt, but he didn't comment on it. He didn't want to make the kid self-conscious. "How's it going?" he asked.

"I need Ruby to sneak something into Addison's house again," Zachary said. "At least, I'm pretty sure this is Addison's." He pulled a cheeta-print bra with racer straps out of the pocket of his jacket, then quickly jammed it back in. "It was on the doormat, just like the diary."

Jamie's cat is diabolical, David thought.

"You don't really know it's Addison's, though, right? A lot of things have been turning up in strange places. Maybe you should just drop it off at the fountain," David suggested.

"Squirrel," Zachary said just in time for David to brace for the Shoulder Popper.

"Thanks," David said. "We could swing by the fountain now."

"If it is hers, wouldn't she be embarrassed to have to pick it up there? People would see. And Hud would probably ask her a bunch of personal questions," Zachary answered.

"If anyone can handle Hud, it's Addison. I'd love to see her take him on." Zachary didn't look amused. "I can see why you think she wouldn't want her underwear left out in public, though. Maybe you could tell her you found it on your doorstep and you thought maybe she'd know who it belonged to. You could stick it in a bag, so it wouldn't be as awkward."

"I guess," Zachary said. "You don't think she'll be mad if it's hers? She might not like that I've seen it."

"It's not that much different from a bathing suit top. You've seen Addison in a bathing suit," David pointed out.

Zachary flushed. "Not lately. I haven't gone to the pool that much lately."

David got it. His growth spurt had probably left him feeling uncomfortable in his skin. He remembered that feeling. "I think she'll be fine with it," David told him. "But I could have Ruby say she found it and was trying to figure out whose it was if that would be better."

"No, I'll do it." Zachary patted his pocket. "I'll go over there now." He turned and started down the street.

"Let me know how it goes," David called after him. His cell buzzed, and he grinned when he saw it was another text from Jamie. He checked the time on the phone. About three hours before he was supposed to pick her up. He realized his body had a buzz of anticipation that he hadn't felt in a long time. *This is just something convenient for both of us,* he reminded himself. Sure, he was looking forward to tonight. Why wouldn't he be? He was going to one of his favorite places with a woman who made him laugh.

Although he didn't feel like laughing when she opened the door to greet him that night. He wasn't expecting this. She looked amazing, wearing a shirt that clung to her curves, her hair falling around her shoulders in loose waves. It took him a second to realize he hadn't actually said anything. "You look beautiful."

"Thanks. Thanks," she repeated. "Ruby said that sometimes people wore vintage to the place you're taking me." She ran her hands down the sides of her skirt. She looked nervous.

"They do. You're perfect." He smiled. "Should we slowly walk past Al and Marie's on our way to my car?"

She smiled back. "Of course. I wouldn't mind Helen seeing us together, either. I don't think she gives up any easier than Marie." She stepped outside and locked the door.

"I realized my tax forms are in my other jacket. But I promise I can afford popcorn, as long as we can share a small," he told her.

"I realized I left my tats on my other body," Jamie answered. She took his hand as they started toward the sidewalk. "Is this okay? I've never had a fake boyfriend before."

"Fine by me." He gave her hand a light squeeze, and was hit by how long it had been since he'd touched someone. Yeah, he occasionally brushed hands with someone if he subbed in at the cash register at work, and he gave Lucy a quick hug now and then, but this was different. They were putting on a show, but it was still different.

Al gave an approving grunt as they passed by. He was watering his lawn the old-fashioned way, with a hose. "I think I saw the curtain twitch in the kitchen," David whispered into Jamie's ear. He caught a faint whiff of her perfume, something woodsy, maybe sandalwood with a little citrus mixed in.

"Even if Helen doesn't see us, I'm sure Marie will pass the intel along," Jamie answered softly. "When I moved in, it was like they'd both memorized my rental application."

"You said you'd never seen a silent movie?" David asked as they walked toward the side street where he'd parked his car. The bad thing about Storybook Court was that none of the houses had garages.

"Just some clips on TV," Jamie answered. "Chaplin. Buster Keaton."

"It's a whole different experience live," David said. "When I first started going to the Silent Movie Theatre, the man who played the piano and organ, Bob Mitchell, was in his eighties. He'd actually accompanied some of the movies when they first came out. I loved watching him as much as the movies. He'd get so into it. He even dressed up to play for the Halloween screening of *The Cabinet of Dr. Caligiari*."

"I wish I could have seen him," Jamie answered. "I've been thinking about people and their jobs a lot lately, since I'm trying to figure out what I want to do. Can you see yourself still wanting to bake when you're in your eighties?"

"I think so, yeah. I don't think I'd want to be working full-time. But I bet I'll still be coming up with recipes for family dinners or to bring to parties."

They reached his Ford Focus, and he let go of Jamie's hand and opened the door for her, realizing as he did that they'd kept holding hands even after they'd been out of sight of Helen and Marie. He hadn't even thought about that until now.

"How's the search going? Have you gotten any ideas about what you might want to do?" David asked as he pulled out onto Gower.

"Not yet, at least not for a career. But I found out I love surfing. One lesson and I was a goner. Ruby's been encouraging me to try things I've never done. She thought I was making my search too narrow, and she was right. Now I'm all about the new, which is why it was so great you suggested the Silent Movie Theatre."

"Maybe you'll end up wanting to be an accompanist for silents," David said. "A very practical career choice. Lots of room for growth."

Jamie laughed. "I really do have to think about that practical stuff. But not right now. For now, I'm in the exploratory phase."

"I admire that," David told her. "It's easy to get locked down and do the same things, go to the same places. I've been especially bad about that since . . . the last few years," he said. He'd been about to say since Clarissa died, but he didn't want to talk about Clarissa tonight, even though Jamie already knew he was a widower. "I hang out with Adam and Lucy, the friends I told you about who have been shoving me into online dating; I walk Diogee; I go to movies; I read. Then repeat."

"Nothing wrong with liking what you like," Jamie answered. "Do your friends have kids?"

"Yeah. Two. I'm the youngest one's godfather," David said.

"And you've been able to keep your friendship up?" she asked. "After my friends had kids, we sort of drifted apart."

"Maybe it helps that my schedule is different. I'm free in the afternoons, and Adam, he's a TV writer, and there are at least some times during the year when he's off then, too," David explained. "We take the kids to the park together. And a lot of times I do things with him and Lucy. It works somehow. I don't end up feeling like a third wheel. Also, I think Lucy actually insists that Adam go out with me for drinks sometimes. She worries about me."

That was something David wouldn't have said if this was a real date. He'd be in that stage where all he wanted to show was the positive stuff. Which didn't include being pathetic enough that his best friend's wife worried about him.

"Worries about you?"

"Just about me being alone too much. After Clarissa died." And here he was talking about her.

Jamie nodded. "I can't even imagine losing someone like that. With a parent, you expect it. It's horrible and heartbreaking, but your whole life you know it's coming."

"Yeah. Have you done any more searching to find out how Mac's escaping?" David asked.

"Holy screeching subject change, Batman," Jamie said. "If you don't want to talk about her, I completely get it. But if you do, it's all good. Sometimes talking about my mom makes me feel better, just talking about the little stuff."

"Like what?" David asked.

Jamie tilted her head. "Mmm. How she thought I was perfect." She laughed. "I guess that's not a little thing. She wasn't delusional or anything. She knew I wasn't really perfect. But she was always on my side, even when I did stupid stuff."

"She sounds great," David said.

"She was," Jamie answered. "Tell me something about your wife."

"Clarissa listened to me. And she remembered little stuff I said. Like, I told her about a Christmas when I was about five. I got this Ghostbusters Proton Pack that I really, really wanted, then my brother broke it before I even played with it once. It wouldn't even make the proton stream sound," David said. "Years after I told her that story, I opened a Christmas present—and there was the proton pack. From the eighties. And it made the sound."

"She sounds great," Jamie said.

"She was." Jamie'd been right. It had felt good to tell her that Clarissa story.

David found a parking spot near the theater. "Let's get seats first. There are a couple couches near the front that are a lot more comfortable than the rest of the seats." He led the way inside and down the aisle. "Great. There's one open." They sat down. "Now, I think I promised you a small popcorn. There's a drinking fountain in the lobby, so drinks won't be a problem."

"I saw they had cupcakes at the concession," Jamie said.

David shook his head. "No. My fake girlfriend can't eat someone else's cupcakes. I won't have it. You want cupcakes, I'll make you cupcakes. How about if I try to win you some candy?"

"Win? How?" Jamie asked. "Maybe I can win some."

"You have a good memory?" David asked.

"Pretty good," she answered.

"Okay. To win you have to be able to name the star in each of the photos on the walls. I'll coach you. Let's start with the easy ones. You know Charlie Chaplin and Buster Keaton. Anyone else you recognize?"

"Uh, Louise Brooks, but just because of the hair," Jamie said.

"Okay. Over there we have Fatty Arbuckle." He ran through all the portraits again and again until Jamie could recite them. When the host for the night walked up to the stage and asked who wanted to accept the star challenge, David jumped up and pointed to Jamie.

"All right. You," the man called to her. "Stand up and speak loud."

Jamie stood, cleared her throat, then gave every single name correctly. The host tossed her an assortment of candies. "I call the Hot Tamales," David told her.

"Hey, I'm the one who won them," Jamie protested.

"Without me, you wouldn't have had a chance," he said.

"Fine. We'll share." She opened the box, took out one of the candies, and held it up to his lips. They locked eyes for a minute, and Jamie looked as surprised as he felt. She started to move her hand away, but he opened his mouth and she popped the candy in.

That hadn't felt like a fake date move. It had felt real. And as sexy as hell.

*　*　*

"Mac, there is seriously something wrong with me," Jamie told her cat. She was lying on the couch with her feet handing over the arm. Mac was sitting on her stomach, kneading her Minion-tee nightgown, which was too thin for kneading. His claws kept nicking her, but she didn't try to stop him. She didn't want him to jump down and leave. They were in the middle of a conversation.

"See, it was supposed to be a pretend date. Pretend. I made him hold hands with me, which was okay, because it was to convince Marie and Helen that the date was the real deal. But then I didn't let go. It didn't even occur to me to let go. He was probably wondering why I didn't, but was too polite to pull away."

Jamie scratched Mac under the chin and his purring got so loud, she could feel its vibrations. "Then I fed him a piece of candy. You might not know this, being a cat, but feeding a guy is a flirty move. It's not like when I give you a Salmon Bite. Not at all. When a woman puts a treat directly into a guy's mouth, that's sending a signal. And I don't want to be sending signals. Because I don't want a boyfriend. And David, he doesn't want a girlfriend. That's the whole reason we went out in the first place."

She sighed, Mac rising and falling with the deep breath. "Like I said, there's something wrong with me. But you don't care. And that's one of the many reasons I love you."

Mac rubbed his cheek against Jamie's stomach. She smelled a lot less lonely tonight. There was a little anxiousness in her scent, but nothing that worried him. He was sure if he went to David's house, David would smell better, too.

He'd done well. He was giving himself the night off. Tomorrow he'd get back to helping the other people who lived around him. There were so many who didn't have the sense to figure out how to help themselves. But tonight, he was staying right here, with Jamie scratching that spot he loved under his chin. He hadn't really been listening to her, but he'd heard the words "Salmon Bite." That was an extra reason to stay where he was. He loved Salmon Bites.

CHAPTER 14

David smiled as he began adding black pawprints to the vanilla buttercream frosting on a batch of cupcakes. Jam cupcakes. He was planning to take them over to Jamie's after work. Because if he was going to be a fake boyfriend, he was going to be a good fake boyfriend. He'd give Al and Marie a few cupcakes and make sure they knew he'd made them special for his Jam. He was sure Jamie would get a kick out of him being so devoted.

He heard steps on the stairs leading down to the bakery kitchen and looked over to see Lucy. Perfect. He could use the cupcakes to show her that he was really excited about going out with Jamie, and that would trickle down to Adam. It wasn't that David never wanted to go on a real date again, but he was done with counterpart.com. And he was done with having his friends help him find somebody. Now that he was feeling ready to meet someone, he figured he'd keep noticing women more, picking up on cues like the girl at the vet flirting with him. It would happen when it happened.

"What's up?" he asked Lucy as she headed over to him. As if

he didn't know. He was sure she wanted to know more about this woman David had decided to go out with.

"Dropped one off at kindergarten, one off at preschool. I now have a few brief precious hours to myself, and decided to start it off with sugar and caffeine," Lucy told him. "Whatcha makin'? And can I have one?"

"Sure. They're vanilla cupcakes filled with blueberry jam. I'm actually making them for Jamie, the woman I met in my housing complex. We went out last night, and I met her cat. I thought she'd like these." He started creating another icing cat pawprint.

"Bringing out the big guns, huh? No woman can resist your cupcakes." Lucy took one off the closest wire rack. "It's almost unethical. Like using a love potion."

"My cupcakes are good, but they aren't that good," David answered.

"They're damn good." Lucy licked a little frosting off her top lip. "We both know I want details. Give it up. How'd you meet? What's she like? Where'd you go on your date?"

"Remember how I told you I talked to a woman in the pet store?" Lucy nodded. "Well, she was that woman. I didn't know we were basically neighbors," David continued. "Then we ended up at the same bar after I had the date with the scary pyramid-scheme lady. Jamie, her name's Jamie, had just had a really bad date, too. We talked, had a drink. I still didn't know she lived at Storybook Court. Until her cat went through my bathroom window and stole my jockstrap. Jamie was trying to catch the cat, because he's not supposed to go outside. She gave me my jock back, and I ended up asking her out."

Lucy gave a hoot of laughter. "I love it! And now I understand the pawprints." She started to sing. "Tell me more, tell me more."

David held up his hands. "No *Grease* before noon. She just moved out here from a little town in Pennsylvania. She was a teacher, but she wants to make a change and is trying to figure out what she wants to do next. She's trying all kinds of things—surfing, acting, special-effects makeup."

Lucy raised her eyebrows. "She sounds a little flaky."

"Yeah, I can see how it would seem that way. But it's not like she's thinking she's going to make a career out of any of those things. She just exploring. It's pretty cool," David said. He really admired the way she just flung herself into things.

"So, is she pretty?" Lucy asked.

David thought of the different times he'd seen her. In her bare feet wearing only her sleep tee, hair mussed. As the fifties-style Hollywood starlet she'd turned herself into to go to the movie. In her regular clothes at the pet store. "Yeah, very pretty."

"This jam filling is amazing," Lucy said. "Keep talking. I want to know everything."

"Got the jam at the Hollywood Farmer's Market. It's from Forbidden Fruits Orchard. Their berries have an especially long ripening time, because the east-west mountains—"

Lucy punched him in the arm. "You know I wasn't talking about the jam. Where'd you take her?"

"We went to see *The Parson's Widow*. She'd never seen a silent movie before, and she was curious," David answered.

"Wait. Just wait. You took her to the Silent Movie Theatre on your first date? What about that thing where you might ruin your favorite place if you took a woman there and you ended up hating each other? That's what you said when I suggested it," Lucy reminded him.

David shrugged. "She's just not someone I see myself hating. Even if at some point we stop going out, I can see us as friends." Since friends was actually what they were.

"When do Adam and I get to meet this woman whom you decided was Silent Movie–worthy, whom you're already making cupcakes for?" Lucy demanded.

"Let me at least go out with her a few more times before she has to face the inquisition," David answered.

"I'm not an inquisitor. I'm just interested in people," Lucy protested. "And I want to make sure she's good enough for you."

"She's good enough for me," he told her. "But you can meet her at some point."

"At some point," Lucy repeated. "That sounds like a long time from now. But I guess you aren't really quite at the meet-my-friends stage." She picked up a flat bakery box and started to fold it. "You know I'll be taking a few."

"Just no more of the cat-paw ones. Try the coffee ones with the mini donut toppers." He nodded toward the tray.

"A cupcake topped with a donut. You are evil. And that's why I like you so much," Lucy loaded up the box. "I'm glad you had a good date, sweetie. You deserved one." She hurried back up the stairs.

A few hours later, he was walking toward his place, carrying a box with the cupcakes he'd made for Jamie. When he spotted Zachary on his front steps with Diogee at his side, David felt a spurt of disappointment. He'd been looking forward to getting over to Jamie's, and it was clear Zachary needed to talk.

"Hey, Zachary. Hey, Diogee."

"She thinks I'm a perv," Zachary announced, voice flat.

"What?" he asked, staggering back a few steps as Diogee leaped on him in greeting.

"I did what we talked about. I put the bra in a bag and asked Addison if she knew whose it was. She looked at it, called me a perv, and slammed the door in my face," the boy explained. "It's not fair. When she gave me my T-shirt, I just said thanks."

"She'll get over it," David said, silently adding "probably."

"You know her. She has a short fuse." He ruffled Diogee's ears, then scratched his belly when the dog flopped down onto his back.

"It's just when we were talking about *Adventure Time* and Ms. Marvel and everything . . ." Zachary let his words trail off.

"Yeah. You don't expect to have a decent conversation one day and get the door slammed in your face the next," David said. "But you read"—he decided to give the kid a break—"a few pages of Addison's diary. You know she's emotional. She'll get over it."

Zachary looked a little hopeful. "Maybe because her boyfriend is such a jerk, she just assumes all guys are jerks. But she'll realize I'm not. If I ever get to talk to her again."

"So, you want to talk to her again?" David asked. He was curious to hear whether Zachary would admit it.

"Well, we're like neighbors. And we like some of the same stuff. It would be cool to have someone around here to hang out with sometimes." A guilty expression flashed across his face. "You and Diogee are great. I didn't mean that."

"No worries. We aren't offended," David told him. "Hey, you want to make a few bucks and walk Big D for me? I need to deliver some cupcakes, and if I try to walk him and keep the box upright, it could go badly."

"Go get your leash, Diogee," Zachary said, and the dog scrambled through the dog door. "You don't have to pay me."

"I'd pay a dog walker, so I should pay you. It's always good to have a little extra cash, right?" He gave Zachary a twenty.

"This is too much," Zachary protested.

"Tire him out and you'll have earned it," David said. It took a lot to tire the beast.

Diogee slammed back through the dog door, and Zachary clipped on his saliva-dampened leash. "See you later," he called as Diogee pulled him toward the gate.

David went inside. Baking could be surprisingly sweaty work. He wanted to grab a shower before he went over to Jamie's.

* * *

Jamie couldn't stop grinning as she parked her car. She'd been grinning the whole drive home. Her jaws actually ached, but she just couldn't stop. She'd spent hours in an actual video arcade. She hadn't been in a video arcade since she was thirteen and used to go to the one near her middle school with her first-ever boyfriend, Bobby Martin.

Wonder what he ended up doing? she thought as she walked toward her little Snow White cottage. He'd moved when they were near the end of seventh grade. Heartbreaking. She spotted David heading away from the house when she turned onto her street. "Hey! Hi! Were you looking for me?"

He turned and waved. "I was. I am," he answered. "I made you some cupcakes."

"You did? Really? That's so sweet of you," Jamie said when she reached him.

Al gave a grunt. He was planting bulbs in his little garden.

"I brought a couple extra for you and Marie," David told him.

Al put down his bulb-planting thingie—Jamie wasn't sure what it was called—and hollered, "Marie!"

A few moments later, Marie opened the door. "What?"

"He brought us cupcakes." Al jerked his chin toward David.

"I'm glad to see you don't have that dog with you," Marie said. "Don't think I didn't notice how close it got to pooping on my lawn a while back."

"But he didn't," David answered. He held up a bakery box tied with string. "I made some cupcakes for Jamie and thought I'd bring you and Al a few, too. Do you have something I can put them on?"

Without a word, Marie disappeared back into the house. David looked at Jamie. "Do you think that means she has no interest in cupcakes, or that—"

"She'll be back," Al said, pushing himself up to his feet. He wiped his hands on the knees of his jeans. A moment later, the door opened and Marie came out with a glass platter. She set it on the porch rail.

David walked over and transferred four of the cupcakes. "They have jam in the center. Jam for my Jam." He looked over his shoulder and winked at Jamie.

Jam for my Jam. She couldn't believe he'd said that. He'd really committed to convincing Marie that Jamie didn't need any more matchmaking. David put another two cupcakes on the platter. "For Helen. I know she has a sweet tooth." He hadn't forgotten that the two of them needed to show Helen they were going out, Jamie thought.

"Helen, cupcakes!" Al yelled.

"She doesn't need any cupcakes," Marie said. "She and Nessie are twins. There's no reason Helen couldn't be just as slim and attractive." Helen opened her door. "You don't need any cupcakes, but David brought you some."

David returned to Jamie's side, and she kissed his cheek. She knew it was because if she was his real girlfriend, that's what he would have done. Her body didn't seem to have gotten the memo that she and David were just faking it. A little jolt of heat zapped through her.

"I put pawprints on them, in honor of Mac," he said. He opened the box to show her.

"I love them. You want to come in and have some with me?" Jamie asked.

"Sure," David said. "Hope you enjoy them," he called to Al, Marie, and Helen, who had joined the Defranciscos on their porch.

"They're going to have to stop matchmaking now," Jamie told them as they walked into her house. "You've proven you're the best boyfriend ever. Thanks for making such a big effort."

"You're welcome," David answered. Mac fell into step behind him and Jamie as they headed to the kitchen. "I'm probably going to need some payback."

"Payback?" Jamie asked.

"Lucy is already pushing to meet you. She wants to make sure you're good enough for me," he explained. He sat down and Mac immediately jumped into his lap.

"I don't think I am," Jamie said. "I definitely can't compete with a gift of cat-paw-decorated jam-filled cupcakes. I don't even have a cute little nickname for you."

"And thanks for that," David said, scratching Mac between the ears.

"You want coffee?" Jamie asked. "I love coffee, but I have to have milk with cupcakes. Or I have juice or beer."

"Coffee would be great," David told her. "What have you been up to? You looked especially happy when I saw you coming down the street."

"You'll never guess in a million years," Jamie teased.

"I'm intrigued," David said. "Cave diving?"

"Close. It was even more exciting and dangerous." She started the coffee. "I was playing Mortal Kombat II, Crazy Taxi, and Skee Ball."

"You found a time machine?" David asked.

Jamie thought of the arcade, and her grin reappeared "Close. I found the Royce Arcade Warehouse."

"Seriously? You went there?" David shook his head. "Adam and I are always saying we're going to go, and you've been here two minutes and you've gone?"

"And it was so cool. It really is like a garage, with a big rollup door. All the machines are crammed together. Dads and grampas, with a few moms and grandmas, hanging out, teaching kids what it was like back in the day," Jamie told him. "And I met Mr. Royce! Well, that's what people call him. Royce is his first name. Royce D'Orazio. He started the business in his actual garage. Actually, before even that, he was collecting arcade games. Then he started repairing arcade games and renting them. He still does that, plus, like, you know, opening up the place on Saturdays. I played for hours for just the three bucks it took to get in. It's the first time I didn't have to worry about how many quarters I had left."

"I'm jealous," David told her.

"Next time I go, I'll take you," Jamie promised. Yikes. Was that too much? They didn't have an audience in the kitchen, and she'd just sounded like a non-fake girlfriend. Or maybe just like a friend. She and David were becoming friends.

"Any time," David said. He wasn't acting like she'd over-stepped. Good.

Jamie handed him coffee, and sat down with her glass of milk. After the first bite of cupcake, she closed her eyes with pleasure. "And I thought nothing could top the arcade."

Mac stood up on David's lap and gave an aggrieved meow. "Oh, I'm sorry, Your Highness." She looked at David. "He doesn't approve of me having milk if I don't give him some first." She got a saucer, poured in a little milk, and set it on the floor for Mac. He jumped down and started lapping it up. "When I got him, I didn't know most cats couldn't digest milk well. But he loves it, and he's never gotten sick, so he's one of the minority of cats that are lactose-tolerant."

"He's unique in many ways," David commented.

Jamie snorted. "Yeah. That's one way to put it. Where's your beastie? I meant it when I said you could bring him whenever," she added.

"Zachary's walking him again. He needed something to do. I found him sitting on my porch looking like he was waiting for the world to end," David answered.

"What was wrong?"

"Remember how I told you he found Addison's diary, then his shirt got left on her doormat?" David asked.

"Yeah, and they ended up having a good conversation about the show that was on the shirt," Jamie answered. She took another bite of the cupcake letting the buttercream frosting melt on her tongue. David was seriously talented.

"Right. But then Zachary found a bra he was pretty sure was Addison's on the doormat," David continued.

"He recognized her bra?" Jamie asked.

"He said he was pretty sure it was hers. Maybe her bra strap was showing once and he saw it. When you're fourteen, seeing the bra strap of a girl you have a crush on can set your imagination going, especially if it had a cheetah print, which this one did," David said. "Anyway, Zachary decided to try to return it—in a paper bag so it wouldn't be embarrassing. But Addison called him a perv and slammed the door in his face."

"Oh no. Poor guy. Do you think there's a chance she might like him, too? Door slamming and name calling don't necessarily mean she doesn't. It might actually mean she does. Teenage girls are hard to decode sometimes."

"I'm not sure they completely grow out of it," David said.

"I used to spend all this time trying to figure out what boys were thinking." She started speaking in a high singsong, trying to imitate her teen self. "What did it mean when he asked to borrow a piece of paper? He could have asked Sarah, who sits on the other side of him. It has to mean something that he asked me." She laughed. "It took me a long time to realize that most men don't think that much before they do something."

"Are you saying men are like dogs again?" David asked.

"Maybe," Jamie admitted. "But not in a bad way. I have way too much internal chatter."

"Tell me some of it."

"No way." Jamie shook her head so hard her hair flew around her face, curls bouncing. "You'll think I'm insane."

"Come on," David urged. "We're in a unique situation here. We're fake boyfriend and girlfriend, so we can tell each other stuff a real couple wouldn't, at least not for a long time."

Why not be honest? There was no reason not to, not with him. "Okay. Okay, here's an example. When I said I'd take you to the garage arcade the next time I went, my brain immediately started throwing out crazy thoughts. Like, what if that sounded like I was trying to turn myself into your real girlfriend? What if it sounded like I was just assuming I could make plans for you?"

"If I don't like something you're doing, I'll tell you," David said.

"See?" Jamie exclaimed. "That's more of a guy thing. Guys don't analyze what they're going to say until they make themselves crazy."

"Wanna try not thinking for a while? Watch some mindless TV, maybe order some pizza?" David asked. "And just so you don't have to analyze any of that, I wasn't attempting a Netflix and chill."

"Sounds good," Jamie answered. "And by that I mean, yes to TV and yes to pizza later. How do you feel about pizza crusts?"

"I think pizza crusts are the second-best part of pizza, right after the cheese," David told her.

"Excellent. You can have mine. They're too doughy for me, but I don't like to waste them," Jamie said.

"We're the perfect fake couple," David told her. "And by that I mean, it's turning out to be fun faking out our neighbors and friends with you."

"Agreed," Jamie said. "By which I mean I think so, too."

Mac jerked awake, disoriented. He thought he heard his Jamie crying from someplace where he couldn't reach her. Then he realized he was curled up on the couch between David and

Jamie, and she smelled good, content, with none of the loneliness tang. David smelled the same way.

Still, something pulled at him. He had other missions. Later tonight, when Jamie was asleep, he'd go out. He wouldn't rest until he'd helped everyone who needed him.

CHAPTER 15

"I was just thinking we're like a current-day Mary and Rhoda, except I think we both might be Rhoda," Jamie told Rudy when she showed up for coffee the next morning. "I used to love how they were always just dropping by each other's places."

"You're way too young to even know who Rhoda and Mary were," Ruby said. "Even I only watched that show in reruns."

"My mom loved it. I did, too. We watched it together on Nick at Nite. You know what? Maybe I am kind of a Mary. Moving to a new town, ready to make my mark. I just need to get a hat to throw in the air."

"I'll find you one," Ruby told her. "Have you seen David since the movie?"

"Actually, yes." Jamie wouldn't have thought it was possible, but she felt like she was grinning more widely than she'd been on her way home from the arcade. "He made me jam cupcakes. That's his pet name for me. Jam. Jam, short for Jamie. And the cupcakes had pawprints on them."

"Let me guess. Because you have a cat," Ruby said dryly.

"I deserved that. But pretty sweet, no?" Jamie asked.

"Pretty sweet, yes," Ruby answered. "David's a good guy."

"He is turning out to be a peerless fake boyfriend," Jamie agreed, taking a sip from her reindeer coffee cup.

"He could be—"

Ruby was interrupted by a knock on the door. "I'll hold that thought," she told Jamie. She returned to the kitchen a few moments later with Riley and Addison. "Teacher in-service day for Addison, and Riley wanted to stay home with her sis," Ruby explained. She poured a cup of coffee and handed it to Addison. "There's milk and sugar and whatever you want."

Addison gave a grunt that sounded very much like one of Al's. "Is it okay if she hangs out with you for a while?"

"Of course, Riley can stay. We're thinking of making a schoolhouse for Paula."

"Thanks." Addison took a long swallow of the coffee, black. "Hey, Ri-Ri," she said, making her voice more bright and cheery than Jamie would have thought possible. "Have you seen Zachary hanging around our house lately?"

"I saw him with the big dog," Riley answered.

"By our house? Or on the sidewalk?" Addison asked, her tone getting a little sharp.

"Sidewalk," Riley said. She dug into the peanut butter toast Ruby set down in front of her.

"You want some toast, Addison?" Ruby asked.

Addison shook her head. "I think Zachary might be a creeper," she announced. "A T-shirt of his showed up by my front door, so I gave it back. This morning it was there again. And yesterday he said he *found* a bra he thought might be mine. Which, why would he think so? It's not like he's ever seen my underwear."

"Strange things are afoot at the Circle K," Ruby said.

Addison scowled and dropped her bright, cheery voice completely. "What?"

"Never mind. I just meant that weird things have been going on around here lately. That's why Hud set up headquarters over by the fountain, because so many things have turned up in the wrong places."

"If it makes you feel better, my cat is probably the one who left the T-shirts and took your bra, not Zachary. I caught him in the act once. I thought I'd figured out how he was escaping, but he must have another way, because stuff is still getting taken," Jamie said. "On my way over here this morning, I saw Helen's sister. She couldn't have been anyone else. She's thinner, and she hasn't let her hair go gray the way Helen has, but it's clear they're twins. She was leaving a little doll on the edge of the fountain, and Hud was taking notes in his little book."

"I guess then maybe Zachary isn't some sicko," Addison conceded.

"What's a sicko?" Riley asked, as she held the toast up to Paula's plastic mouth, getting peanut butter in the pony's hair.

"Forget it. I guess I'll just give him the shirt back—again," Addison said. "Bring Riley back when you get tired of her," she told Ruby, then left.

Jamie pulled out her cell. "Riley, would it be okay if I took a picture of Paula?" she asked.

Riley smiled. "Paula loves getting her picture taken."

Jamie started taking pics, making sure to get in the peanut butter smear and the place on the side of Paula's head that looked like it had been used for teething. "How long have you had your pony?"

"Always. Paula saw Mommy in the store and told her that she wanted to belong to me. I was still in Mommy's tummy, but Paula knew I was there," Riley said. Jamie took more pictures of Riley and Paula. It was clear Paula made Riley very happy.

Riley looked up at Ruby. "Can we play rodeo again?"

"Sure thing," Ruby answered, and Riley's eyes sparkled. It

was clear Ruby made Riley very happy, too. And her crazy cat burglar had brought them together.

Any interest in going to the Museum of Jurassic Technology with me?

Jamie stared at the text she'd just typed for a moment, then shot it off to David. He was only her fake boyfriend, so she didn't have to make herself crazy thinking about whether it would bug him if she took the initiative and invited him someplace.

Another place I know about, want to go to, but never have. When?

She smiled as she sent a reply. *Open from 2-8 today. 12–6 F–Sun. Pick you up at 3?*

Great. Jamie set down the phone, trying to ignore the fluttery anticipation filling her. Fluttery anticipation wasn't a "friend" thing, and that's what was happening at three, going someplace with a friend.

She wandered from the living room to the kitchen, then back. Mac was snoozing in a spot of sun, and he looked so blissed out that she didn't want to wake him up for a play session. Instead, she pulled a big piece of orange poster board she'd picked up at Target out of her closet and put it on the kitchen table. She'd decided to make what an article she'd read called a creativity board, a collection of quotes and pictures and anything else she found inspiring. It was supposed to help her figure out what it was she really wanted to do with her life.

Jamie got out her laptop and started scrolling through pictures of surfers. She'd had two more lessons, and she loved how surfing made her feel. Well, not the sore part, but the rush of it, and the sense of accomplishment. There were some gorgeous photos online, and lots of them caught the thrill of riding a wave. None seemed exactly right for her board, though.

She got her phone and pulled up the pictures she'd been taking since she'd moved to LA. One of Kylie immediately grabbed her attention. Kylie wasn't even out on the water. Her board was on the sand, and she was standing on it, showing Jamie the correct posture. Her face was animated, and it was obvious she was loving what she was doing.

Jamie downloaded all the LA pics onto her computer and pulled up the picture of Kylie again. It was a great shot—if she did say so herself. But what if she enhanced it? Jamie wondered what it would look like if she gave it a Technicolor treatment. Glorious Technicolor. She loved those old movies with the saturated, totally fake-looking colors that seemed hardwired to emotion.

She'd played around a little with digital enhancement techniques in college, but not since then. She definitely needed to brush up. She did a Google search and found a YouTube tutorial, which led to another, and another. A knock on the door startled her. She could hardly believe it when she glanced at the clock. It was a few minutes after three.

Jamie rushed to the door and opened it. David stood there smiling at her. "Sorry, I'm not quite ready. Obviously." She didn't even have her shoes on. "I got caught up in something."

"No rush," David told her. "You said it doesn't close until eight. I don't know how you found out about the museum so fast. It's not exactly mainstream."

"The Internet. Where else?" Jamie asked. She noticed David was holding a small white bakery bag. "For me?" She reached for it, but he playfully pulled it away. "Hands off. These are for the cat burglar. I was feeling in the experimental mood, and I decided to make some cat treats."

By the time he'd said "cat" the second time, Mac was twining himself around David's ankles. David took out a small fish-shaped treat and handed MacGyver one.

"Only two sniffs before he ate it. That's pretty much a five-star rating from him," Jamie said. "Make yourself at home. I'll be ready in a couple minutes."

"No rush," David said again.

Jamie rushed anyway. She hurried into her bedroom and checked herself out in the full-length mirror inside the closet door. Her hair was a wreck. She had a habit of running her fingers through it when she was thinking. But other than that, she looked okay. She was wearing her favorite jeans, and her favorite crazy-patterned Etsy shirt. She put on a pair of sandals, did what she could with the curly chaos that was her hair, put on some lipstick, and returned to David.

He was feeding Mac another treat while studying at the picture she'd been experimenting with on the computer. "I hope you don't mind that I'm looking at this. Is it what you were working on when I got here?"

Jamie nodded. "Sorry again that—"

David waved her apology away. "I like what you're doing with it. Going for that fifties Technicolor. This your surfing teacher?"

"Yep. I thought the color made her natural awesomeness even more awesome," Jamie explained. "The color kind of makes her pop the way she pops in person. She has this wonderful exuberance when she's teaching. And when she's not."

"You caught it," David said. "Got any more?"

"I've been taking a ton of pictures since I moved here, but this is the first one I've been digitally playing around with," Jamie told him. She started a slideshow so he could see the others.

"These are great. You definitely captured the real Ruby with that one where she's working on that pony barn." He paused the slideshow so he could take a closer look. "Seems as if you're drawn mostly to people. I like the one with the rat in the palm tree, too, though. Wouldn't want it on my wall necessarily, but it's eye-catching."

Jamie laughed. "That rat caught me by surprise. I liked the contrast. But, yeah, I mostly end up taking photos of people. Actually, they're all people who really seem to love what they're doing." She clicked to the next picture. "Like this guy, who gives bad advice on Venice Beach. A bunch of people on the Walk seemed happy to be there, painting names on grains of rice or whatever. Probably I ended up taking pictures of them because trying to figure out what I should be doing is always in the back of my mind. If not the front."

"Are you going to do any enhancing on the rest of them?" Mac jumped up on the table and stretched out across the keyboard, blocking most of the screen. David coaxed him away with another cat treat and looked at the next picture. It was the one of Wonder Woman in front of Grauman's Chinese theater.

"I hadn't really thought about it," Jamie answered, but she was already itching to turn Wonder Woman's eyes the shocking shade of a blue-raspberry Slurpee, her lips ruby-slipper red, and her hair the shiny blue-black of a crow's wing. Jamie would pop a few details in the clothes of the tourists surrounding Wonder Woman—like the lavender chucks on the little blond girl and—

"You're thinking about it now, though, right?" David asked. "I can practically see the ideas spinning in your brain. You want to postpone the museum and work some more?"

That was something The Cling-Wrap Man wouldn't have asked in a million years, Jamie thought.

"No, the museum's only open a few days a week. Besides, we're only at the beginning of our fake relationship. We should be together as much as possible. If we want to be convincing."

"Together at a museum? If I wanted to be convincing, I'd never—" David stopped abruptly.

"Never what?" Jamie asked.

"We should get going. It'll take twice as long to get to Culver City if we have to deal with rush-hour traffic," David answered.

"I'm ready." Jamie shut her laptop so Mac wouldn't get back on the keyboard. "But what were you going to say about being convincing? We don't want Helen or Marie or your friends getting suspicious."

"I was going to say that if I wanted to be convincing, I wouldn't let you out of the bedroom for at least the first couple months," David admitted.

"A few jam cupcakes and I'm supposed to be sleeping with you already?" Jamie teased, keeping her voice casual even though her stomach had done a roller-coaster drop at the thought of having David in her bed.

"I also bought you a drink," David reminded her as they headed for the front door. "*And* took you to the movies. *And* we had dinner together."

"No, we didn't," Jamie protested.

"Pizza. Mine with double crusts," David said. "Actually, maybe we haven't slept together yet. I haven't gotten my white truffles and excellent wine."

"You're not easy. That's something I should know about my fake boyfriend," Jamie commented, then let the subject drop. Her stomach needed to get off the roller coaster.

The exhibits at the Museum of Jurassic Technology were bizarre and fascinating, but David found himself looking at Jamie as much as at the strange objects. Ever since they'd had that exchange about whether or not the fake couple of David and Jamie were sleeping together, he couldn't stop thinking about having sex with her. It wasn't like it hadn't darted through his brain sporadically, but now the thoughts were almost incessant. Those jeans she was wearing didn't help. They clung to every curve.

Jamie read the title of the next display aloud. "The World Is

Bound with Secret Knots." She looked up at him. "I love that. It's like poetry." She studied the figures made of white wax that were suspended in water inside glass globes. "There are magnets inside the wax people and that crank turns a central magnet and somehow you can use this machine to divine the future. I think. This place makes me doubt everything and believe everything at the same time. I'm so glad we came here."

"Me, too." It had been great to get her text. He realized that his circle of friends had been reduced to Adam and Lucy—and Zachary. It was his own fault. After Clarissa died, he'd turned down invitations so often they'd stopped coming. It had taken meeting Jamie to realize he was ready to have some more people in his life again.

"Sorry. Excuse me," a twenty-something British guy in a porkpie hat said. There wasn't much space in any of the museum's small rooms. David moved closer to Jamie to let him squeeze past. He got a whiff of her soap or shampoo, something citrusy and sweet. And that was all it took to get him thinking about sex again.

From one of the rooms they'd already visited, came the sound of a high yipping and growling. The exhibit had a taxidermy fox's head inside a glass case, and a special pair of glasses that would let you look inside the head. Instead of showing a larynx with vibrating vocal folds, the view through the glasses showed a holographic image of a man making the supposed fox sounds, which sounded nothing like a fox.

"I can't decide whether that sound is more or less disturbing now that I've seen the man making it," Jamie said over the falsetto growling.

"More. Definitely more," David answered. He forced himself to step away. There was no one they knew around, no Marie and Helen or Adam and Lucy. He had no reason to be putting on the boyfriend show right now. Except that he wanted to stay close to her, keep breathing in that scent.

"I think I might need a break. My brain is starting to hurt. I heard they have a tea room on the second floor. Want to check it out?" Jamie asked.

"Sure." David followed her down one of the dim corridors and up a flight of stairs. The tea room was empty, but a few seconds later, a woman dressed all in black and gray appeared with two glasses of hot tea, as if she'd received some kind of advance alert they'd be needed. She gestured them to a dark wood table with a large doily in the center. Without a word, she set down the tea and disappeared. A few seconds later, she reappeared with a plate of cookies, set it on their table, and vanished again.

Jamie laughed. "I bet she likes her job. I don't think you'd end up working at a place like this if you didn't appreciate it. I'd love to take her picture, but no cell." Cell phones weren't allowed in the museum. "And I'd really love to meet the man who created this place. The museum has to be a passion project."

David nodded. "It's not a place designed to make money. Maybe it's ended up making some, but it feels like he just wanted to make his vision come to life."

"I envy that. I envy someone having that strong a vision," Jamie said. "I'm having fun exploring. But I'm just zipping from here to there. Mostly I've just been seeing what other people have found to do with their lives."

"And taking pictures of them. Noticing them. Appreciating them," David answered. "That's what I see. I see focus, even in just the short amount of time you've been out here. I can see you creating your own kind of *Humans of New York*."

"Really?"

"Really. You could do a series of photos and stories about people doing what they love, whether it's teaching surfing or creating a place like this," David answered. "You've already started. I was serious when I said I thought that Technicolor treatment you were giving that picture of your surfing guru was great. You could start with a blog, or posting on Instagram or Facebook."

"How cool would it be if coming to places like this could be part of my job?" Jamie asked, her brown eyes glowing with excitement and her face pinkening. He wanted to run his fingers over her cheeks and feel the warmth.

"If you saw yourself right now, you'd want to take your own picture," David told her, trying to push away the thoughts of touching her face. And her breasts. And her—They were friends doing each other a favor by pretending to be more than friends. He needed to slap himself around until he could remember that.

Jamie leaned across the table and rested her hand on his. "Thanks, David. Just, thanks. It was right in front of me, but I'm not sure I'd have seen it without you." She squeezed his hand, then picked up her tea. "Who knows if I could turn it into actual work, the way the *Humans of New York* guy did. But who cares? I'm going to start putting the pictures up on some kind of social media, because the people in them inspire me, and maybe they'll inspire someone else." She finally sucked in a breath after the rush of words. "Hey, do you think I could take some photos of you baking? You should be part of the series of people doing what they love for sure."

"Anytime," David told her.

"Now?" Jamie asked. "You've got me all inspired."

"Now works," he answered.

About an hour and a half later, they were in the basement of the bakery. He was stirring a tablespoon of sake into the pan where he was boiling pitted plums. "You put the sake in a tablespoon at a time," he told Jamie as she continued taking pictures. "You want to get a little of the alcohol kick, but not too much." He continued stirring, then spooned out some of the mixture.

"Wanna be my taste tester?" Jamie set down her phone and came over to him. He raised the spoon to her lips. "Maybe blow on it a little first," he suggested.

And as she did, he was focused on her mouth, thinking of sex again. He felt like a teenager. Everything she did was making him think about sex. Although watching her tentatively lick the mixture to make sure it wasn't too hot would probably make an octogenarian hard.

"I think it could use a little more," Jamie told him.

David was glad to have a reason to turn away. He added another tablespoonful of sake to the pan and stirred.

"How do you come up with your recipes?" Jamie asked, returning to taking pictures of him.

"Sometimes I'm inspired to cook something for a particular person," David answered. "Like some jam cupcakes I made recently."

Jamie smiled, but didn't lower her cell. "Ahhh. Interesting. And other times?"

"I like to go to little shops and see what they have that's different," David answered. "For these, I saw wasabi and plum sesame seeds in a little market on Sawtelle Boulevard. I wanted to do something with them, and I decided to do an almond cupcake that would let the other flavors really pop. I'm doing some alcohol-infused cupcakes for a bar near here, so that's where the sake came in. Plum sake to pick up the plum in the sesame seeds." This time he sampled the mix. "Just so you know, when I'm cooking for the public, I use a new spoon each time. But since you're my girlfriend, I figured you wouldn't mind." He put in another tablespoon of sake.

"I guess not. Even though you're refusing to sleep with me until I buy you a nice meal, I suppose we must have swapped spit by this point," Jamie teased. David let that one go.

"Think it's good." David added a mix of cornstarch and

sugar to the pot. "I need one more taste test. Sweet enough?" He held out the spoon.

Jamie sipped. "Little more," she said. He added a bit more sugar and turned off the heat, then he opened the top oven to check the cupcakes. "Just about ready. We'll need to wait until they cool a little to start cutting out holes, actually more like cones, for the filling. Sake while we wait? In a glass instead of off the spoon this time?"

"Sure." Jamie set the phone down.

"I actually don't have any real glasses down here." He found a clean glass measuring cup, poured about the equivalent of a shot's worth of sake in, and handed it to Jamie, then got himself one. "*Kanpai!*" He clinked his cup with Jamie's.

"*Kanpai!*" she repeated, swinging up to sit on one of the wooden tables. "Is it okay that I'm sitting up here?"

"Absolutely." He swung up next to her. "Did you know that there's a traditional Japanese toast that translates to 'you're tired'? It's a big compliment, because working hard is valued."

"Makes more sense than 'here's mud in your eye'," Jamie said, taking a sip of her drink, and he noticed her eyes were locked on his face.

"You're staring," David told her.

Jamie blinked. "Sorry. Just trying to decide what kind of technique I'd want to use on your photos. I don't know if I want to do the Technicolor thing on all of them. I saw this one effect that makes everything look kind of dreamy. . . . Maybe that." She shook her head. "Okay, no. From your expression I can tell that has zero appeal."

"I didn't say that," David protested. Although she was right. Some soft-focus, dreamy pictures of him sounded pretty embarrassing. Definitely nothing he'd let Adam see.

"There was also one I saw that you can use to give kind of an eighties vibe, all fluoro colors," she said.

"Much more me. Billy Idol Baker," David answered, then shout-sang the "more, more, more," from "Rebel Yell." While she was still laughing, he kissed her, just one fast kiss.

"Uhh . . ." Jamie didn't seem to know how to react.

"You're the one who said the fake couple of Jamie and David have kissed," David reminded her. "If I have to kiss you in front of Marie and Helen, I don't want it too look awkward, like we've never done it before." It was a better reason than that he just couldn't help himself.

"Ahh." She nodded. "And under what circumstance do you think it would be necessary to kiss me in front of Marie and Helen?" She sounded amused, but was still looking a little startled.

"Like if I walk you to the door after we have dinner, and they're standing on their porches or peering out their windows," David told her.

"They *are* always watching," Jamie agreed. She slid a little closer, pulled his head down to hers, and kissed him. Not fast. A long, sweet kiss that lit up his entire body. When she released him, she jumped off the table and poured herself some more sake. "That's more of a good-night kiss, don't you think?" she asked over her shoulder.

He jumped down, took the measuring cup out of her hand, put it down, and pulled her tight up against him, then he kissed her the way he'd been wanting to kiss her all day, letting his hands run down her back. When one hand slid down over her ass, she stepped away. "Nope," she said, sounding a little breathless. "You can't grab my butt in front of our little-old-lady neighbors."

"Right. Right," David said again. His brain wasn't able to come up with more words than that. Finally, he managed to add, "Let me see if the cupcakes are cool enough to work on."

* * *

Mac began to purr before Jamie even opened the door. There wasn't even a whiff of the loneliness that had clung to her for so long, even when she'd had another human living with her.

He butted her leg with his head when she stepped inside, and she scooped him up and twirled around. He could tell that she'd been with the bonehead's person, David. He could smell that, too. He'd chosen well. Jamie should let him make all the decisions about her life. For starters, she should eat a lot more sardines, and share them. He loved the crunch of their little bonesies.

He'd completed his mission. Jamie was happier than he'd ever smelled her, and that made him feel like he'd been rolling in catnip. Mac wanted more of that feeling. Much more. And he knew how to get it. All he had to do was wait until Jamie fell asleep.

CHAPTER 16

A knock on the front door the next morning pulled Jamie away from her work. She'd been fooling around with turning one of the pictures of David into something out of a Billy Idol album cover, coloring half his face in red on a diagonal. She'd been watching tutorials on hidden iPhone camera features, and she'd downloaded some apps to give her more techniques to play with.

When she opened the door, Ruby was standing there. "I brought iced coffees. I can't drink hot coffee after noon," she said.

Jamie saw that the sun was already high in the sky. "What time is it?"

"A little after one," Ruby answered.

"I thought it was only about ten. I got up around six. I can't believe I've been working this many hours," Jamie said.

"Move aside and let me in, or we're both going to get interrogated by Hud," Ruby ordered.

Jamie obediently stepped back. When Ruby moved past her, Jamie's mouth dropped open. The edge of the fountain was covered. There were usually a couple things, but today there were probably more than twenty. In just a quick glance, she saw underwear of an array of sizes, styles, and colors; a cloth doll; a Kanye T-shirt; and a long, dangly earring sparkling with what she hoped were fake jewels. She didn't want Mac to start taking anything that was truly valuable. A couple people wandered around the fountain, looking at the array of items.

"Hurry up and shut the door," Ruby told her.

But it was too late. "Hold up there, little lady," Hud called as Jamie started to swing the door shut. "I was wondering where you, and your *cat*, were last night from, say, sundown to sunup," he said when he reached her. He looked over her shoulder. "Your accomplice, too."

"I was home from about ten thirty on," Jamie answered. "My cat—" She looked at all the new things on the edge of the fountain. "My cat was probably out stealing stuff. I'm trying to figure out how he's getting out, so I can stop him. But so far, no luck."

The divorced man who owned the orange Speedo hurried across the courtyard and dropped one silk stocking on the edge of the fountain. "It was on my porch this morning," he called to Hud as he walked away.

"Why don't you just tell me the truth? We both know your cat can't possibly be behind all this." He gestured to the fountain. "Not without help." He pulled down his sunglasses and gave her a long look, then looked at Ruby.

"You're the detective. Or at least you played one on TV," Ruby said. "Aren't you supposed to get clues and evidence? You shouldn't need us to tell you anything. Not if you're as good as you think you are."

"You think you can nibble the bait and leave the hook bare. And maybe you can—a few times. But one little miscalculation, and you're supper," Hud answered. "I'll see you two at suppertime." He sauntered away.

Jamie shut the door. "I've got to figure out how Mac is getting out. I keep trying to stay awake and catch him. But he's too sneaky."

"Don't worry about it. It's harmless. Mac's giving the Court some entertainment." Ruby set the coffees down on the kitchen table. "What were you working on that made you lose complete track of time?

"This." Jamie turned her laptop so her friend could see the photo of David.

"I. Love. It," Ruby announced.

"I took some pictures of David at the bakery yesterday. He gave me this idea. He saw this picture of Kylie I'd been playing with, and he said I should think about doing a series of photos of people with different jobs. People who love their jobs. Kind of a spin on *Humans—*"

"*Of New York,*" Ruby finished for her. "That's brilliant!" Her phone neighed and she checked it. "Addison wanting to know if Riley can hang with me this afternoon." She typed in her answer.

"I'm sure that's a yes," Jamie said.

"Of course. I love it when she comes over. It's such a kick to get a four-year-old's view of the world. So, you're going to keep taking pictures of people at work?"

"Yeah, I want to go back and talk some more to everyone, try to find out how they got into doing what they do," Jamie said. "I can talk to Kylie at my next lesson, and I thought I could hit up the other people I photographed at Venice Beach then, too. As long as I bring enough singles. They all expect to get paid. And why not?"

"David came up with the perfect idea. How many times have you gone out with him now?" Ruby asked.

"I'm not going out with him," Jamie protested. "I'm just hanging out with him. So his friends and Marie and Helen will stop trying to set me up. I mean, you and I have seen each other almost every day since you invited me in for gingerbread man decapitation. It's not any different from that."

Except for those kisses. Jamie felt heat flood her face—make that her whole body—just thinking about it.

Ruby pointed at her. "You slept with him!"

"I did not!" Jamie cried. Ruby raised her eyebrows, waiting. "I did kiss him a few times," Jamie admitted. "But only so that if we had to kiss in front of anyone, it would look natural."

Ruby cracked up. When she finally managed to stop laughing, she said, "You two are ridiculous. When are you going to admit that neither of you is doing this to keep people from matchmaking?"

"When's the last time you tried to say no to Marie?" Jamie countered. "Or got in the middle of a competition between her and Helen? David and me pretending to go out has solved the problem."

"News flash. You're not pretending," Ruby told her.

"Yeah, we are. You know I want to focus on myself this year," Jamie said. "I have this amazing new project—"

"Thanks to an idea from David," Ruby reminded her.

"Right, David. Who isn't ready to go out with anyone yet. He's still grieving." Jamie picked up her coffee and took a long swallow, almost choking on an ice cube.

"Jamie, I was friends with Clarissa. She was a wonderful woman. It broke David's heart to lose her. But he wouldn't be *practice*-kissing you if he wasn't ready to start another relationship. And you wouldn't be *practice*-kissing him if you absolutely didn't want a guy in your life. You have to know that."

"Look, I enjoyed kissing him, and it's always fun hanging out with him. I like him, and it's great to have a new friend out here. But that doesn't mean I want to have to think about whether or not he'll be jealous if I want to track down the puppet guys some night to interview them. Or worry about whether he ate dinner because I wasn't around to cook for him."

"You wouldn't have to think about those things with David," Ruby said. "And anyway, I'm not talking about you two moving in together or anything. I'm talking about more of a friends-with-benefits kind of thing—with the potential to upgrade."

"I'm fine with how things are," Jamie insisted. "David is, too. It's working for us."

"Are you're fine with not kissing him again?" Ruby pressed. "Since you've gotten your practice in, there's no reason to kiss him anymore, right?"

Jamie tried to pretend that the idea of never kissing David again didn't make her body feel several degrees cooler. "Right."

When David came home from work, Diogee greeted him leash in mouth, as always. David didn't bother trying to convince the beast to give him two minutes to relax. He always lost that argument—even though David was absolutely the alpha dog.

He snapped on the leash and allowed Diogee to haul him outside. A few seconds later, Zachary burst out his front door and trotted over to them. "I can't hang with you guys today," he said, twisting his face to one side to avoid getting kissed on the lips by Diogee, who had his paws planted on the kid's shoulders.

"What's the up?" David asked, then he gave a pull on Diogee's leash. "Diogee, knock it off," he ordered. The dog usually just gave a lick or two, but today it was like he wanted to give Zachary a bath. Maybe it was because of the smell coming off the kid. It was like he'd doused himself in umbrella drinks and coconut suntan oil.

"Oh, gross, he got me on the mouth." Zachary backed up until Diogee's paws dropped back to the ground. "Addison and I are going to do our English homework together."

That explained the sweet stench. Zachary had clearly discovered cologne. "I guess this means she's reconsidered and doesn't think you're a perv anymore." David gave Diogee a knuckle rub on the top of the head as a thank-you to the dog for keeping his tongue to himself.

"My shirt turned up on her doormat again, and she brought it back," Zachary answered. "She said since a bunch of other things have gone missing and turned up on other people's doormats that she shouldn't have blamed me for the bra. I still don't know why she was blaming me in the first place, since I was the one bringing it back. Why would I have brought it back if I was the one who took it? Anyway, we started talking about this English assignment and decided to work on it together."

"Does that mean she dumped the boyfriend?" David asked.

"No. Not from what I saw at lunch. But it's not like we're going out or something. We're just doing homework together," Zachary said. "I can walk with you as far as her house. Come on, Big D!"

"Uhhh." David tried to think of a tactful way to say what needed to be said. "You might want to wash off a little of the cologne." That was the best he could come up with.

Zachary blushed. "Does it smell bad?" He sounded horrified.

"No. It's not that. It's just that a little of that stuff goes a long way," David answered. "Not that I know much about it. Clarissa wasn't a fan of cologne. She said she liked my 'natural manly odor'." He could still hear the smile in her voice when she'd say that to him, which was almost every time he came back from a run.

"Really? I thought all girls liked it," Zachary said, pulling out the collar of his shirt and taking a whiff of himself.

"Not all," David answered. "But if you wear it, it's not something everyone sitting around you in class should smell. A girl shouldn't smell it unless she gets close to you."

Zachary blushed again. He checked his cell. "I have time to wash some off. I'll see you later." He took off for his house.

"Do you remember when he thought she was a shrew?" David asked Diogee as they started down the sidewalk. He decided to head over to Jamie's and give her an update on the Storybook Court teen romance.

When they turned onto Glass Slipper Street, Diogee gave a happy woof and broke into a gallop. David ran alongside him, and they both skidded to a stop in front of Ruby, who was walking across the courtyard.

"How are you two big idiots?" Ruby asked, leaning down to give Diogee a hug before he could plant his paws on her shoulders.

"Hey, we may not be the brightest bulbs, but 'idiots' is a little harsh," David protested.

Ruby shook her head at him. "Not from what I've been hearing," she answered.

"What have you been hearing?" he asked.

She just smiled, gave Diogee a pat good-bye, and walked away.

"Come to look for stolen items?" Hud asked. David hadn't even noticed him—or the dozens of things spread out on the edge of the fountain. "It's still not too late to file a report on the item we both know was stolen by our friend over there." He nodded toward Jamie's house, where both Jamie and Mac were looking out the window at them.

"Not missing anything new," David told Hud. "And Jamie's welcome to my jockstrap or anything else." He let Diogee pull him over to the largest palm tree in the courtyard so he could mark it as his, then he pulled Diogee over to Jamie's door.

"You said it was okay to bring him," he told her when she opened it.

"It's more than okay. It's great."

Once they were inside, David unsnapped Diogee's collar. The dog immediately dropped to the ground and rolled onto his back so she could scratch his belly. She got the message, and crouched down beside him. Diogee's eyes drifted shut and his tail thumped on the floor as she got to work.

David saw a streak of tan. It took him a second to identify it as Mac, moving fast. The cat pounced on Diogee's wagging tail, grabbed it between his paws, gave it a bite, and raced away. Diogee took off after him. A few seconds later, they heard Diogee give a wail.

"Mac, bad kitty!" Jamie called as they rushed toward the sound. She looked over at him.

He and Jamie followed the sound and discovered that somehow Diogee had trapped himself in Jamie's closet. Mac sat on the bed, calmly licking one paw. "What's wrong with you? You were so good the last time. Did you forget Diogee's our friend?" Jamie asked her cat as she released his dog. Diogee immediately ran into the living room. "I guess we should keep them in separate rooms for now." She shut Mac in the bedroom, and leaned against the door.

"Hi," she said.

"Hi," David said.

He wanted to kiss her, of course. It was like was coming out of suspended animation. He wanted to kiss women again. Well, Jamie. He wanted to kiss Jamie. He hadn't really thought about kissing anyone else. But that made sense. She was really the only woman besides Lucy and Ruby that he had any real interaction with.

In a few more months, who knew? Maybe he'd be ready to date somebody for real. Right now, he liked what he had going with Jamie. He liked hanging out with her. It was distracting thinking about kissing—and sex—every other second when he was around her, but it was good to have that impulse back. It was kind of like being a teenager again. And he could just keep pushing those impulses away. He and Jamie had a deal. She was his real friend, and his fake girlfriend. That meant no kissing, unless it was necessary to keep up their charade. Or practice for the charade, which they'd already done. And no sex, ever. Until his brain and not just his body was ready to start up an actual relationship with someone.

"Uh, you're staring," Jamie told him.

"Sorry. Just thinking." She raised her eyebrows. "About Zachary. And Addison. You should have smelled the cologne on the kid. At least I convinced him to go wash some off before he went over to study with her. I wonder if he's the only one who's thinking of it as more than just studying."

"Well, I know that Addison made sure Riley would be out of the house when he came over," Jamie said. "Which could mean she wanted quiet for studying or that she wanted her little sister out of the way for hanging out with a cute boy. Although, last I knew she had a boyfriend."

"A boyfriend she seems to break up with every couple of days," David answered. "He seems like a jerk, at least from what Zachary read in her diary."

"I can't believe he read her diary," Jamie said. "Although if it showed up on his doorstep, it would be pretty hard to resist taking a peek."

"And reading it is at least part of why he no longer thinks she's a shrew," David answered. "Although methinks the boy protested too much about that. I'm pretty sure she was behind Zachary starting up an extreme grooming routine, and that was back when he was still ranting about how horrible she was."

Diogee gave a loud woof. "What's he want?" Jamie asked. "Should I get him a bowl of water?"

"I think he's feeling cheated by the shortness of his walk," David answered. At the word "walk," Diogee ran into the hall and skidded to a stop in front of them.

Jamie laughed. "How about if we walk down to Grauman's? I'm hoping Wonder Woman will be there. I want to ask her some questions about how she got into being one of the characters who takes pictures with people outside the theater."

"Great." David snapped Diogee's leash on. "Have you thought any more about getting your stuff up on Instagram or some of the other sites?"

"I spent most of the day working on one of the pictures I took of you," Jamie answered. "I'll send it to you. I think Diogee's head will explode if we don't leave right now. I showed it to Ruby, and she thought it was cool."

David opened the door, and Diogee bolted out. He and Jamie trotted after him. "I saw Ruby as I was heading over. She called me and my dog 'big idiots'. I know why she'd call Diogee an idiot, because he is, in fact, an idiot. But she said she'd been hearing things that made her think I was an idiot. Any idea what that was about?"

Jamie hesitated.

"What did you tell her?" David asked.

Jamie hesitated again, then answered. "What happened was somehow it came up that we'd kissed a couple times—as practice. And Ruby thought we were being ridiculous. I'm sure that's why she called you an idiot."

"Ridiculous to think we need practice?" David asked as they left the Court.

"Ridiculous for not admitting that we were kissing each other because we wanted to be kissing each other, not because we were worried about making our thing look authentic to Marie and Helen and your friends," Jamie answered.

David wasn't sure exactly what to say to that, so he went with, "Huh."

"Yeah, Ruby thinks we should stop pretending we're just helping each other out, and just suck it up and have sex, because we clearly want to and that it doesn't mean we're getting all serious, it could just be a friends-with-benefits kind of thing," Jamie said, speaking so quickly her words ran into each other.

A bolt of heat shot through David's body. "Huh," he managed to say. "What do you think?"

"I think the idea of benefits is . . . appealing. But I promised myself I'd give myself this year to figure out what I want to be doing with myself and my life, with no distractions," Jamie answered, speaking even faster. "I think you have your own reasons for not wanting to get involved right now. And no matter what Ruby thinks, friend with benefits is still involved, even if it's less involved than a full-on relationship or whatever. What do you think?"

He liked the idea of benefits. A lot. But there was a "no" in all those words she'd just spewed out, and he had to respect that. "I think things are great the way they are," he told her.

The next morning, Mac sat on the windowsill, staring out at the courtyard, waiting for the right moment. He preferred to do his missions at night, under the cover of darkness, but this one could only be done during the day. He had no doubt he could pull it off. He was MacGyver.

He heard Jamie clicking around on her computer. She was smelling good. He knew he should have been merciful to Diogee yesterday to make sure nothing interfered with Jamie and David being together. But when he saw that big rope of a tail flopping around, he had to give it a bite. Had to. And it didn't end up ruining anything. And it was fun.

He heard the target before he saw her. She always made a *jingle-jangle* when she walked. And she always smelled of loneliness. But there was someone who replaced the lonely smell with another scent, the scent of blood rushing close to the surface of the skin.

Mac didn't quite understand the female's reaction to the male. Her body went tight, and she froze, the way some cats reacted to big dogs. Some cats who weren't Mac. When Mac saw a big dog, the big dog had better get ready to talk to the paw—*whap, whap, whap*. But the way her scent changed told him that she wasn't afraid of the male. And the male was the only one who caused the reaction in the female. She clearly needed his help.

Luckily, Jamie always went outside when the female came into the vicinity. He leapt off the sill and positioned himself by the door. Just as he expected, Jamie opened it a few moments later, and Mac slipped out.

"MacGyver, no!" his person cried.

He ignored her. He had a mission to complete. He needed one of the jingle-jangles. The female set down her bag, leaving it unguarded. It took Mac a few seconds to figure out the mechanism, then he got one of the shiny things free, snatched it up between his teeth, and ran. He followed the scent trail to the male's house and left it for him. He hoped the male wouldn't be as slow to figure things out as Jamie and David had been. But he understood that humans were slow. It was their noses. Mostly.

CHAPTER 17

"I blame you," Jamie told Ruby. "Ever since you said David and I should be friends with benefits, all I can think about is sleeping with him. That means I've been obsessed for almost two weeks. It's making me insane. And don't tell me not to think about it. It's impossible. You put it out there, and I hate you."

Ruby laughed. "You know my solution. Start doing, and you'll stop making yourself crazy with the thinking." She continued using the curling iron to tame Jamie's curls into loose waves. Mac sat on the edge of the sink, playing with the trickle of water coming out of the faucet.

"No, I'm actually getting a lot done, even with the obsessing. Maybe even because of the obsessing. Working on the pictures helps distract me."

"I love what you've got going on MyPics. I want to change careers every time I visit," Ruby said.

"I still can't believe the one of the guy who charges a buck for bad advice has gotten viewed more than sixty thousand times. Most people are probably just clicking by, but still."

"You're a rock star," Ruby told her, pulling one last lock of

Jamie's hair through the curling iron. "And you look gorgeous."

"Thanks for fixing my hair," Jamie said. She pressed her hands to her stomach. "I can't believe how nervous I am. Why should I be nervous? I'm sure Adam and Lucy are great."

"They are. I don't know them that well, but they've come to a bunch of my Christmas parties. You'll like them," Ruby assured her.

"It feels different pretending to be David's girlfriend in front of them. They're so close to David. Adam's known him since they were kids. It's not like faking it in front of Marie and Helen." Jamie tightened the taps, stopping the trickle of water. Mac made a throaty sound that some people might have thought was a purr, but Jamie knew was a complaint.

"Nobody who sees you together is going to have a hard time believing you're really a couple. You two—" Ruby didn't finish. Jamie knew why. She'd asked Ruby about a billion times to quit saying how perfect she and David were for each other.

"I think I need a glass of wine. David's not supposed to pick me up for another half an hour. You want to have a glass of wine with me?" Jamie asked.

"I would, but Riley's mom is working late tonight, and I told Addison that Riley could come over while she and Zachary study," Ruby answered, heading for the door.

"Again? Are they studying, do you think? Or are they *studying?*" Jamie asked.

"I'm not sure. But I haven't heard any Addison rants about the boyfriend, so I'm thinking maybe she dumped him," Ruby said. "Have fun tonight, okay?" She opened the door, then grabbed Jamie's hand. "Hud just took something out of his pocket and put it on the fountain. I think it's time for us to do the questioning." She rushed outside, tugging Jamie along with her. "Sweet cheeks," Ruby drawled. "Hold up there a minute."

"Are you speaking to me, Toots?" Hud asked, without his usual bravado. He looked pale under the bright floodlights that he'd set up around the fountain to make it convenient for people to look for missing items after dark. There were new things dropped off every day. And Jamie still hadn't figured out how Mac was doing it.

"Yes, I'm speaking to you," Ruby said when they reached him. "I saw you add that little keychain to the missing stuff. That means the thief must have gone right up to your front door, am I right? That's where everyone finds things—right by the doormat."

"Maybe the reason the thief was able to get so close is because Hud is really our thief." Jamie couldn't resist teasing the TV detective. "He has motive—everyone knows he wants to prove he's a great detective. What better way to do that than create an unsolvable mystery, then solve it?"

The color rushed back into Hud's face, and he turned and strode away. "I think I actually hurt his feelings," Jamie said, feeling a prickle of remorse as she watched him go.

"He's said basically the same kind of thing to both of us," Ruby reminded her. "But his ego is so tied up in playing at TV detective. I guess we should take it easy on him." She picked up the keychain Hud had set on the edge of the fountain. "This looks like one of the ones Sheila keeps on her mailbag."

"Yeah. She has a bunch on her purse, too. David and I ran into her at the Thirsty Goat the other night. She and her trivia team had a competition. It was all TV questions, so I thought Sheila would be a star. Once I heard her rattle off everything Hud Martin has done, even guest spots. But she was having an off night. The Trivia Newton-Johns went down—hard."

Ruby set the keychain down. "Maybe it just looks like something of hers. Everything else that's been taken has belonged to somebody who lives here, right?"

"I think so. Mac had better not be leaving Storybook Court," Jamie answered. She didn't like her kitty being outside at all. But the streets in the complex all had low speed limits. If he left the Court, he could be in real danger. She bet he thought he could just whap a car with his paw to make it stop.

"Sometime I'll spend the night, and we'll take turns keeping Mac under surveillance. We'll put a stop to his roaming," Ruby promised.

"That would be great," Jamie answered.

"I've got to get home for Riley." Ruby gave Jamie a quick hug. "Have a fab time tonight. I know you will."

David didn't think he could do it. When he'd made plans for him and Jamie to go out with Adam and Lucy, it had sounded fun. He'd wanted his friends to meet Jamie and vice versa. He'd been sure they'd hit it off. He was still sure.

But when he was getting ready, his heart had started pumping as hard as it did at the end of a run, and he knew he wasn't ready. Going out with Adam and Lucy was something he'd done a bunch of times by himself, and even more times with Clarissa. It wouldn't feel right with Jamie.

He grabbed his cell and shot Adam a text. *Gotta cancel. Jamie's sick. Another time.*

A few seconds later Adam answered. *Come anyway. Be our third wheel.*

Nah, David typed back. *Gonna go see if she needs anything.*

A few seconds later, Adam sent another text. *Lucy says you're sweet. I say you're whipped. Another time.*

Yeah, David answered. He couldn't do it tonight. It had felt like he was about to have a panic attack. Maybe at some point, he'd tell Lucy and David that he and Jamie had just been fake-dating to give themselves a break, and then the four of them could go out.

He grabbed his keys and tossed Diogee a massive rawhide. "You're in charge, big guy," he told his dog on his way out. It felt like the sidewalk had become rubberized, giving his walk a bounce. Canceling with Adam and Lucy was a huge relief. Now he could enjoy the night with Jamie.

He grinned as he turned up the walkway to her house, thinking of the perfect place—places—to take her. He couldn't go to the restaurant he and Adam had picked. Adam and Lucy would probably still go there. They wouldn't want to waste the sitter.

"You up for walking?" he asked when Jamie opened the door.

"I thought we were going to Santa Monica," she answered.

He'd already almost forgotten they were supposed to be double-dating. "Lucy isn't feeling well," he told her, mostly managing to ignore the jab of guilt he felt lying to her. It wasn't like it was a big lie. "We'll have to reschedule."

"I'm kinda glad," Jamie admitted as she and David started down the walkway. "I was a little nervous about meeting them."

David looped his arm around her shoulder. "For Helen and Marie," he said. It was a reasonable precaution, he told himself. They did spend a lot of time looking out their windows. "You don't have anything to be nervous about. You'll like them, I know."

"I'm not worried about liking them. I'm worried about them not liking me," Jamie told him.

"Not possible," David answered, pulling her closer to his side.

"You going to tell me where we're going?"

"Nope. It's a surprise," he said. They walked a few blocks, then David cut across the parking lot of a run-down strip mall and over to a video store.

"Did I miss something? Has VHS become the new vinyl?" Jamie asked as they walked inside.

The dimly lit place didn't have a DVD in sight, just wire racks jammed with VHS tapes.

"There are a few movies that never got transferred. Take a look back here." He headed toward the pink neon ADULTS ONLY sign in the back.

"Are we already so bored in our fake sex life that we're renting porn?" She sounded a little wary, but looked willing to play along.

"Well, it has been a few weeks." David pulled back the black velvet curtain, revealing a grimy little room stuffed with X-rated videos.

Jamie glanced at the closest shelf. "*Womb Raider*? That's just wrong. 'Womb' is not a sexy word," Jamie commented. "Or is that a girl reaction? What do you think of the word 'womb'?"

" 'Womb' is all about babies," David answered.

"Exactly!" Jamie exclaimed.

"The really good stuff is back here." David swept back a second curtain at the other side of the room, revealing a bar with high ceilings, soft ambient light, cushy sofas, and stained-glass windows. *Barbarella* was playing on the large screen above the archway leading to the billiards room.

Jamie laughed just the way David hoped she would. He was getting addicted to the sound. He'd chosen the place because he thought she'd get a kick out of it. And because it hadn't even opened until after Clarissa died.

"Welcome to LA's speakeasy scene," he told her. "There are places like this hidden all over. To get to this other one I go to sometimes, you have to go through a barbershop. You can actually get your hair cut there, too."

They settled in on one of the empty sofas. David picked up one of the VHS boxes that served as the drinks menu and handed it to Jamie. "I usually get this one, with the mescal and cilantro." He pointed to one of the cocktails on the list.

"Sounds good," Jamie said. "Hey, look. They have a photo booth! We have to get pictures. I might need hard evidence of our couple-hood for Marie and Helen."

"Do they ask a lot of questions about us?" David asked.

"Helen, not so much. But Marie asks a lot of questions about everything. We share a trash can, and she's actually asked me questions about the contents of my trash. Like I had a Lean Cuisine box in there, and she said she saw I was trying to lose weight. I've never had a neighbor who was so . . . let's say *involved* in my life," Jamie answered. "On the upside, she does make the best coffee and sends Al over with a cup any time I'm out in the yard in the morning. She can be annoying, but she has a good heart."

"She does. But I'm still afraid to see what will happen if Diogee ever manages to poop on her lawn." The waitress came by and David ordered two of the cocktails. "We're going to swing by the photo booth, but we'll be back," he told her.

"It might be fun to do some pictures of my happy job people as strips from a photo booth," Jamie said as they walked across the room, past a DJ who was getting set up.

"That story about the Grauman's Wonder Woman you put up on MyPics was great," David told Jamie as they waited for the booth to free up.

"You saw that? I just added that this morning."

"I have an alert," he said.

Jamie smiled at him. "That's so sweet."

"You're racking up some nice comments. I'm assuming you saw the one from John Schuller."

"I did. And don't think I don't know you had something to

do with that," she informed him. "I know he's the star of the show your best friend writes for."

"I told Adam to check out what you were doing. He probably tweeted about it," David said, pleased that he'd help get her some extra attention.

"We're up," Jamie said as a twenty-something couple came out of the booth. They both looked flushed, and he suspected they'd been using the booth for more than getting their picture taken. Jamie shot him a wink, and it was clear she was thinking the same thing.

They got inside the booth and sat down in the two seats upholstered in well-worn plush. The little space was done up to make it look like the people getting their photos were part of the audience in an old-timey theater. Rows of other people were painted on the backdrop behind them.

"Ready?" Jamie asked.

"Ready."

She pushed the button and cried, "Duck face!" David obediently pushed out his lips into an exaggerated pout. "Watching a scary movie!" He widened his eyes and pretended to scream, while Jamie gripped his arm with both hands and buried her face in his shoulder. "Heart hands!" He wasn't sure what she meant by that one, and she didn't manage to get his fingers curved into half a heart before the picture snapped. "Lovey-dovey for Marie and Helen," Jamie called out. He didn't know what she was expecting, but he grabbed her face in his hands and kissed her.

A few moments after the sound of the photo being taken, Jamie pulled back. "Good one," she said. She sounded a little breathless. He'd probably sound a little breathless, too, if he tried to talk. One kiss from her was all it took. They got out of the booth, and as they waited for their strip of photos, the DJ started playing "Total Eclipse of the Heart."

"This was my dad's prom theme song," David said. "My brother and I used to look at the pictures and crack up. There were all these black hearts with a neon yellow glow around them hanging from the ceiling. My dad wore this pale blue tuxedo with a ruffled shirt, and his date had on a metallic pale blue dress with a short poufy skirt."

"I didn't even go to my prom," Jamie said as she took the strip of pictures the booth spit out. "My boyfriend did that classy move where he broke up with me about two weeks before. I had the dress and everything."

"Okay, we're dancing. This wouldn't have been your prom song, but it's *a* prom song." David grabbed her hand and pulled her out onto the dance floor. He took her by the waist, and she wrapped her arms around his neck. "What was your dress like?"

"It was beautiful." Jamie gave an exaggerated sigh. "Dark purple. Spaghetti straps. Long. Really simple."

David pulled her closer, until her body was flush against his, and she rested her head against his chest. It felt so good to hold her. "I bet you would have been the prettiest one there. The guy was a jerk."

"He was," Jamie murmured without looking up.

Why was he doing this? Why was he slow-dancing with her when she'd made it clear she just wanted to be friends, no benefits? Why had he kissed her in the photo booth? It hadn't been a long kiss, but it had been long enough to leave him aching for more.

David pulled in a deep breath, trying to get control of himself, but instead he was flooded with the scent of her. He had to stop this. He had to get them off the dance floor. Instead, he slid his hands lower down her back. She didn't pull away. She hadn't seemed to mind when he kissed her, either.

"Friends with benefits works out for some people," he murmured in her ear. He hadn't been planning to say that. It was like the words had come out of his mouth without getting an okay from his brain.

Jamie jerked her head back and stared at him. "What?"

"Someone I work with was talking about how he and this girl he was friends with started sleeping together. Neither one of them was with someone else, and they just fell into it. But he said it's working out." Total lie. But he had to say something.

"Okay. So you just decided to share this conversation. While we're dancing," Jamie said. "Or . . ."

"Ever since you said that Ruby thought that's what we should do, that's all I can think about," David answered, deciding it was time to start telling the truth.

"Me, too," Jamie answered. The song changed to "Let's Hear It for the Boy," but they didn't pull apart. They continued to sway to the fast music, staring at each other. Then they both spoke at the same time.

"You thought that it wouldn't—" David began.

"You aren't ready to—" Jamie said.

They both broke off and danced in silence for a few moments. "We're good friends," Jamie finally said. "I think we could handle, um, more without it getting messed up."

"You want to go?" All David wanted was to get out of there and get her home, get her in bed.

"Yeah."

They started for the exit. David stopped to drop some bills—probably way too many, but who cared—on the table next to their untouched drinks.

Their pace picked up with almost every step they took on the few blocks back to Storybook Court. By the time they got to the courtyard, they were jogging. Then, laughing, they both broke into a sprint. While Jamie fumbled with the key, David shot Zachary a text asking him to walk Diogee. He had a dog door, but he was used to a before-bed walk.

Jamie got the door open and pulled him through. She shut the door fast. "Don't want Mac to—"

David didn't let her finish. He couldn't. He had to taste her—now. He backed her up against the door and caught her mouth with his.

He had to stop to kiss her six more times between the front door and her bed.

Mac scaled the inside of the chimney with ease. He'd used the escape route many times since his person had repaired the screen. He paused on the roof to enjoy the feel of the breeze ruffling his fur and the sense of accomplishment filling him. It was like he'd eaten a whole can of sardinesies and then played with Mousie until his head felt lighter than his body. Jamie had her packmate in the house, and they both smelled like they had been eating sardinesies and playing with Mousie for hours.

He opened his mouth and flicked out his tongue. There were two scent trails that were so similar it was hard to separate one from the other. But he'd done it before, and he'd do it again tonight.

But first, some fun.

He scrambled down the sloping roof, leapt down to the bushes below, and from there to the ground. He gave the biggest palm tree by the fountain a good clawing—the bonehead had been peeing on it again—then began to run across the complex. He needed to run. Every muscle was begging to be used.

He heard the bonehead whining before he got to the mutt's home. He slowed down to a creep in case whatever had caused the dog to make such a pathetic sound was still around. Cautiously, he moved closer. He didn't sense any danger. There probably wasn't any. The dog was a wimp. He couldn't even take a little swat with the paw without whimpering.

He moved even closer. No, there was nothing anywhere

near the bonehead that was threatening. He was probably just crying because he couldn't get out and have a good time the way Mac could.

Mac was feeling so good that he decided to do Diogee a favor. He sprang to the top of the gate and gave the latch one expert flick of the paw. He leaned his body halfway over the gate to get it to swing open.

Even though he was free, the dog just sat there. He really was a bonehead.

Obviously, he needed some help getting started. Not a problem. Mac jumped from the gate to the dog's back. The mutt stopped his blubbering and let out a howl. Then he barreled through the gate with Mac riding him. Yee-haw!

The mutt raced down the street, then skidded to a stop and looked around. He turned his head to the left, then to the right. Then he seemed to finally realize he had freedom. He gave two happy barks, then ran over to the closest tree and peed on it.

Mac didn't need to hang around for this. He dismounted and picked one of the two nearly identical scent trails to follow. He hadn't gotten far when he heard a high "yip, yip, yip." It was a dog, but it wasn't the bonehead. There was another yip, then a sound Mac had heard before. The sound the bonehead made when Mac gave him a dose of the paw.

Mac spun around and ran toward the yipping and howling. A little, almost-hairless dog in a polka-dot sweater was chasing the bonehead, biting the big, galumphing dog's ankles.

Not on Mac's watch. The bonehead was *his* toy.

Mac let out a battle cry and launched himself at the little yipper. He rammed his head against the thing's sweater-covered belly and the yipper toppled. Mac got in its face and gave it a warning growl. That was all it took. The yipper ran away with his tail tucked between his legs, going home to Mommy, Mac was sure.

Clearly the bonehead couldn't handle himself in the big world. Mac herded him back into his own yard with a few paw whaps, then latched the gate behind him. The big dog wagged his tail like he was happy to be in prison again. Pathetic.

Well, he'd tried. Now he had to get back to his latest mission.

CHAPTER 18

David stared up at the ceiling of Jamie's bedroom. Her head had been resting on his upper arm so long it had gone to sleep. His body was tense with the need to move. Move, move, move. He needed to lace on his sneakers and run until he dissolved into a puddle of sweat, even though his heart was beating as fast as it would have been if he'd been about to cross the finish line in a marathon.

What the hell was wrong with him? He'd almost had a panic attack when he'd thought about Jamie and him going out with Adam and Lucy, because it would have felt wrong to be on what was pretty much a double date without Clarissa.

So, what did he do? Genius that he was. He'd slept with Jamie. Like that would get to him less than sitting with her at a dinner with Adam and Lucy.

He looked over at Jamie. She was sleeping soundly. He began to slowly ease his arm out from under her head, while simultaneously sliding a pillow in as a new headrest. It was that or chew his arm off at the shoulder. He had to get out of there.

Adrenaline was surging through his body. He could feel it

jolting through his already-pounding heart. It felt like it was going to explode. He had to get out of there.

He continued transferring Jamie's head from his arm to her pillow. There. Got it. He stood up, and just getting off the bed sent a burst of cool relief through his veins. He quickly, and quietly, pulled on his clothes and picked up his shoes. He could put them on outside.

David took three steps toward the door, then stopped. As much as he wanted out, he couldn't go. Not like this. He slowly slid open the drawer of Jamie's nightstand, praying she wouldn't wake up. He found a pencil and a scrap of paper and wrote her a quick note: "Had to go check on Big D. Glad we're friends." He added a smiley face. Disgust at his behavior almost got him climbing back into bed with her, but he couldn't make himself do it.

He crept out the front door, making sure it locked behind him, then ran for home without even bothering to put on his shoes.

When Jamie woke up, the bed was empty. It took her a minute to remember why that felt wrong. Then it hit her. She'd slept with David. And it had been wonderful, maybe because they'd been such good friends before taking the plunge.

What had she been thinking? It was crazy to think David would keep her from exploring all the things she might want to do with her life. She felt like she'd received a jolt of adrenaline, like she was ready to take on the world. David had been so supportive about her photos. It wasn't like he was going to turn into another person now. Ruby had told her that. What had she been thinking, ignoring her friend's advice?

David must be foraging for coffee, she decided. She got up, pulled on the Minions T-shirt she used to sleep in, and practically skipped to the kitchen. The earth seemed to have less gravity than it did yesterday.

But David wasn't in the kitchen. Or the bathroom. Or the screened-in porch. He wasn't there. Jamie rushed back to the bedroom and ran her hand over his side of the bed. It was cool. How long ago had he left?

She spun around in a circle as if he was going to pop out from behind the dresser and yell "surprise," then she sank down on the bed, the euphoria draining out of her so quickly it made her dizzy. "David wouldn't just take off," she said, speaking aloud. "He'd leave a note."

Jamie looked on the nightstand, and—yes!—there it was. The note said he had to go check on Diogee. Which made sense. Diogee was probably crossing his legs, waiting by the door for David to let him out. Except David's place had a dog door. Well, maybe he wanted to make sure Diogee had water. Or maybe his dog was like her cat. Maybe he would be extremely displeased if his breakfast was late.

Yeah, that had to be it. She returned to the kitchen. "Mac, food," she called. With a "mmmrow," he trotted in and began twining himself around her ankles. No matter what, she could always count on Mac. Jamie opened a can of a salmon/chicken mix and served it up with a sardine on top. Mac loooved sardines.

As he ate, Jamie realized she was just standing there, staring down at Mac, but not really seeing him. She'd completely zoned out. Coffee. She needed coffee. That's what she did every morning, have coffee, and that's what she'd do now. And probably by the time she'd had a cup, David would text or call or just come back over.

But as she finished her second cup, she hadn't heard from or seen him. Rattled, she decided to go over to Ruby's. She needed the perspective of a sane person, and she wasn't feeling entirely sane right now.

"Be back, Mac," she called as she left. A few minutes later she was knocking on Ruby's door.

Ruby grinned when she opened it and saw Jamie. "Yay! You're here. I want to hear all about the date, or whatever it is you and David call it when you go somewhere together. I was right, wasn't I? Adam and Lucy are great."

"They had to cancel," Jamie said. "Lucy got sick."

"Nothing serious, I hope." Ruby ushered Jamie inside.

"I don't think so."

"You sound like you need coffee," Ruby said as they headed to the kitchen.

"No thanks."

"No thanks? I don't think I've ever heard you turn down coffee before." Ruby studied Jamie as they sat down at the table. "What's wrong?"

"Probably nothing," Jamie answered. "I slept with David last night."

Ruby jumped to her feet and flung her arms heavenward. "Hallelujah!"

Jamie tried to smile. It must not have come out looking right, because Ruby sat down again and leaned toward her. "I guess my 'hallelujah' was premature. I just got carried away for a second. There's something wrong, isn't there?"

"It's just that David was gone when I woke up this morning," Jamie said.

"Did he leave a note or text you or anything?" Ruby's eyes scanned Jamie's face.

"He left a note saying he had to check on Diogee. But I've been up for more than an hour, and who knows how long he's been gone. Shouldn't I have heard something else by now?"

"Yesss," Ruby said slowly. "Especially because it's David we're talking about. But he does have to get to work really early. Maybe he meant to say he had to check on Diogee before he headed to the bakery."

Jamie dropped her head in her hands. "I didn't even think of that. That makes complete sense." She lifted her head and gave a real smile. "He's at work. He'll probably call or text once he gets all the morning muffins and stuff made. He does them fresh every day."

"It does make sense. Now, get to the good stuff. How was it?" Ruby asked, waggling her eyebrows.

"It was as good as I could possibly have imagined," Jamie answered. "Times a hundred."

David stared at the little screen on the phone. It was almost noon. He had to get in touch with Jamie. It was unacceptable not to. But he didn't know what to say.

Maybe the best thing to do was just say nothing. Nothing about last night. Maybe he could just shift them back into the friend zone without some big explanation. They'd only slept together once. And it wasn't like either of them thought it was going to make them a couple. Friends with benefits, that was the deal. Did friends with benefits even sleep together regularly, or was it just once in a while? Maybe if they just didn't sleep together for a while, the whole idea of benefits would fade away.

Like he was ever going to forget last night. Until that attack of heart-exploding panic had hit him after Jamie had fallen asleep, it had been amazing. But he clearly wasn't ready to be with anyone.

David started a new text. *Hey, Jam. Want to watch a movie suitable for 17 and under tonight?* He definitely didn't want her to think he was suggesting porn. He read the message over, decided it was the best he was going to do, and hit send.

Jamie held out her cell to Ruby so she could read David's message. Ruby raised her eyebrows and gave a "hmmm."

"I've never had a friend with benefits. Is that normal?" Jamie asked.

"It's definitely friendly," Ruby answered. "I'd have thought he'd have said it was a great night or something, but he's asking to hang out. It seems like everything's good."

"I guess. I mean, it's a text. How much can I expect from a text?" Jamie sent back a *sure* with a smiley face, just a plain one, not one with hearts for eyes or anything. She told herself she'd feel better when she saw David face-to-face.

But she didn't. Because even though David's face looked like David's face, David didn't feel like David, not completely. Almost, but not really. He smiled at her, handed her his latest cupcake creation, then kissed her on the cheek. Which upped the feeling that something was off. They were past the cheek kiss after last night. Way past.

He leaned down to scratch Mac on the head. Mac did that weird thing where he opened his mouth and flicked out his tongue, then he gave the meow that was usually reserved for the Fourth of July. Mac hated the boom of fireworks. Jamie reached down to stroke him, but he slipped away from her hand and disappeared into her bedroom.

"What's with him?" David asked.

Jamie shrugged. "I'm not sure. I'm not always able to read him." *Or you,* she silently added. She headed to the kitchen to put the cupcake in the fridge, and David followed her.

"What've you been up to today?" he asked as he sat down at the table.

Back when they were just friends—just great friends—Jamie might have answered truthfully. She might have admitted she spent the morning obsessing about why she hadn't heard from him, and then spent the time after she heard from him analyzing his message and trying to figure out why it felt a little less friendly than the messages he'd sent when they were friends without benefits. She might have admitted that the whole friends-with-benefits deal was a little more complicated than she thought it would be. She might have confessed that she did have different expectations from him now that they'd slept together than when they were friends period. Or maybe they weren't different expectations. Maybe she just expected them to feel as close as they had pre-sex than they did now. Maybe she'd have told him that she was completely confused and off-balance.

Instead, she just said, "I fooled around a little with some of the pics." Which was a lie. She'd pulled the picture of the puppeteers up on the screen, stared at it for about one full minute, then walked away, unable to concentrate.

Jamie opened the fridge and set the cupcake on the top shelf. "You're not going to try it now?" David asked.

That's right. Usually Jamie took a bite of whatever he brought her to sample as soon as he handed it to her. But her stomach was clenched. It didn't feel like it would accept any food. "Big lunch," she told him. Had she even eaten lunch? She couldn't remember.

"Are you okay?" David asked.

"Yes. Why?"

David shrugged.

"Are you okay?" Jamie asked.

"Sure. Great," David said.

Not true. Something was wrong. She could feel it. Jamie told herself to stop being crazy. David was still David, and maybe he was having some trouble figuring out exactly what friends with benefits meant, too.

"So, you said you were up for a movie? Anything in particular?" Jamie struggled to keep her tone light and casual.

"Not really. Anything you especially want to watch?" David asked.

"Pretty much anything is good for me," Jamie said.

"Me, too," he answered.

"You want to go out? Or just stream something?" Jamie asked.

"Either's good for me," he said.

They were both being ridiculously polite and accommodating. This was getting worse and worse.

"I still haven't seen anything at the Cinerama Dome. Let's just walk over there and see what's on. If it's nothing we want to see, we can just go to something else at the ArcLight," Jamie suggested. Maybe the walk would help them loosen up.

"Sure," he answered. Jamie hid a cat treat behind one of the sofa cushions for Mac to find, then they headed out.

"Pssst!" Jamie looked toward the sound and saw Marie on her porch, signaling them over. "Helen and her sister are talking!" she whispered when they reached her, jerking her head toward the fountain. The sisters were sitting on the edge, heads close together.

"It's the craziest thing," Marie continued. "They each had these dolls from when they were little girls and their parents took them to Greece. That was before the divorce. Helen's doll showed up on Nessie's doorstep this morning. Nessie came over to put it on the fountain with the other things, and Helen went out there to accuse her of stealing her doll. They went from yelling to talking, and now they've been out there for hours. I've known them both for more than forty years, and I was starting to think they'd die before they ever spoke again."

Marie's eyes were shiny with tears. Jamie reached out and gave her arm a squeeze. "That's wonderful."

"Isn't it?" Marie asked. "I think I'll make them a little something to snack on." She hurried inside.

"Do you think I should tell everyone what Mac's doing?" Jamie asked. "It's been going on for so long."

"You don't even know for sure Mac's still taking things. Maybe he really can't get out of the house. Maybe someone else thought the whole thing was funny and decided to keep it going. Strange, but possible."

"Strange. Yeah," Jamie said.

They fell into silence. It was a silence that made Jamie feel itchy and edgy, not one of those comfortable silences where you're so in synch you don't have to talk, the kind of silences she and David used to have.

She tried to push the thought away. Silence was silence. She was probably just letting her imagination run away with her. But last night she'd felt closer to him than she ever had, and now she felt further away than ever. Feeling something didn't make it true. She knew that. But she also knew sometimes you had to trust your gut.

"It looks like that new action flick with Chris Pratt is playing at the Cinerama Dome. That should be fun," Jamie said, squinting to see the marquee in the distance.

"Yeah. I'm up for that," David answered.

Jamie was relieved when it turned out the movie was starting a few minutes after they arrived. She could use a few hours of sitting in the dark with no need to talk and something on the screen that she hoped would pull her away from the craziness jittering around in her brain.

"They have great caramel popcorn here," David told her. "I'll get us some." He also got her a Diet Dr Pepper without having to ask what she wanted. *See?* she told herself. *Still considerate David.*

But when they were settled into their seats and they both dipped their hands into the popcorn at the same time, David jerked his hand back. The motion seemed involuntary. An instinctive reaction to touching something dangerous or disgusting.

He was repulsed by her.

Finally, they were crossing the courtyard of Storybook Court. The movie had felt endless to David, even though he usually enjoyed a good mindless action flick. But sitting next to

Jamie for those two hours had been brutal. He'd been so aware of her physically, the warmth of her body when her arm brushed his, the scent of her shampoo, everything. If his body had been in charge, he would have taken her home to bed before the last trailer ended. But he couldn't go through the heart-busting anxiety he knew would follow. Or the rush of devastating grief, that grief that felt fresh and raw, that followed it.

"Wow. Helen and her sister are still at it," Jamie said. Through Helen's front window, David could see the sisters sitting on the sofa.

"A happy ending," David answered. He followed Jamie up her front walk to her door. She unlocked it and stepped inside, clearly expecting him to follow. "I can't come in. I'm sure Diogee is dying to get out."

"But you have the dog door. He can get out whenever he wants," Jamie said.

"Yeah, but he has a little separation anxiety," David told her.

Jamie raised her eyebrows. "You've been gone, what, not even four hours."

Why couldn't she just accept that he didn't want to come in? "Yeah, but you know I have to get up crazy-early for work," David answered. "I'll be in touch," he said as he started to walk away.

With every step he took toward home, he felt a little tension drain out of him. When he got there, he'd have a game of tug-of-war with Diogee, read a few pages of *Infinite Jest* and a few dozen of its footnotes, then watch TV until he fell asleep. That was all he wanted. His old routine. His old life.

The sound of footsteps coming up fast behind him made David look over his shoulder. It was Jamie. Rushing toward him. "Did you actually just say you'd 'be in touch'?" she demanded. Her face was flushed, and her eyes were blazing.

"Yeah, I said something like that," David answered.

"I guess I should be expecting a Christmas card from you? Is that the translation?" Jamie asked.

"Jamie, we've seen each other every few days since that night we met in the bar," David answered. "And we just finished seeing each other about three minutes ago—because *I* asked if you wanted to see a movie. What are you so pissed off about?"

She shook her head. "Don't pretend you don't know. Don't pretend I'm being crazy. We had sex last night, and today you're acting like I'm contagious and you're telling me you'll 'be in touch'."

"I told you I wasn't ready to get into a relationship, and you told me the same thing," David shot back, even though he knew exactly what she meant. All he wanted was to get home. "We said we were going to be friends who had sex sometimes. That's what happened last night. And tonight we went out—like friends."

Jamie stared at him for what felt like a full minute, but could only have been a few seconds, then she turned away. "See ya! Don't be a stranger!" she called, and he could hear the anger and pain in her voice.

He knew he should call her back, try to explain. But he knew he wasn't going to be able to hang out with her as friends. Tonight proved that. So why not just let it end right there?

Mac watched as Jamie lay on her bed. She was crying, and he didn't know how to help. Finally, he walked over to her and lay by her side, as close as he could get. She continued to sob.

The scent coming off her was worse than the loneliness he used to smell on her, the loneliness that had made him decide to make it his mission to find her a packmate. Something had gone wrong. He'd sensed that when David had come into the house earlier. But Jamie's scent was much worse than it had been then.

Her sadness pressed down on him, making it hard for his lungs to take in enough air.

Mac had chosen David for his person, and Jamie had ended up crying. He had failed her.

Mac stood and jumped to the floor, then crawled under the bed and curled into a tight ball. He should stay away from her. He should stay away from everyone.

CHAPTER 19

When Jamie woke up the next morning, she had about three blissful seconds before she remembered what had happened the night before. She pulled the blankets higher and squeezed her eyes shut. All she wanted was to go back to sleep, to escape the memory of David jerking his hand away from hers in the movie theater, and the cold way he'd explained that his behavior was exactly what the two of them had agreed on. But what they'd agreed on was friends with benefits, and last night David had acted like a stranger.

She struggled to will herself back into oblivion, but her brain was pounding with questions: Why had David acted like that? What was wrong with him? Was something wrong with her? Why had he acted like she disgusted him? Why had he even suggested going to the movies when he obviously wanted nothing to do with her? Why? Why? Why?

She held out for a few minutes, then gave up. There was no way she could sleep with these thoughts ricocheting in her head. Her body felt heavy and cold, but she forced herself to climb out of bed. Maybe coffee would help. Coffee made everything at least a little better.

Belatedly, Jamie realized the room was lighter than usual. She checked her alarm clock. It was after nine. Mac never let her sleep this late. He expected breakfast at seven thirty. He should have been meowing his head off by now. "Mac?" she called. There was no answer. She did a search of the bungalow, but didn't see her kitty anywhere. Had he gotten out again? She checked the screen enclosing the porch and the window screens. No new rips. Not that that proved anything.

"Mac?" she called again. She started a more thorough search, opening cupboards, checking under the couch, looking in the corners of her closet. She finally found him curled up under the bed. "What's up, Mac-Mac?" She stretched out her hand and managed to brush her fingers down his back. "You okay?" He didn't react. He didn't move or mew or purr. "What's wrong, baby?" There had to be something. Mac never acted like this. He'd always loudly demanded breakfast and dinner if she was late serving it up, even by a few minutes. His internal clock was amazingly accurate.

She hurried to the kitchen, got his water bowl and a bowl of food, then returned to the bedroom and set them next to the bed. Maybe the smell would tempt him. He didn't react. *Don't panic,* Jamie told herself. Mac's breathing seemed normal. He hadn't vomited. She would have noticed when she searched the house for him. She checked his litter box. Didn't seem like he was having any problems like diarrhea. She decided to wait and see if he decided to eat in the next few hours. In the meantime, she'd hunt down the name of a good vet.

Usually she'd have called David and asked who he took Diogee to. She was sure—pretty sure—David would still take her call. He'd probably give her the answer with that same chilly politeness he'd used on her when he explained that all that had happened was that they were friends and they'd had sex, just the way they'd agreed. Then he'd probably tell her to keep in touch. She couldn't deal with that. She'd go ask Marie. Marie knew a billion people.

She pulled on a pair of cargo pants and a long-sleeved T-shirt. "Right back, Mac," she said, then hurried out the front door. She saw Al testing the soil of his little flower patch. "Do you know a good vet in the neighborhood?" she called as she waked toward him.

"Ask Marie." He jerked his head toward his house.

Jamie rushed up to the front door and knocked. Marie's eyes widened with surprise when she opened the door. "Are you all right?"

Belatedly, Jamie realized that she hadn't brushed her hair or her teeth, and partially cried-off makeup had to be streaking her face. She'd managed to hold off tears until she'd gotten safely inside her house last night, but she'd started crying as soon as her door was shut behind her.

"I'm fine." Jamie started scrubbing her face with her fingertips, then stopped, figuring she had to be doing more damage. "I'm worried about Mac, though. Do you know a good vet around here?"

"What's wrong with him?" Marie asked, her forehead furrowing with concern.

"Maybe nothing. He's just acting weird and not eating. I want to know where to take him if he gets worse," Jamie explained.

"Why don't you ask David who he takes the dog to?" Marie said.

"Don't you know anyone?" Jamie practically begged.

"Did you have a fight?" Helen called from the sofa in the

living room. Her sister sat beside her. Jamie hadn't even noticed them.

Jamie didn't want to discuss the David situation with the three women, but Marie was already asking, "Did you break up with him?"

"Did he break up with you?" Helen and Nessie asked in unison. "Jinx!" they said together, grinning.

"No. We weren't—No. But I don't think we'll be seeing each other as much," Jamie said. It was pointless to try to keep it from them. They'd see he wasn't around.

Marie shook her head. "He's not over his wife. If you're having problems, that'll be the reason. I'm going to have you meet my—"

"We should introduce her to—" Helen and Nessie began, talking over Marie.

"No!" Jamie's voice came out loud and horrified. All three women closed their mouths and stared at her. "No," she repeated, more softly. "No more setups from anyone. I mean it. You try, and I walk out." Jamie sucked in a deep breath. "All I want is the number of a reliable veterinarian. That's all."

"I'll get you the number for the Gower Animal Clinic. Dezzy used to take his little Pom there," Marie said with uncharacteristic gentleness.

"Thanks." She tried to smile at the twins as she waited for Marie to return.

"This is my sister, Nessie," Helen told her.

"I figured," Jamie said. She wondered if she should congratulate them on making up after so many years, or if it would be rude to mention their feud. Helen had never actually told Jamie about it. She only knew the sisters' history because Marie had filled her in.

"We haven't spoken in—" Nessie began.

"Fifty-eight years," Helen finished for her. "Isn't that—"

"Ridiculous?" Nessie concluded.

Alternating back and forth, the twins gave their story. A doll that had belonged to Nessie had turned up on Helen's porch, and almost as soon as Helen gave it back, a doll of Helen's had appeared on Nessie's doormat. They'd accused one another of being a thief, but that had gotten them talking. And then somehow they were talking about the county fair where they'd gotten the dolls, and they'd been pretty much talking nonstop since then.

"With time out to—" Helen said.

"Sleep and use the facilities," Nessie said.

"That's wonderful," Jamie told them. And she really was happy for them. It was a great story. But she couldn't actually feel the happiness. It was buried under the pain of David shoving her away and worry about Mac.

The twins chattered on, sharing memories of the time before their estrangement, before their parents divorced and they each stayed with one of them. Jamie pretended to listen, but kept glancing toward the kitchen, hoping for Marie's return.

Finally, the kitchen door swung open, and Marie reappeared with a slip of paper in her hand. "It took me a minute to find it. Al's been rummaging in my things again. I keep telling him to let me get whatever he wants, but he doesn't listen." She handed the vet's number to Jamie. "I hope your Mac is feeling better."

"Thanks for this. I'm going to go check on him."

The women didn't wait to start discussing her. Before Jamie was able to shut the door behind her, she heard Marie say, "I knew David wasn't the right—" Simply hearing his name sent an extra jab of pain through her. She ignored it. Well, she tried to. She needed to focus on Mac.

When she returned home, he seemed to be in exactly the same spot under the bed where she'd left him. It didn't look like he'd come out for a bite of food. She decided to give him a few more hours, then she'd call the vet.

Jamie took off her shoes, but crawled back into bed fully

dressed. She wanted to stay in the same room with Mac, and if she fell asleep for a while, all the better.

Two days after the breakup, David was hanging out with Adam. He knew he shouldn't be thinking of what happened with Jamie as a breakup, since they had never officially been together, but that was what it felt like.

He hadn't wanted to come over, but it was Lucy's book group night, which meant it was pizza night for Adam, the kids, and David. The kids expected to see him, and so did Adam, so here he was. At least Maya and Katy were finally in bed. It was hard being fun Uncle David—they both called him Uncle David, even though he was Maya's godfather and not any kind of actual relative—when he was feeling like crap.

"You getting whatever Jamie had?" Adam asked. "You don't look so hot."

It took David a minute to remember he'd said Jamie was sick when he'd wanted to get out of the double date. That felt like it was a hundred years ago. Back when he'd been excited every time he knew he was going to see Jamie. Now every time he thought of her he felt disgusted with himself.

"Maybe," he answered. Adam had given him the perfect excuse for being off, and David might as well use it.

"You better not have infected the kids," Adam warned. "One kid gets sick and it circles through the family, around and around, until we've all had whatever at least a couple times."

David shoved his hands through his hair. Maybe he should tell the truth. Maybe it would help to talk it through with Adam. "You don't have to worry. I'm not actually sick. I'm just kind of messed up. I broke up with Jamie."

Adam took a swig of beer. "Unexpected. What happened?"

Before David could answer, the front door opened and Lucy came into the living room. "How're the girls?" she asked.

"They're great. Asleep. But David's not so good. He just told me he broke up with Jamie," Adam answered.

Lucy sank down on the sofa next to Adam. "What happened?"

"That's what I just asked," Adam said. "You want a beer before we hear the whole sad story?"

Lucy slapped his arm. "Don't say it like that."

"It's okay," David said.

"No, it's not," Lucy insisted.

"How's this? You want a beer before David starts telling us what went wrong with his relationship?" Adam asked.

"Better. And no. Grace made sangria." Lucy took off her shoes.

"Which means she's drunk," Adam told David. "You know she loves sangria."

Lucy gave Adam's arm another slap. "I'm not drunk. I am simply slightly tipsy. I couldn't say 'simply sligthtly tipsy' if I was drunk." She turned to David. "What happened?" she asked again.

David realized he couldn't actually answer that without admitting he'd lied to them. "We were never actually together. We were just pretending to be together, because her neighbors were trying to fix her up and she didn't want to be fixed up. And you two were nagging me about Counterpart and I wanted to take a break from it."

"You lying liar!" Lucy burst out. She did sound sort of drunk.

"I don't get it. If you weren't together, how come you're so upset about breaking up?" Adam asked.

David groaned. "I have so totally screwed things up. I think I really hurt her and I feel horrible."

Lucy pointed at him. "What did you do?"

"Things were going great. We had fun, a lot of fun. We had good conversations. We were both enjoying it. Then we decided to sleep together," David began to explain.

"Makes sense. You like each other. You're spending all this time together. She's cute, you said. Of course you slept together," Adam said.

"How was it?" Lucy asked. Yeah, she was definitely drunk. She'd have wanted to know if she was sober, but she wouldn't have been so blunt about it.

"Details," Adam said.

"No details. It was amazing. That's all I'm going to say," David answered.

"I'm so confused." Lucy took a sip of Adam's beer. "You like her. You have fun with her. You have fun with her," she repeated. "And what else did you say?" She concentrated for a second. "You talk. And you had amazing sex. Really confused."

"It is confusing, even when you're not simply slightly tipsy." Adam took his beer back.

"I had a panic attack. That's all I can think to call it," David admitted. "I knew this guy who went to the emergency room because he thought he was having a heart attack, and it turned out to be a panic attack. I had a hard time believing something emotional could feel that bad. But it did. It does. I had to get out of there. I left in the middle of the night."

"Without saying anything?" Adam asked.

"I left a lame-ass note," David said. "It was all I could do. It felt like my heart was going to slam out of my chest."

Lucy sat up straight and rubbed her face with her hands, like she was trying to sober herself up.

"You haven't been with anyone since Clarissa. It's understandable. Just tell her what happened," Adam said.

Lucy nodded in agreement. "Just tell her what happened."

"We had a big fight. It was obvious she never wants to see me again. I think I want to just let it fade away. It's not like we've known each other that long," David said. "And it's not like I want to try it again. I'm obviously not ready."

"That is a chicken-poop move, and you are not a chicken poop," Lucy told him. Even drunk, she kept her language kid-appropriate. "You're a grown-butt man. Act like it."

"You're not going to feel any better until you do," Adam told him.

"It's been three days," Jamie told Ruby. They both sat on the floor next to the bed, peering at Mac, who lay beneath it. "The vet said there's nothing wrong with him. She gave him some intravenous liquids, but that's all she could do."

Ruby rubbed Jamie's shoulder. "I'm so sorry. But at least he's physically okay. And you can get him more fluids if he's still . . . like he is tomorrow."

"I just don't understand." Jamie's eyes filled with tears.

"Animals are sensitive. Do you think he could be upset because you're upset?" Ruby asked.

"I shouldn't be upset. I shouldn't," Jamie said. "David sent me that e-mail explaining everything. It makes total sense that he had that reaction. We shouldn't have tried having sex. He didn't think he was ready. We just let ourselves get carried away. It's no one's fault. And now I'm back to where I want to be. I have time to work on my photos without the distraction of a relationship. I even got a comment from an editor asking how many more pictures I'm planning to do in the series. She called it a 'series'."

"And that's great," Ruby told her. "But it doesn't mean it doesn't hurt that David's out of your life. I know you weren't together very—"

"We weren't together," Jamie interrupted.

"Okay, you weren't together. But you spent a lot of time together. You liked each other. And now you're missing him."

Jamie angrily wiped her tears away with the heels of her hands. She leaned farther down so she could get a really good look at her cat. "MacGyver, if you're upset because you think I'm upset, don't be. I'm okay." It was a lie. A big part of her wished she could curl up under the bed with Mac and never come out. Ruby was right. She missed David. No, "missed" was too mild. She yearned for him, longed for him, grieved for him, and she couldn't have him. She couldn't believe her feelings went so deep after such a short time, but they did. From almost the beginning, it had felt like she'd known him forever.

But she had to get over it. And she would. She wasn't going to waste the rest of her year. She wasn't going to throw away her mother's gift.

She cleared her throat. "You're my good Mac-Mac. All I need to feel fine is for you to be okay."

Mac opened his eyes, filled with determination. He'd realized the truth. He hadn't been wrong about David. He *was* the packmate for Jamie. Mac knew when Jamie was happy, and she had been happy with him. David had been happy with her too. Mac's nose was never wrong. The two of them had messed things up. Or maybe it was the bonehead's fault. But Mac would fix it. He couldn't stay under the bed anymore. He couldn't abandon his person. She needed him, and he loved her.

He slipped out into the sunlight streaming through the windows, then lapped up a little of the water Jamie had left for him. The food dish was empty. He gave a loud meow. He was hungry. He need fuel to continue his mission.

"Mac! You're out!" Jamie cried as she rushed into the room. She gently lifted him up and held him against her chest. He allowed her to cuddle him for a few minutes, then gave another meow. He needed his food!

"Food! You want food! You want food!" Jamie carried him into the kitchen, set him down, and began opening a familiar can.

Mac purred until he felt his fur vibrating. With a stomach full of sardinesies, he could do anything!

CHAPTER 20

Jamie slowly opened her front door and looked down. A sasquatch sock lay on the mat, along with a worn copy of *Infinite Jest,* an A's baseball hat, and a *Ghostbusters* proton pack.

Every day for the last week, things belonging to David had appeared on her doorstep. Other people were still getting things, too. The rim of the fountain always had new objects displayed. Hud was about to lose it.

"Mac, this has to stop. I know you like David. I like David. But it just can't work."

Mac didn't even give an "uh-huh" meow. He was too busy playing with Mousie. He'd been as frisky as a kitten since he came out from under the bed. And he'd gotten back to playing cat burglar. She was sure of it, even though she still hadn't caught him escaping the bungalow. There hadn't been any new thefts when he was sick, but as soon as he was well—*bam.*

Jamie sent David a text. *You around? I have stuff for you, including the proton pack. Don't want to leave it on the fountain until I know you're coming. I know it means a lot to you.*

She remembered the story he'd told her about Clarissa replacing the proton pack that his brother had broken back when David was a little boy.

Coming now. Thanks. I have things to drop off, too, he texted back.

Jamie put everything into a shopping bag, wrote David's name on it, then took it to the fountain. Hud was talking to one of her neighbors, and Jamie was grateful she could avoid at least one conversation with him. She hurried back inside. She wasn't ready to see David face-to-face, and it was clear he felt the same way about her.

She retreated to the kitchen and her laptop. She'd gotten the owner of the Museum of Jurassic Technology to allow her to photograph him, and she was experimenting with different effects, trying to find one that matched his personality. Mac jumped down from one of the kitchen chairs with an annoyed huff and stalked out without acknowledging her.

Jamie didn't mind that he was sulky. She was too happy to see him walking around. He was still a little too thin, but the all the sardines had gotten him almost back to his fighting weight. She'd been so afraid she was going to lose him.

Mac could tell by Jamie's breathing that she was just pretending to be asleep. He also knew when she stopped pretending. Then he ran to the chimney and climbed up. He sat on the roof, unsure what his next move should be. What he'd been doing hadn't been working.

Jamie and David took his gifts and left them at the fountain. He was starting to think they really were as boneheaded as the bonehead. He knew they should be packmates, why didn't they?

Wait, the bonehead. David loved the bonehead. Mac didn't

understand why. All the dog did was drool and howl and pee on things. But David loved him the way Jamie loved Mac. Diogee was David's packmate. That meant he was more important to David than anything.

Now Mac knew what he needed to do. He leapt from the roof to the bushes to the ground, then loped to David's house. Luck was on his side, because the bonehead was in the yard. Mac unlatched the gate and swung it open.

Time for the good part. He ran over to Diogee and gave his tail the *whap! whap! whap!* with one paw. The bonehead whirled around and let out a howl. Mac took off—like he was afraid of the big, galumphing thing. As if!

He ran for home, but not too fast. He wanted the bonehead to keep up. When he reached his yard, Mac let out his loudest yowl. That got the dog barking. And *that* got Jamie barreling out the front door.

"Mac! Diogee!" she cried. "Get in here. Mac, sardines! Diogee, treat!"

Mac didn't have to be asked twice. He raced through the door. Diogee came right behind him. Mac headed for his under-the-bed hideout. He thought he might have gotten the mutt a little too riled up. The bonehead might think Mac was the treat!

Jamie shut the bedroom door, and he heard her scolding the dog. Ha!

Mac had done what he could. He'd have to wait and see if it worked. If it didn't, he'd come up with another plan. He was never giving up.

At first David thought the beeping was his alarm, then he realized it was his cell. He checked the time. A little after one. He grabbed the phone. Jamie was calling him. He hesitated, but only for a second, then answered.

"I've got your dog," Jamie said.

"What?"

"I heard him barking outside my house, so I brought him in," she explained.

"The gate was locked."

"Well, I don't know how he got out, but he's here," Jamie told him. Her voice was brisk.

"Okay, well, I'll come get him." David hung up and pulled on his clothes. He jammed on his sneakers, not bothering with socks. When he stepped outside, he saw the gate swinging in breeze. He was always so careful about latching it. But he'd been distracted lately. Screwing up recipes at work. Even burning two dozen cupcakes.

His chest started feeling tight as he headed to Jamie's. He'd only have to see her for a minute. There was no reason for a freak out. But by the time he knocked on her door, he was struggling for every breath. His ribs were like a vise crushing his lungs.

"It's like Diogee's been taking lessons from Mac. They were both out there, and—" Jamie said when she opened the door. Then she broke off abruptly and stared at him. "Are you okay?"

"Yeah. Still half-asleep," David managed to say, panting. He needed to get home. He'd be okay if he could just get home. Diogee barreled toward him. David managed to grab the door frame before Diogee jumped on him in greeting. "Come on, D." He'd forgotten to bring a leash, but the dog should follow him home. He turned to leave.

Jamie grabbed his arm and pulled him inside. She shut the door behind them. "David, you're hyperventilating," she said, speaking slowly and deliberately. "Hold your breath, okay?"

David shook his head. "Already can't get enough air."

"You're breathing really fast and really hard," she explained, without releasing his arm. "You're getting too much air. Hold your breath and you'll feel better. I'll do it with you." She pulled in a breath and locked her eyes on his face.

He managed to hold his breath along with her, even though it increased the pace of his heartbeat, the drumming of it loud in his ears.

"Okay," Jamie finally said. "Take a breath. Just a regular breath. Not a big one."

Diogee whined and pawed David's leg. "It's okay, dude. It's okay." David took a breath. He patted the dog's head.

"Better?" Jamie asked.

"Better," David answered.

"Panic attack?"

"Yeah."

"Come sit down for a minute," Jamie said. "Or is it making it worse being here?"

Now that he was a little calmer, the urgency to get home had drained out of him. His legs had gone to jelly, and he felt exhausted. He let Jamie lead him over to the sofa. "I'll get you a drink of water."

Diogee jumped up onto the sofa next to him, and then Mac leapt up onto the sofa back and gave David a head butt. "I'm okay, guys," he said. His heart rate was slowing down a little.

"Here you go," Jamie said as she came back into the living room with the water. She handed it to him, then sat down in the chair across from the couch.

David's hand shook as he raised the glass to his lips, but he managed to get some down. "Sorry. I just need a couple more minutes, and then—"

"Don't be stupid," she told him.

He leaned his head back and focused on pulling himself back together. When he felt ready and lifted his head, he found Jamie looking at him, her eyes full of concern. "Is this how you felt that night?"

"Pretty much," David answered.

"I wish you'd woken me up," she told him. "But I guess that would have made it worse."

"Probably," David admitted. "I'm actually going to see someone. A therapist. Lucy nagged me into it." After she'd apologized repeatedly for pushing him too hard to get into online dating and for being drunk when he told her what had happened after he slept with Jamie.

Jamie nodded, but didn't say anything. She probably didn't know what to say. Was there a right thing to say to someone when they were about to start therapy? He still couldn't believe he was going to do it. He'd always thought it was fine for other people, but a part of him felt like he'd never need it, that he was smart enough to solve his own problems. But clearly not.

"I don't want to have a panic attack every time I start to care about a woman," David continued. Jamie still didn't say anything. "The way I care about you." Her eyes widened, but she didn't speak. "I think it was getting close to you, not just us having sex, that got to me." He choked out a laugh. "I sound like I'm in therapy already." Mac leaped down onto his lap. It put him inches away from Diogee, but they didn't start another staring contest. They just pressed themselves close against David.

"Looks like you're getting a little pet therapy right now," Jamie said. "It's really late. Do you want to just stay here tonight? On the couch, I mean," she added quickly.

"Yeah. Thanks," David said.

"I'll get you a blanket and a pillow." Jamie disappeared into her bedroom.

David felt wrung out, but not like he couldn't breathe or that his heart was going to burst. He pushed off his shoes and stretched out, forcing the animals to resettle themselves, Mac on his stomach, and Diogee curled up at his feet. He closed his eyes, and began to drift off almost immediately. He was only vaguely aware of Jamie covering him with the blanket.

Jamie checked the clock. Almost ten, and David was still asleep. She'd called his boss at the bakery and told him David was sick. She hoped he wouldn't mind. He seemed to need the rest so badly.

When he'd e-mailed her and told her he'd had a panic attack, she'd understood—intellectually. But seeing him last night made her understand in her gut why he'd taken off the way he had. He must have felt like he was dying. It was actually kind of brave of him to ask her to the movies the next day. He had to know it might bring on another attack, and maybe it almost had. Maybe that's why he had jerked his hand away from hers in the theater. Maybe touching her started bringing the panic back.

Mac gave a yowl, bringing her out of her thoughts. He sat on the sill of one of the living room windows, staring out into the courtyard. "Shhh!" Jamie hurried over to him. Mac yowled again. Jamie glanced at David. Still asleep, with Diogee lying at his feet, awake, watching over him.

"What's the problem?" she whispered to the cat.

Mac started clawing at the screen. Jamie batted his paws down. She looked into the courtyard to see what had gotten him so riled up. She was expecting a squirrel or another cat, but all she saw was Sheila, the mail carrier, heading across the courtyard, and Hud at his usual spot by the fountain.

"There's nothing out there," she told MacGyver.

He leapt to the ground and ran to the door, then yowled again, like he wanted to go out. As if she would ever just open the door and let him go. He paced back and forth, then streaked across the living room and climbed up the chimney!

Jamie bolted outside. She stared at the roof. Would he come out up there? Or could he have gotten stuck? No, there he was. Trotting down the roof, jumping down to the bushes, and then taking off toward Sheila. Before she could open her mouth to call him, he leapt up and managed to free one of the keychains on her mailbag. Then without a second's hesitation, he raced over to Hud and dropped the keychain at his feet.

"I didn't tell him to do it!" Jamie exclaimed, holding up her hands as Hud stared at her.

Hud leaned down to pick up the keychain. "I'll get it!" Sheila cried, rushing toward him.

He beat her to it, studying the silver fish dangling at the end. "The whole crew got one of these when the *Catch of the Day* pilot got picked up. They were specially made." He pulled down his sunglasses and stared at Sheila.

"I bought it on eBay," she admitted. Her cheeks were flushed. So was her neck. So were the tips of her ears.

"You're a fan?" Hud couldn't keep the elation out of his voice.

"I've seen every episode a million times," Sheila admitted, speaking to the ground instead of Hud. *She likes him,* Jamie realized. *She* likes *Hud. That's why she knew every guest spot he ever had, but didn't know any TV trivia that night at the pub.*

"Which was your favorite?" Hud reached over and tilted Sheila's chin up so that she was looking at him.

Jamie suddenly felt like she shouldn't be standing there watching them. She scooped up Mac. He didn't protest. Then she returned to the house. David was sitting up, putting on his shoes. "I've got to get to work."

She shook her head. "I called in sick for you. I hope it's okay."

"Thanks."

Jamie didn't know what to say, now that he wasn't in the middle of a crisis. "Oh! Hud is going to have to accept that Mac is behind the burglaries at Storybook Court. He just witnessed Mac stealing something with his own eyes. And I wasn't there giving Mac signals and sardine bribes. Also, I know how he's been getting out." She pointed to the chimney.

David looked at MacGyver. "Impressive."

Jamie looked at her cat, too. "Not the word I'd use."

David stood. "You think you might want to get some breakfast?"

"I . . . don't know," Jamie answered. "I'm not sure I can shift into friends again without a little more time. I know I was completely onboard with the whole friends-with-benefits thing, but I was fooling myself. We were too good at being a fake couple. It felt too real."

David nodded. "To me, too. I don't want to be friends with benefits. I want to be friends with the possibility of taking it to the next level—for real—once I get my head on straight."

"Oh. Well. Hmm." Jamie hadn't been expecting that. But it was exactly what she wanted. Even if it happened during The Year of Me. It wasn't men who had gotten in the way of her dreams. It was the particular men she'd gotten involved with in the past. That and the way she'd turned herself inside out to please them. She hadn't done that with David, because they'd been friends first. And because he'd never have wanted it.

She looked at him for a long moment, then nodded. "I've been thinking about checking out Roscoe's Chicken and Waffles."

"Another place in LA I've always wanted to go, but never have," David said.

Mac began to purr.

One Year Later

The doorbell rang, and Jamie rushed to open it. "Happy Moving In Together Day!" Lucy exclaimed, handing her a doormat that said HOME IS WHERE THE PETS ARE.

Jamie gave her a hug. Getting to be friends with Adam and Lucy was a huge side benefit to her relationship with David. "I'm putting this out right now," she announced. "Go out to the backyard. David's getting the barbecue fired up."

She'd just finished laying out the doormat in front of the round Hobbit hole door when Ruby, plus Riley, Addison, and their mom—and, of course, Zachary—strolled up the walkway. Zachary and Addison were pretty much always together. They'd been going out for a little more than a year and were working on a graphic novel together. They hadn't broken up once.

Diogee galloped toward the door, and Jamie barely managed to shut it before he made it outside to greet, and possibly knock down, the new guests. "You look fabulous," she told Riley, kneeling down so she could take in every deal of the little girl's fuchsia cowgirl outfit, which Ruby had been working on for months.

"I do!" Riley gave a little twirl and everyone laughed.

"Okay, I'm going to open the door now. Get ready to be Diogee'd," Jamie said, then ushered them into the house, where they were all enthusiastically licked.

"He kisses better than you do, Zachary," Addison joked, but her tone was light and affectionate.

"More tongue. Got it," Zachary asked.

"Not hearing this," said Addison's mom.

Ruby wrapped her arm around Jamie's waist as they headed through the house to the backyard. "I'm so thrilled for you. I knew from the beginning you and David were perfect for each other."

"Marie and Helen are both trying to take credit for getting us together. They're out there right now arguing about it. Nessie is trying to referee. They've managed to completely forget about the dentist and the godson. Also, they've each somehow decided to take credit for Hud and Sheila falling in love, too, even though the credit for that has to go to Mac."

"Mac does get all the credit for that. But I can see Helen's point about you and David," Ruby answered. Jamie stared at her. "Well, the godson did lead to you going to the bar, where you had drinks with David," Ruby explained. "So I think Helen deserves a little credit. But don't tell Marie I said that."

Jamie veered toward the kitchen. "I've got to show you something. You'd see it soon anyway, but I can't wait." She opened the lid of a large cake box. "David made me this." The cake—jam-filled, of course—had a perfect replica of the cover of Jamie's book on top. "Can you believe my pictures are going to be published?"

"Not really," Ruby answered. "I didn't think there was any possible way you'd get a book together with a clingy, needy, controlling guy like David around."

"Funny. You're very funny," Jamie said. "Come on. Let's get out there." She looked over her shoulder. "Not you, Mac," she warned. "You are an indoor cat. The chimney is closed."

Mac stared at the young one, Riley, until she came over and opened the glass door leading to the backyard. Who needed a chimney? There were lots of ways to get out of a house if you were MacGyver.

He sauntered toward the grill, enjoying the smell of the cooking meat and the scents of the happy people, especially Jamie and David. The tip of his tail gave a little flick. He'd done good. He took in another breath, using his tongue for a deeper exploration of the air. There were people nearby who needed him. He'd start following the scent trails tonight.

He jumped up on the table next to the grill. A platter of cooked hamburgers sat on it. He gave a meow and Diogee trotted over. Mac flipped him one of the burgers. He might need muscle on some of his missions. The bonehead could handle that. Mac had enough brains for both of them.

Connect with

Visit us online at
KensingtonBooks.com
to read more from your favorite authors, see books
by series, view reading group guides, and more.

for sneak peeks, chances to win books and prize packs,
and to share your thoughts with other readers.

facebook.com/kensingtonpublishing
twitter.com/kensingtonbooks

Tell us what you think!
To share your thoughts, submit a review,
or sign up for our eNewsletters, please visit:
KensingtonBooks.com/TellUs.